Books by
Vicki McBee Irwin

A Journey for Rebecca

By Grace

Love by the Master

Praise for By Grace

"We all meet people like Diane in life. Bitter and no hope. Just pure mean. I just wanted to slap her sometimes, she was so mean. So ungrateful. God doesn't give up on us like we give up on people. God keeps coming after us like he did with Diane until we relent. Everywhere she turned, God had a believer in her path. We must humble and accept the forgiveness of those that do us wrong. Again, great book." —Francis

"I love Vicki's books. They're so uplifting and encouraging. She is a master of taking a bad situation and showing how it can be not only overturned by God's love, but also made into something even better. This second of her books has several stories that are woven together, making it even harder to put down. I can't wait for #3. Thank you, Vicki."—Rebecca

"By Grace is another book by Vicki McBee Irwin that captivates you from the beginning until the very end! The characters are intriguing, in real life situations, and the overall theme is forgiveness and redemption. A must read by anyone who struggles with life situations and how to handle them. Vicki is an excellent writer." —Mama K

"This is such an inspiring story that will put a smile on your face and love in your heart. It tells how you can have a difficult life with one problem after another, but when you let God into your life, you can see things differently. The love of God in one woman's life touches and changes so many people. I loved this story and pray that I can be more like Leah." —Annita

"Vicki did an amazing job on this book… Once I started reading, I didn't want to put it down! If you are having a difficult time in your life, pick up her book and it will lift you up and inspire you… Love you, Vicki… I am ready for a sequel!!!" —Kathy

By Grace

Vicki McBee Irwin

Knoxville, Tennessee, USA
crippledbeaglepublishing.com

Cover design by Jody Dyer

Follow Vicki Lynn McBee-Irwin on Facebook

Scriptures marked NIV are taken from the NEW INTERNATIONAL VERSION (NIV): Scripture taken from THE HOLY BIBLE, NEW INTERNATIONAL VERSION ®. Copyright© 1973, 1978, 1984, 2011 by Biblica, Inc.™. Used by permission of Zondervan.

Paperback ISBN 978-1-958533-32-1
Hardcover ISBN 978-1-958533-33-8
Paperback ISBN 978-1-958533-34-5
Hardcover ISBN 978-1-958533-35-2

Library of Congress Control Number: 2023904796

Printed in the United States of America

"Love is patient, love is kind.
It does not envy, it does not boast,
It is not proud.
It is not rude, it is not self-seeking,
It is not easily angered,
It keeps no records of wrongs.
Love does not delight in evil but
Rejoices with the truth.
It always protects, always trusts,
Always hopes, always perseveres.
Love never fails."
1 Corinthians 13:4-8 (NIV)

Acknowledgments

I want to thank my brother, Jerry McBee,
Who took my books and shared them
everywhere he went.
You will never know how much you mean to me.
Love you,
Sis

Also

Linda Albert, my editor.
I cherish our friendship, your wonderful
sense of humor, and your guidance with this book.
Couldn't have done this without you.
Love you, sweet friend.

Scripture given to me by my Mother before she
went home to heaven on October 31, 2020

Joshua 1:9 (NIV)

"Have I not commanded you?
Be strong and courageous.
Do not be afraid;
Do not be discouraged,
For the Lord your God will be
With you wherever you go."

I would like to dedicate this book to my great grandson,
Isaac Russell.

One

The gloomy, rainy weather mirrored Diane Baker's emotions as she thought back over the past few hours, hours that revealed an upending in her world that she had not seen coming.

Jake Simpson was the love of her life and had been since the first time she saw him; it was love at first sight. They had been together almost a year, and he had made so many promises, promises Diane now saw that he had no intention of keeping. They moved into a tiny apartment, for he had promised once they saved up enough money, they would buy a home.

The apartment living room had space for only a love seat, television, and a floor lamp. The bedroom was large enough for only a regular-sized bed and a small chest of drawers. The kitchen was compact as well, with room for a small table and two chairs. Whatever Jake asked of Diane, she did, no questions asked.

Jake worked several aisles over from Diane at Murphy's Manufacturing, and the only time they saw each other was at lunch. Ruby Young had transferred from another department and worked beside Diane. The three of them soon became close friends and spent as much time together as they could.

One Wednesday after work, Jake said, "Diane, some guys and I are going camping this weekend to get away and have some guy time."

"That sounds like fun. Who all is going with you, Jake?"

"Oh, just some guys from work. This will give you some time to yourself to do whatever you want."

"Will you be leaving the car? Remember, you had me to sell mine so we could save more money. If you take it, I'll be stuck at home unless I walk."

"Oh, Diane, I will need the car to put some of the camping equipment in. I'm sorry, it slipped my mind that we only had the one vehicle. Next time I'll leave the car for you."

"Do you guys plan on going camping often? Say, why don't we go camping sometime? It might become a way for us to get away from this tiny apartment."

"I don't know, Diane, guys like to get out to themselves. I'll think about it."

On Thursday at work, Diane asked Ruby, "Do you have any plans for the weekend? Jake is going to be gone, he's taking the car, and I'm stuck at home."

"Oh, Diane, this weekend I already have plans. Wish you had said something sooner. Seems like I'm always at your place, and I thought I would give you guys a break from me hanging around all the time."

"Ruby, you know we don't mind. You seem like family to us and you're always welcome. By any chance, will you be using your car this weekend?"

"Yes, I will. I'm so sorry, Diane, wish I could help you out. If only it was any other weekend."

Diane began to notice Jake had to go somewhere after dinner nearly every night and that Ruby was coming over less and less. Today she found out why. After work, Jake walked Diane to the car as usual.

"Diane, here are the keys, take the car on home. I'll be coming by this weekend to pick up my things."

Looking at Jake in disbelief she said, "What are you talking about?"

"Things are over between us. I'm moving out."

Still in shock, Diane could feel tears in her eyes. "Jake, why, what's happened?"

"Diane, someone else is in my life, and I am much happier with her. There is nothing between us anymore. Things were good with us for a while, but now that's over, and I need to move on." Then he turned and walked away.

As Diane pulled up in front of the tiny apartment, she sat in the car trying to figure out what went wrong. Everything Jake had asked of her she had done, even things that she didn't want to do. He always had a reason, and he would say if she loved him, she wouldn't question his decisions, just do it.

When she walked into the apartment, it felt like the walls were closing in on her. She had never liked this place, but to save money, she endured it. Jake had said they would only have to live here a year and then they could move into something much nicer. Diane was unsure of how much money they had in the bank. She hoped it would be enough so she could move to another place.

The next morning at work, Diane did not see Jake at all. She wondered if he had taken the day off, or if he had changed jobs.

Ruby was already at her station when Diane arrived. She asked, "Diane, are you alright this morning? Did you not sleep well last night?"

"Oh, Ruby, Jake is moving out. He said he has found someone else."

"Diane, where is he going, did he say? Did he say who it was?"

"No. I don't have any answers, and I don't know who it is. I'm thinking, the times he was supposed to be out with the guys, he was with this other woman. I can't talk about it anymore right now or I'll start crying again. It's so hard to think about what I'm supposed to be doing here at work. My mind and heart are so torn."

After work, Diane decided to go by the bank. Hopefully, she would be able to withdraw her half of the money so she could look for a bigger apartment. When she gave the teller the account number, the teller informed her the account had been closed.

Diane clutched the cold marble surface separating her from the teller in disbelief as a wave of nausea washed over her. Her voice was a whisper as she said, "There must be some mistake. My boyfriend deposited my check every week."

"This account was closed out a week ago," the clerk replied in a clipped, all-business tone with a hint of impatience.

"But how could the account have been closed without my permission? My name was on it."

The teller peered at the computer screen again and told Diane, "There was only one name on the account."

Diane not only turned pale but also felt like she was going to faint. How could Jake have done this to her? Had he been planning this all along? Turning back to the teller, Diane asked, "Was the name on the account Jake Simpson?"

"I'm sorry, but I can't give out that information. I have never seen you here in the bank, so you are not a familiar face to us."

"Well, this bank had no problem accepting my paycheck. I signed it every payday and gave it to Jake to deposit. He said my name was on the account, and I believed him. He paid all the bills and took care of the banking. I had no idea he was lying to me. Now, you're telling me I have no money at all?"

"I wish I could be of more help to you," the clerk said, looking behind Diane for the next customer. "Have a good day."

Turning away, Diane could not believe what she had been told. What was she going to do? Getting in the car, through sobs, she finally made it home. When she pulled up in front of the apartment, Jake was standing in the yard. Diane got out of the car and walked up to him.

"Jake, how could you? I just came from the bank, and you have closed out the account. Half of that money is mine and I need it."

"Diane, I need that money. Besides, you will have to prove that you deposited money in that account. You will need an attorney, and I don't believe you can afford one right now."

Jake took a step closer to Diane and snatched the car keys. "I believe you are driving my car, which I need."

"Jake, you had me to sell my car. What am I supposed to drive and how will I get to work?"

"Now, that's your problem, not mine."

Then he turned, walked to his car, and left. Diane could not believe this was happening to her. She was unable to control her tears; turning, she went inside, only to receive another shock. Jake had taken the television and the bedroom furniture. Walking over to the kitchen, she found that he had taken the good pots and pans, dishes, towels, food, everything. What had she done to deserve this?

Going over to the love seat, as it was, she sat down and called Ruby. She needed someone to talk to, someone to listen as she cried. Instead of Ruby's voice, Diane heard Jake's.

"Diane, if you are looking for Ruby, she's busy. We are trying to get our place fixed up and we don't have time for you."

Then he hung up.

Diane sat back in the seat as another shock came over her. Jake and her best friend together. She curled up in a ball on the love seat and cried and cried until at last, exhausted, she fell asleep.

Two

Leah Conner sat at her kitchen table, trying to make a grocery list. It was so hard to cook for only one person. Looking around, she knew she had way too much house, but the thoughts of selling were more than she could bear. A knock came from the back door, and Nora Perkins from next door popped her head in. "Leah, you home?"

"Hey, Nora, I'm in here. What are you up to this morning?"

"Wanted to stop by and see how you are doing. Have you thought any more about what we talked about the other day?"

"Yes, Nora, I have. I've given it a lot of thought, but I can't sell the house. Everywhere I look I'm reminded of the girls and David. I know the girls are grown and have moved away to live their own lives now, but David and I built this house. I feel as if he is still here with me."

"Leah, I've never lost a husband, so I don't truly understand your feelings, but I think David would want you to move into something smaller. Something you can manage."

"You're probably right, Nora, but now is just not the time for me to move. I have been praying and asking God for a sign on what I should do. Until I feel God leading me to move, I'm going to stay here. I can't put my finger on it, but I don't think moving is the thing I need to do."

"Leah, David has been gone a little over a year. You work yourself to death trying to keep this place up. You need to think of yourself. You don't go anywhere but to the grocery store, church and to pick up supplies to work on the house or in the yard."

Leah sighed and then tried to explain her feelings to her friend "Nora, I'm happy working around here. David and I did everything together, and what I'm doing brings me happiness. I can't move away, not now anyway. I need more time."

Nora was still unconvinced. "I'm going to visit my sister in Florida in a few weeks. Why don't you come with me? It might do you good to get away for at least a few days. Don't say 'no' yet. Think about it, okay?"

"I'll think about it, and I do appreciate you looking after me. You are a good neighbor, and I don't know what I would do without you. I was making a grocery list before you came. Can I pick anything up for you while I'm out?"

"Thanks, but I went to the store the other day and spent way too much. Went in for only four items and came out with a shopping cart full. If you make a list, better stick to it or you will end up like me." With that, Nora was gone, laughing as she went out the door.

Leah walked through the house, observing each room. Yes, everywhere she looked, she could see things David had made. He could look at a picture of anything and make it. He was gifted in woodwork. He loved people and life. Why did God have to take him so soon? She went over to a window and could see the flower bed David had been working on. He had made a swing for them to sit on outside near a tree they had planted when they first built the house, which was now a big shade tree. He had said it needed some flowers and a fountain to make it complete. When he had finished, he called for her to come out to see how it looked, wanting her approval. They had just sat down on the swing when David clutched his chest and fell over. She was told he had suffered a massive heart attack. He had not been sick and never complained about feeling badly. One minute they were happy, and the next David was gone.

No, now was not the time to sell and move away. Leah felt God would let her know when the time was right. For now, she was going to the store to hopefully buy only what was on her list.

The store was not as crowded today, for which she was grateful. Pushing her buggy down an aisle, a lady came up to her and said, "Excuse me, could I ask a favor of you?"

Leah looked at the lady and asked, "How can I help you?"

"I really need to go to the bathroom, but I have four boys here and can't take them in with me. Would you mind watching them long enough for me to use the bathroom? I won't be long."

Leah smiled. "I don't mind at all. We will stay right here until you come back."

With that, the lady made a dash toward the bathroom. Leah turned to the boys and asked them if they enjoyed shopping, but they just looked at her and never said a word. Then she asked them what school they went to. Again, total silence. Looking the boys over, Leah noticed their clothes were worn and dirty. She asked the boys if they liked ice cream and what flavor was their favorite. Still no reply. Then she said to the tallest boy, "My name is Leah Conner. You look to be the oldest, what is your name?"

The boy replied, "Daniel."

Turning to the next boy, she asked, "What is your name?"

"Stephen." How about you, what is your name?

"Caleb." The youngest child smiled at her and said, "My name is Benjamin."

"Well, boys, it is nice to meet you. Do any of you play ball?" They just looked at her and said nothing. Leah wasn't sure what to do at this point and began looking around to see if she could see their mother. She was nowhere in sight.

Then she asked the boys how old they were. They stood looking at her and saying nothing. "Okay, Benjamin, how old are you?" Leah asked. He looked at the biggest boy, and Daniel said, "He's five." Then she asked him how old his brothers were. For a few minutes Daniel didn't say anything, then he said, "Caleb is six, Stephen is eight, and I'm nine."

Leah said, "I bet your little brothers look up to you. You seem protective over them." Back to silence again, with the boys looking at her.

Thirty minutes went by and still no sign of the lady. Taking the boys up front where the bathrooms were, Leah asked a clerk if she would go inside the bathroom and check to see if a lady about medium height with long brown hair was in there. The clerk came out and said, "I'm sorry, but there is no one in there."

Looking back at the boys, Leah didn't know what to do. Then she asked, "Do you know where your mother may have gone? Was she sick? Would she have gone back to your car?"

The boys just looked at her.

Turning to the clerk, Leah explained about the boys. "What do I do? I don't know them or who the lady was."

The clerk took Leah and the boys to the back of the store and called the police. She brought out chairs for them to sit in until the police arrived.

When the police officer finally arrived, he looked at Leah and said, "Are you Mrs. David Conner?"

Smiling, Leah replied, "Yes, I am. How do you know me?"

"I'm Officer Kyle Kelley. Your husband used to come to the station twice a week to witness and counsel the inmates. He was respected and well-liked by all. I remember you coming in with him some, and you always brought cookies, cupcakes, or some little treat. I'm terribly sorry about his passing. He has been greatly missed."

Fighting back tears, Leah said, "Thank you so much for your kind words. David loved visiting the station."

"Well, now, Mrs. Conner, what can I do for you?"

Leah explained about the lady needing to go to the bathroom and asking her to watch the boys. Only the lady has never come back, and she didn't want to walk off and leave the boys.

"This is sad," said Officer Kelley. "Did you get the name of the lady?"

"No, I'm sorry, I never thought about her not coming back. We can ask the boys."

Officer Kelly walked over to the boys and looked at Daniel. "What is your mom's name?"

The boys just looked at Officer Kelley and never said a word.

"Boys, I'm here to help you. If you could give me some information, we can hopefully find your mom."

Still not a word was spoken.

"If you won't help us, we will have to call child services. Do you boys understand? We are only trying to help you. You boys have done nothing wrong, and you're not in any trouble."

Still the boys never said a word.

"I'll have to call Child Services and see if they can find some foster parents to take them in," the officer told Leah.

"Officer Kelley, do you mean the boys will be spilt up? Can't they stay together?"

"Mrs. Conner, it's hard to find a foster parent that will take in four children at one time. They will be split up for a while anyway, at least until we can find out who their mother is and if she wants her children back."

Leah turned to look at the boys, and her heart broke. "Officer Kelley, is it possible that I could take all four boys home with me until you can locate their mother?"

"Mrs. Conner, I don't think you realize what you are asking. You don't know these boys. To take them into your home is not a good idea, especially since you are a widow."

"I have plenty of room, and you could call or stop by anytime to check on them. Please, let me try. I don't think separating them would be good."

"If Mr. Conner was alive, things would be different, but since it is just you, it's too risky."

"I understand what you're saying, and I appreciate your concern, but Officer Kelley, I promised their mother I would stay with them till she returned and besides, God is with me, and I have a peace about it. Let me at least try tonight and see how it goes."

"I still need to call Child Services and report this. This is not my decision it will be up to them where the boys will go. Besides, to be a foster parent has many requirements."

"Are you saying I don't qualify to be a foster parent?"

"No, I'm not saying that. I don't know all the rules and regulations, but I do know you have to complete a program of some kind to become a foster parent, a background check is required, you will need a physical, and some other things. I don't know if they will let you take the boys without first meeting the requirements."

"Once the person from Child Services comes, could you speak on my behalf that the children would be safe in my care? I really want to take the boys home with me."

"Let me call Child Services, and we can go from there."

"Will it be alright if I take the boys over to the food bar and get them something to eat while we wait? Would you like for us to pick you up something also?"

"Don't go anywhere else other than the food bar and no, thank you. Appreciate you asking."

Leah took the boys to the food bar and told them they could order whatever they wanted to eat. At first, they just looked at each other, not sure what to do. Then Leah explained they could put anything from the food bar on their plate. Still a little uncertain, the boys put little food on their plates, then went and sat down to eat.

They ate their food in no time. "Would you boys like to go back and fill your plates up again?" Leah asked. "Don't worry about the cost. I'll take care of the bill."

The boys went back, and this time put more food on their plates. They ate like they had not eaten in days. Leah felt so sorry for them and more than ever wanted to take them home with her. Folding her hands, she bowed her head and asked God to please make a way that she would be able to keep the boys together and for as long as necessary.

After they had eaten, they went back to Officer Kelley. He was talking to a lady they had not seen before. You could tell the conversation they were having was a little heated. Leah and the boys stayed back until they motioned for them.

Officer Kelley said, "Mrs. Conner, this is Julie Knight from Child Services. I have explained everything to her, and she has some questions for you."

Leah and Ms. Knight shook hands. Julie said, "Mrs. Conner, if you can step over here away from everyone, I would like to go over some things with you. Officer Kelley will watch the boys while we talk."

Leah took a deep breath and quietly prayed, "Lord, on behalf of those boys, please help them to stay together. They are just children, please have mercy on them."

As Julie started asking questions, Leah knew she was not

going to meet the requirements, yet she answered the questions honestly. Julie asked the names and ages of the boys. Leah was trying to remember their ages, but all she knew was their first names. She never thought to ask what their last name was.

"Officer Kelley said they would not answer his questions at all. He seems to think you might be able to get some answers from them. Mrs. Conner, I need to know what their first and last names and ages are. It's important for my report," Julie said.

Leah went over to the boys to get this information and at first, they didn't want to talk. Finally, Daniel gave her the information she needed.

Going back to Julie, Leah said, "Daniel Taylor, age nine, Stephen age eight, Caleb age six, and Benjamin, age five."

"I take it the other boys' last name is Taylor also?" Julie asked.

Leah, with tears in her eyes, replied, "Daniel said he thought so, but they have different dads."

"By any chance, did they say what their mother's name was?"

Leah said, "Daniel said all he knew was everyone called her Missy. He didn't know if her last name was Taylor. She never told them."

After Julie had finished questioning Leah, she got up and went to a room to make some phone calls.

Leah looked at Officer Kelley and said, "I'm afraid I won't be able to get the boys. Ms. Knight has gone to make some phone calls and will be back in a few minutes."

It seemed like it was taking days for Julie to return. Finally, she came out from the room and said, "We are short-handed on foster parents. I have talked to my boss, and he has agreed to let the boys stay with you tonight, provided I can go to your house and do a walk-through. Officer Kelley gave you a high recommendation. He also said you might consider becoming a foster parent for the boys."

Leah was so excited, she hugged Officer Kelley and Julie Knight. "This is wonderful. Let me know what I need to do to be a foster parent for them. I'll put the boys in the car, and you can follow us home.”

“Mrs. Conner, if everything checks out, you will have to take classes and go to some meetings. There is a lot you must do to become a foster parent, and there is a great need for people to become foster parents. Some do it out of love for the children, while others do it for the money.”

“Oh, it's not about the money,” said Leah. “My reason is purely out of love.” With that, she turned to the boys. “Okay guys, you’re going to my house at least for the night. How does that sound?”

The boys looked at each other, and then Daniel spoke up. “Is our mom not coming back?”

Julie told Daniel, “At this point we are not exactly sure of anything. We are going to try to find your mom and see what happened. When we get to Mrs. Conner's, we can all sit down and go over some things. We are here to help you.”

Leah then took the boys to her car and headed to her house. Benjamin asked, “Do you have a house with beds?”

Leah smiled, “Yes, Benjamin, I have a big house. I think you will like it when you see it.” The rest of the drive home was a quiet one. Pulling into the driveway, Leah opened the garage door to pull her car in. The boys looked out the car window in amazement.

Caleb said, “Your car smells so nice, and your seats are soft. I like your car.”

Leah thanked him, then took them inside the house. They just stood in the kitchen looking around, taking it all in, and Leah heard a soft, collective, “Wow,” from the boys. The doorbell rang and Leah went to let Julie Knight in. The boys stayed put in the kitchen and never moved.

“Boys, Ms. Knight is here. Come on into the den so we can all talk.” When they walked into the den, again the boys froze.

Leah said, “Come take a seat anywhere.”

Daniel said, “Mrs. Conner, your house is really nice and our clothes, well, we probably should just stand.”

“Nonsense, boys, come on over and have a seat. We will take

care of your clothes later after Ms. Knight is finished." After taking their seats, the boys sat still.

Julie Knight went over several things that Leah would need to do and then asked the boys questions about their mother, where they went to school, where they lived. The answers they gave broke Leah's heart that much more. Her home was an average home in an average neighborhood, but she soon realized to the boys, it was a mansion. When Julie Knight left, Leah got the boys back in the car and went clothes shopping. Each boy picked out two shirts, two pairs of pants, five pairs of underwear, five pairs of socks, and one pair of shoes. They also picked out a pair of pajamas, toothbrush, combs, and deodorant. They were so excited; it was like celebrating a birthday.

Back at the house, Leah showed them where their rooms were. Daniel and Stephen shared one room, and Caleb and Benjamin shared another room. Then she showed them the bathrooms, and where she kept the towels, soap, and shampoo. When they had showered and put on fresh clothes, they came into the kitchen where Leah was cooking.

"Oh, my, look at you boys. Don't you look sharp!" Leah said. "How do you feel, and how do you like your rooms?"

Benjamin came up to Leah and said, "Smell me. I smell good." Leah leaned down to sniff Benjamin, and here came the others.

"Are you boys hungry? I have cooked dinner for us. If you're ready, take a seat at the table, and I'll bring you each a plate."

The boys hurried to get seats at the table. As soon as Leah set the food down, they started eating. "Boys, wait just a minute. Before we eat, here at this house, we always say grace."

The boys looked at each other, and then they all said, "Grace," and started eating. Leah said, "No, that's not exactly what I meant. We must first pray and thank our heavenly Father for our food."

Stephen asked, "Who is our heavenly Father? Has he always been around?"

Trying to explain, Leah had the boys put their hands together and bow their heads. Then she prayed, ending with "Amen."

Benjamin smiled at Leah, "That was nice. We've never done anything like that before."

After dinner, Leah took them all through the house to show them where everything was. Then they went to the den to talk. Daniel, being the oldest said, "I haven't got to sleep in a bed in years."

"Where do you guys normally sleep, Daniel?"

"Mostly in our mom's car, or if she had a new guy in her life, we had to sleep on his floor."

When it was time for bed, she had them brush their teeth. Not used to doing this, they brushed and brushed. Finally, Leah went to check on them. "What is taking so long to brush your teeth?"

Daniel said, "Our teeth feel so good we just want to keep brushing."

Benjamin gave Leah a wide, toothy smile and said, "Look! What do you think?"

"My, they do look nice," Leah told him. "You boys have done a really good job."

Next came bedtime, and Leah explained that they needed to pray every night before they went to sleep. She first asked if they had anyone they would like to pray for or if they were thankful for anything.

Five-year-old Benjamin, the youngest of the boys, climbed up in Leah's lap and said, "I'm thankful for you. I'm glad our mom picked you to watch us today." Leah felt tears in her eyes.

Giving Benjamin a hug, she said, "I'm glad your mom picked me, too."

Stephen and Caleb said at the same time, "We are glad we get to stay with you." Caleb added, "We've never been this happy or clean in a long time."

Daniel added, "We have a bed to sleep in tonight, and our stomachs are full."

Having the boys hold hands and stand in a circle with her, heads bowed, Leah thanked God not only for the boys, but also gave thanks for what each boy had said. Tucking them in, Leah kissed each one on the forehead, and then turned out the lights. As she walked through the house, she stopped and looked around. Now she knew why she hadn't heard from God about selling the house. He had four little boys who needed a home and someone to love them coming her way. Lifting her hands high, she said, "Thank You, Lord. Now my house is full again. Show me, Lord, what I need to do to help each boy. I pray that they will grow to have a desire to serve You, always. Thank you for your many blessings you have given us today."

Three

Diane woke up about eleven o'clock that night. She decided to freshen up her face and go for a walk. She needed to get away from the apartment and try to clear her head. She had no idea what she was going to do. The street was empty and before she realized it, she had walked several blocks from her apartment. A small cafe was open, so she went in to order a soda. She heard a man say, "Pardon me, you look familiar. I can't place where we have met."

Looking at the man, Diane said, "I'm sorry, you must have me confused with someone else. This is my first time in here."

"Mind if I join you? You look like you could use a friend."

"Sir, I do mind. Now if you will go away and leave me alone…"

The man then said, "How would you like to make some money on the side?"

Diane never said a word, trying to ignore the man and hoping he would go away. Then he took a napkin and wrote down a dollar amount and pushed it in front of her. "I personally guarantee you this amount tonight."

Looking down at the amount on the napkin, Diane couldn't believe what she was seeing. Turning to the man, Diane asked, "For that kind of money, what do I have to do?"

"My name is Bo. I have businessmen come in from all over the world. They stay in nice hotels, and all you are required to do is make them happy for the night. You will be paid the next morning, and sometimes they give you a little extra if they are really pleased."

"Do I have to split my money with you? If so, forget it. Been there, done that, bought the T-shirt."

"No, the businessmen pay me to find them a nice lady. If you are good, they will ask for you when they come back into town. They let me know if I send them one worth their money. If I get a bad report, I never hook you up again. Then you are on your own."

Diane was desperate for money. Could she do this? What all would be required of her? She knew she couldn't face going back to her job and seeing Jake and Ruby together.

Bo said, "Hey, try it once. If it's not your bag, forget it. If it appeals to you, let me know, and I'll keep you in business. What do you say?"

"Where do I have to go, and what does this guy look like?" Diane was so unsure of this.

"Come with me and I'll show you. Again, if you don't like what you see, I'll bring you right back here."

Diane thought she had nothing to lose, so she followed Bo to his car, a fancy red sports car parked just outside the cafe. He drove her to Hotel Copeland, one of the finer hotels in this area of Virginia. Bo parked across the street from the hotel and said, "In a few minutes the man you are to meet will be pulling up."

Just as Bo had promised, in a few minutes, a guy in a Jaguar pulled up. Diane could see he was handsome. As he got out, Bo said, "There's your man. What do you think?"

Diane couldn't believe someone like him would want to be with her.

"I'll call and tell him you will meet him in the lobby if that's okay. Are you ready?"

"I'm ready, I think I can do this." Still, in the back of her mind she wasn't sure.

Bo made the call. "Hey, this is Bo, I have you a sweet one. She can meet you in the lobby. She will have on jeans and a blue top. Catch you later, man."

Turning to Diane, he said, "He's all yours. Make the best of it, and you could have yourself a full-time job."

"Bo, if it works out, how do I find you?"

"I'll be down at the cafe. I'm in and out so if I'm not there, just hang loose and I'll be in soon."

Diane opened the car door and walked across the street to the hotel. When she turned to look back, Bo was gone. Walking into the hotel, she looked around to see if she could find the handsome man she had seen earlier. Someone from behind her said, "I believe you are looking for me!"

Diane nearly jumped out of her skin. Sure enough, standing behind her was the guy from the Jaguar. Taking her arm, they went to the elevator. Once inside, she said, "Bo didn't tell me your name."

"What name would you like for me to have? You pick one, and that is what I'll go by."

Looking at him, Diane said, "You mean you won't tell me who you are?"

"Bo knows, and that's all that matters. I don't ask for your name unless I decide to make you my regular when I'm in town. Then and only then will our true names be shared."

When the elevator door opened, his room was directly in front of it. He unlocked the door and held it open for Diane. She walked in and noticed the luxurious room was bigger than her whole apartment. From that point on, Diane did not think about Jake and Ruby. She was in a different world than what she was used to.

When Diane woke the next morning, on the man's pillow was some money. He was nowhere in sight. She got up, showered, dressed, and was just getting ready to leave when a knock came on the door.

She opened it, and there stood a waiter. "Good morning, Miss. I have your breakfast ready for you. Where would you like for me to set it?"

Not expecting this, Diane said, "Put it here on the table. Who ordered this?"

The waiter said, "The gentleman in this room gave instructions to bring breakfast up to you before you left."

Hoping to find out the man's name, Diane asked "What did you say the gentleman's name was?"

The waiter smiled, "I didn't say his name. I said he asked that we bring you breakfast. Hope you enjoy it." With that he left the room.

Taking the lid from the plates, Diane said, "Oh, my," and what a breakfast she had. Never in her whole life had she sat down to something like this. With no one around, Diane ate till she was stuffed. Thinking back to last night, and now breakfast, yes, she could get used to working like this. Jake had really done her a favor, but she hadn't realized it at the time. After finishing breakfast, Diane left the room and went downstairs. As she walked outside, she realized she didn't have any transportation. Bo had dropped her off last night and she wasn't familiar with this part of town. Diane stood at the edge of the sidewalk, looking around and considering her options, when a car pulled up in front of her.

"Need a ride, lady?" It was Bo.

Diane smiled, "I'm so glad to see you. How did you know I needed a ride?"

"I knew after I dropped you off last night that you would need a ride home. Besides, the clerk at the front desk called and told me breakfast had been delivered to your room. So, I estimated about how long it would take you to eat, and here I am."

"Bo, you have people spying on me?"

"Not exactly, Diane. I knew you would need a ride home and asked that they let me know. Besides, you did good last night. The gentleman you were with would like to see you the next time he is in town."

"Really? I was so scared last night. He was nice, but I take it he is married?"

"Diane, I'm here to help the guys out. They pay good money for my services, and I make sure they get a nice lady. You see, I have been watching you for some time. I have seen your boyfriend out with other women besides you, so I knew it was a matter of time before he got caught. I also noticed you were only with him. I also watched him carry nearly everything from your apartment, so I knew he didn't leave you much, and you would need extra cash to refurnish the place. Did I assume correctly?"

"Yes, Bo, you are much correct, except I didn't know Jake was with other women. I thought he left me for Ruby."

"Well, my dear, I'm not sure who this Ruby lady is, but Jake has been out with other women, so things between them may not last long. Seems he can't decide who he wants to be with."

"That's all behind me now, Bo. Yesterday, at this time, I was a mess, but thanks to you, I feel like I'm ready to move on with my life."

"Good, glad to hear this. So, Diane, meet me tonight at Henry's Cafe. I'll have everything set up for you, and we'll go from there. Oh, and here's your money for your work last night."

Taking the money, Diane replied, "When I woke up this morning, there was some money on his pillow. It wasn't the amount we had discussed last night, so I was a little confused."

"Remember, I said sometimes they will give you a little extra. That's what he did."

Getting out of the car, Diane said, "Thanks, Bo."

Turing to go to her apartment, she stopped, turned to Bo, and said, "I must admit when I first met you, I had reservations about you. Maybe I was wrong." Smiling, Diane went up the walk to her apartment.

Four

Leah got up early to prepare breakfast for the boys. Not sure what they might like, she fixed a little of everything. Just as Leah was getting ready to go wake up the boys, Nora knocked at the door. Letting her in, Leah said, "Oh, Nora, I have so much to tell you. I know now why I didn't want to sell the house."

Looking around the kitchen, Nora turned to Leah, "Who are you fixing all this food for? An army?"

"That's what I want to tell you. I know you are going to think I have lost my mind, but it's really a blessing from God."

About that time, Daniel walked into the kitchen. "Something smells so good."

Nora looked at Daniel and asked, "Who are you?"

About that time, Benjamin came in and said, "I'm hungry, and it smells good in here."

Then Stephen and Caleb walked in.

"Where did these boys come from?" Nora asked in amazement. "Are they family?"

"Let me get the boys fed, and I'll explain everything to you. I'm so happy, and these boys need me as much as I need them."

Smiling, Leah turned to the boys and said, "Boys, remember to pray before you eat," then motioned for Nora to follow her into the adjoining room.

The women were barely out of the boys' sight when Nora said, "Leah, I don't think you realize what you are doing. We have been neighbors for years, and I know you have a big heart, but if you are thinking of taking on four boys, we really do need to talk."

"Nora, we'll talk later. Right now, I need to get the boys fed and ready for the day. Ms. Knight will be by soon, and I want the boys looking their best."

"Leah, who is Ms. Knight? Is that the boy's mother?"

"No, she is a social worker who is going to help me become a foster parent. I'm taking these boys in and hopefully will raise them."

"Leah, have you lost your mind? What are you thinking? You are a widow and not a young widow, might I add. You have grown daughters with children of their own. Taking on one child would be bad enough, but four?"

"Nora, these boys are brothers. They need to stay together, and I intend to see to it that they are not split up. We'll talk about this later. Right now, I have things to do, if you will excuse me."

Nora turned and went home, mumbling as she went.

Daniel looked at Leah and said, "I don't think she likes us."

"Now, don't you boys worry about Nora. She is really a sweet neighbor. I'll talk to her more, and then she will understand what we are doing. As soon as you finish your breakfast, brush your teeth, change into your clothes for the day, and make sure you make your beds."

The boys looked at each other, then Caleb asked, "What do you want us to do with the bed?"

Realizing the boys had never had a real bed, Leah said, "I'll show you."

The boys could not understand why you needed to fix the bed up all nice and neat since you would be sleeping in it that night, but they agreed that it did look nice and made the room look better, too.

The doorbell rang, and Leah went to let Ms. Knight in.

"Mrs. Conner, before I speak with the boys, I would like to have a few minutes alone with you."

Leah had the boys go outside and sit in the chairs on the patio until she called for them.

"Mrs. Conner, have you taken time to go over the task before you? The boys may seem well-behaved now, but that could change in a few days or weeks. You know nothing about them, where they came from, any health issues they may have, and the list goes on. We are grateful for what you are doing, but you are a widow and retired. Like I said yesterday, you are required to take some classes and have a background check. In fact, here is a sheet listing what is required of a foster parent.”

“Ms. Knight, Officer Kelley talked to me yesterday about some of this. I’m willing to do whatever it takes to keep those boys here with me. It’s not about the money. Any money that comes in for those guys will be spent on them. I’ll make sure they are in school every weekday and in church every Sunday, and I’ll try to get them involved in sports if they choose. Those boys need a solid home life filled with love, and I need this house to be filled with laughter and happiness. My children are grown and moved away. I could easily sell this house and move into a smaller home, but if I did that, those boys would be split up. I’m happy here. I think this is where God wants me, and I think He wants those boys here also.”

“Mrs. Conner, read over the papers while I talk to the boys. I need some information and, hopefully, they can help me out. We are grateful for what you are willing to do, but give it some serious thought.”

“I have been praying about what I need to do. God gave me my answer yesterday, and I have peace with this. I plan to take whatever classes I need to. Those boys have a home right here as long as they need one.”

“Again, Mrs. Conner, if at any time it becomes too much, let us know, but do give us some time to find another home for them.”

Ms. Knight got up to go talk to the boys when Leah asked, “Have you noticed the boys all have Bible names? My husband and I and our girls have Bible names. I think God planned it this way. I’m sure He has a special plan for those boys.”

Ms. Knight smiled at Leah. “You know, I have been doing this job for over ten years and never have I ever had the privilege of working with someone like you. I’m positive these boys are in a good, godly home. They don’t realize just how blessed they are. But I still need to speak to them. This isn’t my decision alone. I have to return to the office and give them a report.”

After Ms. Knight finished talking with the boys, she came back inside to talk to Leah. "Mrs. Conner, the boys need to be enrolled in school. Unfortunately, we don't have much information to go on. Daniel is the only one who was of any help, and that wasn't much. I'm going to talk to the school superintendent and see about having the boys tested to see at what levels they need to be placed. I will let you know more details as I find out. In the meantime, we need you to start your classes so we can get you all set up to become an official foster parent as soon as we can. We really have so much to do, so be sure you and the boys get plenty of rest. For the next few weeks, you are going to feel like you are on a roller coaster. Any questions?"

"Yes, should I make an appointment with a doctor so they can get physicals, and how about having them see a dentist?"

"They will need to have that done, so if you can go ahead take care of those appointments, that would be great. Be sure to save the receipts from their doctor visits, and we will reimburse you. Wish we could find some information of some kind on the boys. From what little Daniel remembers, they basically took care of themselves. You have my number. Call anytime should a problem arise or if by some miracle one of them can recall something. That would be most beneficial for us. I'll be in touch with you as soon as I know what we need to do next."

Walking Ms. Knight to the door, Leah thanked her for all her help and for giving her a chance to help the boys. Leah looked outside where the boys appeared content to explore the back yard. While they were outside, she decided to call her pastor. She needed to talk to someone who could be objective.

"Pastor Harrington, this is Leah Conner. How are you today?"

"Why, hello, Leah, so nice to hear from you. To what do I owe the pleasure of this call?"

Leah explained to him everything that had happened. "Pastor Harrington, I miss David so much, especially how we discussed everything before making decisions. With all I have shared with you, I need someone who can pray with me and talk things over so I will do what is right for those boys."

"Leah, let me get back with you. As you were talking, several things came to my mind. It's a blessing to see God's mighty hand at work. Thank you for calling and sharing this story. You will hear from me soon."

Leah did feel better after talking to Pastor Harrington. Her next order of business was getting enrolled for her classes. Everything was now done online. She knew a little about computers but had a feeling the classes might be a bit challenging.

Soon the boys came in ready to eat lunch. Benjamin went straight to his room, then to the bathroom to wash up. Not sure why, Leah never questioned him. After lunch, Leah took the boys to the park to play. She enjoyed watching them have fun. Later they stopped off for ice cream before going home. She tried to find out if they were interested in sports and if so, what kind, but they showed no interest, perhaps because they never had the opportunity to be involved. After dinner, they talked about the Bible again, and she tried to teach them some songs. This they all seemed to enjoy. She wondered if either of their parents were musicians. As soon as the boys were bathed and in bed, Leah went back to the computer to finish up her first lesson of the day.

After an hour of reading and studying, Leah thought it best to call it a night. She was going over things in her mind while preparing to take a shower when she noticed something moving. Not sure what it was, she slowly raised the bathroom throw rug, and there was a turtle. It was a good size, but how in the world did it get into the house? Then she happened to remember Benjamin going straight to his room when he came in from being outside. She went to his room to wake him up.

"Benjamin, wake up. We need to talk."

Raising up, rubbing his eyes, Benjamin asked, "Is it time to get up already?"

"No, Benjamin, but I need to know. Did you bring a turtle in the house today?"

At that Benjamin snapped wide awake. "Is Chester alright? I

put him in a shoe box I found." Jumping out of bed, he looked under the bed and found the shoe box lying on its side.

"Oh, no, Chester got out of his box. I've got to find him."

"It's okay, Benjamin, I know where Chester is. He is in my bathroom."

When Leah and Benjamin walked into the bathroom, the turtle was gone. "Where did he go?" Benjamin asked. "Did you take him back outside?"

"Benjamin, he was right here before I woke you up. He couldn't have gone far." Having raised girls, Leah was not accustomed to finding turtles in her home. She wondered what other creatures may find their way in since boys now lived here.

They were on their knees, crawling around and looking for Chester when Caleb came in the room and asked, "What are you guys doing?"

"Chester got out of the box. Mrs. Conner found him in her bathroom, but now he is gone again. Come on, Caleb, help us find Chester."

Now all three were crawling around on the floor and looking for Chester.

Leah could not believe a turtle could just disappear into thin air. He had to be in her bedroom or bathroom. Caleb woke up Daniel and Stephen to help with the hunt. The boys were having a great time looking for Chester. They even called out, "Chester, where are you? You are in a lot of trouble, you know." Leah wanted so much to find the turtle and put him outside, then go to bed.

They looked for at least an hour with no luck. Leah made the boys go back to bed so she could take her shower and go to bed herself. It had been a long day.

The next morning, while Leah was cooking breakfast, Nora knocked at the door. "Morning, Leah, thought I would stop in and see how things are going. You never came over yesterday for us to talk."

"I'm so sorry, Nora. Yesterday was such a busy day. Grab a

cup of coffee, and I'll fill you in on a few things."

As Leah was talking, Nora felt something on her foot. When she looked down, she spilled her coffee and let out a blood curdling scream. Chester was trying to get on top of her foot. The boys came running into the kitchen, and there were Chester and Nora, both covered with coffee.

Nora looked at the boys and asked, "Which one of you brought this turtle in the house?"

Benjamin dropped his head, "I did. I've never had a pet before, and I wanted to keep him. His name is Chester."

Nora, realizing the harshness in her voice, went over to Benjamin and put her hand on his shoulder. She said in a kinder tone, "Well, Chester certainly gave me a surprise. I didn't expect to find him in Leah's kitchen! I have an idea. Why don't I go home and see if my husband, Nick, can make a fence for Chester so he can stay outside, move around in the grass, and be in an area he is more familiar with?"

"Wow, can he do that? That's great! Can we do it now?"

"You need to get dressed for the day and eat your breakfast. I'll go home and talk to Nick so he can gather up the things needed to make Chester a home."

As Nora passed Leah, she whispered, "Glad we had girls."

Leah just laughed.

Finding a big sturdy box to put Chester in until his new home was made was difficult, but after some searching, they were successful. Leah had Benjamin put Chester and his box outside on the patio.

As soon as the boys could, they went out the door to help Nick make a home for Chester. Leah watched from the kitchen window as Nick and the boys worked on their project. She wondered if David had ever wished for a son. He had never said, but watching Nick and the boys, she figured every man may want a son, just as every woman may want a daughter.

David had been a real trooper with the girls. He played dolls with them, had tea, let them roll his hair with their rollers, and let them put makeup on him. They even painted his nails, which he took some ribbing over at work. Leah had those pictures somewhere. She was so grateful for those memories. Now she would make memories with the boys.

As Leah was watching, she realized that the boys were chatting away with Nick as if they had always known him. What a difference she saw in the boys since she had first met them. They were no longer shy and withdrawn and were acting more like normal children. What a blessing it was to watch them.

Sunday morning, the boys were so full of questions about what church was. Leah tried to explain, but as soon as she answered one question, they had another. They were met at the church door by Pastor Greg Harrington. Leah introduced them and told Pastor Harrington that she wasn't sure which Sunday School class they would need to be put in.

About that time, Cody Lay, a young man who worked with the youth at the church, walked up. "You boys must be with Ms. Leah. I have heard a lot about you and have looked forward to meeting you. If you guys will come with me, I'll show you around and see what class you belong in." The boys were eager to go with Cody and find out all they could about this place called church. Mrs. Conner was always talking about church, prayer, and her Savior Jesus. Leah was thankful that Cody came forward to help with the boys. He was a talented young man, and if the boys could connect with anyone, it would certainly be Cody.

After church, Leah didn't have to ask how the boys liked church. They were all talking at the same time with so much enthusiasm. Then right out of the blue Stephen asked, "When do we get to go back to church? We loved it, and Mr. Cody is really a cool guy."

Smiling, Leah said, "On Sundays. We go that morning and at night. Then on Wednesdays we go again in the evening. Wednesday nights give you that little boost you need to carry you through your week."

"Is that a drink of some kind?" asked Stephen. "Our mom used to say she needed a boost, then she would drink something from a bottle. She said it really helped her."

Shocked by Stephen's reply, Leah said, "No, that's not what I meant at all. Boost means to lift one up, to help one to feel better. When you go to church on Wednesday nights, hearing God's Word and fellowshipping with your friends is a good way to make you feel better, and that will carry you through your week until Sunday."

"Mom always said her drink made her feel good and that's why she kept her bottle close by. She said it was her boost. So why don't we drink something from a bottle?" asked Stephen.

Caleb spoke up, "Don't you remember, Mom said we should never drink from her bottle. She said it was for adults only. They probably have bottles for kids at church. I'm sure Cody will have it for us."

Pulling into the driveway, Leah told the boys to go to the den, and that she would try to explain about Wednesday nights at church. As the boys headed for the den, Leah took a moment to sit in the car and say a prayer.

Who would have ever thought that the word "boost" would turn out like this? Her world and the boys' world were nothing alike. They could use the same word yet have two totally different meanings.

Just as Leah sat down to talk to the boys, the doorbell rang. It was Cody, wanting to know if the boys could spend the afternoon with him. He would bring them to church tonight, and Leah could pick them up then. Hearing this, the boys were eager to go with Cody.

As the boys went to their rooms to get ready, Leah took Cody aside and explained the conversation they had on the drive home.

Smiling, Cody gave Leah a hug. "Don't worry, I'll explain it to the guys. I have some other things I want to talk to them about."

Having the afternoon to herself was a blessing. This gave Leah some time to go over her lessons on being a foster parent. There is no manual on how to raise children. It's the same for being a foster parent, only you don't know what a foster child has been subjected to. This makes parenting more challenging.

Five

Diane was beginning to like the money she was making. Never had she ever made this kind of money in a month at the factory where she had worked. The men Bo hooked her up with were nice, none were shabby, even a few had requested her again, but she still didn't know their names. Bo told her that the name he used for her was not her real name. The men knew her only as Peyton.

With a month's work behind her, she was able to rent a decent apartment and buy a nice used car that she could afford to make payments on. On the nights she was to work, she no longer met Bo at the café. Instead, he came by and picked her up at her apartment. She was also able to update her wardrobe.

One Saturday morning when Bo had dropped her off at her apartment, Diane thought the day was too beautiful to stay inside, so she decided to spend the afternoon at the park. Changing and packing a few snacks to take with her, she got into her car and headed to the park. To her surprise, the park was not crowded at all. She had made about two laps on the walking trail when she came upon Jake and Ruby.

"Diane, it's so good to see you," replied Ruby.

"I'm sure it is," smiled Diane. "Hope you two are doing well?"

"We are happy together. How is your life going?" asked Jake.

"Well, let me say this, you two did me a big favor. At the time, I didn't realize it. I'm the happiest I have been in a long time, and I have you both to thank. Now if you will excuse me, I need to finish my walk." With that, she proceeded to walk on.

"Jake, Diane didn't seem at all upset seeing us together. She looks good, even happy. What do you think is going on?" asked Ruby.

"I don't know, but she did seem different. Even attractive."

"Jake, what do you mean by that remark? Remember you left

her for me. You're not thinking of trying to get back with Diane, are you?"

"I don't know that she would even consider taking me back after the way I left her. I took everything that was worth anything and cleaned out the bank account. What money she had was whatever was in her purse. Yet, she was so chipper and cordial to us."

"Well, we need to wish her well and hope we never run into her again." Taking Jake's arm, Ruby was hoping Jake wasn't having any second thoughts about staying with her.

When Diane got home, Bo called. "Hey, I know you wanted a night off, but I have this guy in from out west. He will be here a few days and wanted to know if I could fix him up with someone special. I immediately thought of you. Are you interested?"

"Well, do you think he will make it worth my while?" asked Diane.

"He is a wealthy young man. Owns several acres of land and has a ranch. From what I have gathered, he can afford anything."

"Hmmm, this might be worth my time. Okay, what time do I need to be ready?"

"I'll pick you up around seven o'clock. He is staying at the Madison Hotel. It will be a good drive. I don't usually go that far out, but something about this guy has impressed me."

"Anything particular I need to wear tonight?"

"He didn't say anything about going out anywhere with you, but to be on the safe side, you might want to wear a nice pant suit and heels. You can always tuck another set of clothes in your purse."

"Bo, what kind of purse are you expecting me to carry? An overnight bag?"

"No, take some leggings or something, I don't know, I'm not a woman. You women can cram more things in a purse no matter what size the bag is. See you at seven."

As Bo and Diane pulled up at the Madison, she could see that it was truly a beautiful hotel. She could only imagine what the inside looked like.

As she got out of the car, Bo said, "See you in the morning," and then he was off. Looking around, Diane saw that all the men had on business suits, and Bo didn't mention what this guy would be wearing.

"Excuse me, are you Peyton?"

Diane turned around and saw standing before her a man with the bluest eyes she had ever seen, jet black hair, and a well-built body, the best she could tell.

"Yes, I'm Peyton."

"Great. Bo said he had someone attractive for me. He wasn't lying. Have you had dinner yet? I have been in meetings all day and haven't had a chance to eat."

Trying to find her voice, Diane finally said, "I had a snack this afternoon. I hope I am dressed well enough for dinner?"

"You look perfect. The hotel here has a nice restaurant, I have been told. Shall we go find out?"

He took Diane's arm and led her inside to the restaurant. Like Bo had said, there was something different about this guy. Normally, she met a guy and that was it, but something about this one was so different. She wasn't her normal calm self, and she really wanted to impress him.

The next morning when she woke up, she expected to be alone. Instead, he was taking a shower. Diane decided to get dressed and leave before he came out, but just as she was putting on her shoes, he walked in.

"Are you leaving already?" he asked.

Not sure what to say, Diane said, "I thought maybe you were getting ready to leave. I wasn't for sure."

"No, I have some time before my next meeting. Would you like to have breakfast with me?"

Diane smiled at the thought of being invited to breakfast, then looked down at the leggings and T-shirt she had slipped on instead of the pantsuit. "Sure, let me change."

"You are welcome to shower or whatever you need to do. I'll

be in the next room whenever you are ready," he said, picking up his phone and some papers.

When Diane came out, she said, "I wish I knew your name. It's nice to have a name to go with a person."

Taking Diane by the arm, he said, "Call me John." Then they left for the restaurant.

Diane wondered if John was his real name. That's what all the men she met went by.

John was easy to talk to, and after breakfast, he walked her outside to wait for her ride. Turning to her he asked, "Why are you doing a job like this? You deserve much better."

"I have my reasons, and besides, it pays the bills."

"Think about what we have talked about. Maybe you will consider getting a job with benefits and something with a future."

"I happen to like my job. Just think, if I didn't have this job, we would have never met. Who knows, we may meet again."

Turning to leave for his meeting, John said, "Please think about it." Then he was gone.

With her thoughts on this man named John, she wasn't aware Bo had pulled up.

"Hey, are you just going to stand there all day or what?"

"Sorry, Bo, I didn't see you pull up. I'm ready."

"So how was your night with the man from out West?"

"He was nice. By any chance will he be needing anyone tonight? If so, I am available."

"He didn't say anything about tonight, but I do have your money, and he gave me an extra envelope for you."

Looking inside the envelope, Diane nearly passed out. "Oh my, he gave this to you to give to me?"

"Yeah. I didn't ask what it was, but from the feel of it, I'd say he left you a good tip."

Diane counted out the money, and he had left her three thousand dollars. With tears in her eyes, she didn't know what to say.

"Girl, you must have left one good impression with that guy. I was told he had money, so looks like he does."

Bo took her home and said he would give her a call when another job came in.

Diane couldn't believe John had left her that much money. He had told her she needed to get out of this line of work. Maybe he was hoping she would take his advice and the money was an incentive. For some reason, John seemed so different. She always came home and thought nothing about the customer she had been with, but with John, it was different. What was it about him that kept him on her mind? It was like she could think of nothing else but him.

She sent Bo a text and told him she needed to talk to him. Maybe he could help her sort things out. He had told her in the beginning not to read anything into her interactions with any of the men. She had a job and that was what she was to do.

Bo texted back that he was unavailable to talk, and he would check in with her tomorrow.

Getting ready for bed, Diane knew it was going to be a long night. So, she decided to take a sleeping pill to help her rest. She needed something to help get John off her mind.

Six

Leah had managed, with the help of Julie Knight, to get the boys in school, get physicals, and make dental appointments. So far everything was going well. The boys had adapted to living with her, and she couldn't imagine them not being with her. She was so thankful that she had not sold her home and moved into something smaller. They were a blessing to her.

On a Monday afternoon the boys brought home a note from their teachers at school wanting to have a conference with her on Thursday after school. Leah signed the papers for them to take back the next day. Later she saw Nora outside and went over to talk to her. She told her about the notes and was worried there was a problem with boys.

"Leah, surely there's no problem. They have only been in school a little over three months, and school will soon be out for the summer."

"Nora, I know. This is the first time they have brought home a note stating a conference was needed. They always do their homework and here at home they are well-behaved. They don't get into anything. Even in church, Cody says the boys listen to his teachings and get along so well with the other children."

"Maybe it's more of a progress report to inform you on how they are doing. I don't think the boys are in any kind of trouble. I will be greatly surprised if they are."

"Guess I'll find out Thursday afternoon." The more Leah thought about it and prayed, she decided to call Pastor Greg and ask him to be in prayer for her this Thursday and explain about the notes.

On Thursday, Leah got to school a few minutes early but was told she would have to wait in her car till the teachers were ready for her. They would call her when she could come in.

While waiting, she watched as the children either climbed aboard buses or got into cars to go home. When the parking lot was nearly empty, her phone beeped, and she found a text from Cody Lay. "Praying for you and the boys now." Pastor Greg must have shared her request with Cody, since he was so close to the boys.

Then she had another beep; it was Pastor Greg. "Lifting everyone up in prayer. Remember, you are not alone, God is right beside you."

Withs tears in her eyes, Leah was so thankful for the friends she had and could count on. Another beep and it was the school letting her know she could come to the door, and someone would let her in. As Leah started walking to the school door, her phone beeped again with a text from Nora. "Nick and I are praying for you and the boys. Also, the teachers."

Leah drew a deep breath and said, "Thank you, Lord, for the sweet people you have brought into my life."

A lady was waiting at the door to let Leah in. She took her to a conference room and told her the teachers would be in shortly.

In a few minutes, four ladies came in and sat down across from Leah.

"Mrs. Conner, I'm Mrs. Jordan, Daniel's teacher."

"I'm Mrs. Wade, Stephen's teacher."

"I'm Mrs. Mason, Caleb's teacher."

"I'm Mrs. Jefferies, Benjamin's teacher."

Mrs. Jordan began the conference by saying, "Mrs. Connor, we are so glad you could meet with us today. First, we want to thank you for taking these boys in. This is certainly a big undertaking, and we commend you for it. I am going to go over things with you about Daniel, then each teacher will go over with you about the other children. We can all see progress in the boys no longer than they have been here. They seem so eager to learn. I feel like Daniel has had some schooling. We gave each child a test on their first day here so we would know where to place them. Daniel did quite well. Each child was given another test last week to see what progress they had made. Daniel showed much improvement. He is still not at the level he needs to be, but I feel that by working through the summer and testing him again before school starts this fall, he should be close to where he needs to be. I know children don't want to give up summer vacation, but it could truly benefit him."

Leah asked, "What did you mean when you said you think Daniel has had some schooling?"

"Mrs. Conner, when Julie Knight, the social worker, came to get them enrolled, she had no information on them. What Daniel was able to tell her is all she had to go on and that wasn't much. She pulled a lot of strings to get the boys registered here so they could be in school. She should be here in a few minutes and can explain more of what she is doing."

The second teacher began to speak. "Mrs. Conner, like I said earlier, I'm Mrs. Wade, Stephen's teacher. Like Daniel, he is so eager to learn. He came to me one day and told me he didn't understand what I was talking about in math. He asked if he could stay in at recess and would I help him. That child had rather stay in and do work than go play. I keep him in three days a week at recess but told him he needed to go out on the other two days to play and make friends. He told me that when he didn't understand things, Daniel always helped him. Here in the classroom, he doesn't have his brother. As Mrs. Jordan said about Daniel, summer school would be a great benefit to Stephen. The earlier he can learn these things, the more it will help him as he moves on to the next grade. If he doesn't grasp it now, it will only hurt him later."

"Oh, I agree. The boys do their homework every night. I had no idea they were having any problems."

"That's because Stephen goes to Daniel for help. Not to you. Daniel has always been there for him, and he feels comfortable asking him for help."

"Oh, my, I never questioned them for they seemed like they knew what they were doing," Leah replied, feeling like she had let the boys down. She listened with apprehension as the third teacher spoke.

"Mrs. Conner, I'm Mrs. Mason, Caleb's teacher. Like his brothers from the test last week, I can see progress. Caleb has never been in school, so what Daniel has taught him, that's all he knows. Daniel has taught the boys to print their names, tie their shoes, to count, the alphabet, their colors, all that they know. Caleb said Daniel was a good teacher. Summer school for him would be of great benefit."

The fourth teacher's report was similar. She said, "I'm Mrs. Jefferies, Benjamin's teacher. Fortunately, he is not as behind as the other boys, but could still use some improvement. Getting him at an early age has been beneficial."

As Mrs. Jefferies was talking, Julie Knight came in. "Sorry ladies, I am running a little behind. I was with another case. Hello Mrs. Conner, it's so good to see you. Hope the teachers have given you an update on the boys!"

Mrs. Jefferies spoke up, "I was just informing Mrs. Conner about Benjamin. If you would like to fill her in on what you know, it may help her understand a few things."

Taking a notebook from her briefcase, Julie looked at Leah and said, "We have an unusual case here, but we are doing all we can for the boys. It seems Daniel is the only one who has ever been in school, but for a short time. This is based on what he has told us. Where he went to school, we don't know. We have no birthdates, no Social Security numbers, no names of parents. Every direction we turn, we hit a brick wall. The boys have no idea who their daddy is, and the only name they can give us for their mother is "Missy." I asked if this was a nickname and was her real name Melissa. They said they called her mom, and the guys that came around called her Missy. When we ran a check on Missy Taylor or Melissa Taylor, it wasn't the lady we were looking for. We have checked court records, death certificates, hospital records, the list goes on, and nothing was discovered.

"Normally, children don't start school without records of some kind, so I have worked hard to get them in school here. The boys need to have some blood work done, we need to get their blood type, plus a list of other things that I have written out for you. I have sent in forms to try to get them a Social Security number, along with a letter explaining why so many blanks were on the form. The boys will remain in your custody, and we are going to do all we can to find out more about them. We can't thank you enough for what you have done for them. There has been a remarkable change from the first time I met them till I saw them here at school last week."

Looking at Ms. Knight, Leah asked, "What if you never find who the boy's parents are? Could I possibly adopt them? Make them legally mine?"

"For now, Mrs. Conner I wouldn't think about adoption. We still need to do more research. While we are investigating every option we can, what you are doing now not only helps us, but it helps the boys. I will admit, when we first met, I was afraid you wouldn't be able to handle all four boys. You have certainly proven me wrong. In fact, it would be a blessing if we had more foster parents like you," replied Ms. Knight.

"Mrs. Conner, how many computers do you have at home?" asked Ms. Jordan.

Leah said, "We only have the one. Would the boys not be able to share, or will I need to purchase another one?"

"No, no, don't buy one. I have two at home that are not being used, and what I can do is set up a program for Daniel. He will receive an assignment every day, Monday through Friday. At the end of the day, he will send in his homework, and someone will grade it. There will be times he will have a Zoom class, which is helpful. This will give him a chance to see other students studying and doing the same work as he is doing. I'll loan Ms. Wade here the other computer so she can do the same thing for Stephen."

"Oh, Ms. Jordan, that is so thoughtful of you. At home with the one computer, could it be useable for Caleb?"

Ms. Mason spoke up, "Is it a laptop? If so, bring it to the school, and we can get the program he needs loaded into it. He, too, will have days that he will get to Zoom and see other children working on the same things he is."

Leah looked at Ms. Jefferies. "Will Benjamin need one also?"

"It would be helpful. Also, he wouldn't feel left out."

Leah thought for a minute then said, "I think I know of a place

I can borrow one for the summer. A young man at church has taken such an interest in the boys, and he has all kinds of things. I'm sure he would be more than willing to help us out."

Ms. Knight spoke up. "This is wonderful. If we can get all the laptops here at school by Monday so they can get the proper programs loaded into the machines and go over some things with the boys, then we should be set for the summer. Now if only things on my end would go so smoothly."

The boys were brought to the room, where everyone waited. Stephen went up to Leah and asked, "Are we going to get to stay with you?"

Putting her arm around Stephen, Leah gave him a hug. "Yes, you boys will be staying with me for as long as you want. That house is our home. We are a family."

With that the other boys came over to hug Leah. Daniel said, "We were afraid you didn't want us anymore. We don't want to leave. We want to stay with you."

With tears in her eyes, Leah wrapped her arms around the boys. "As far as I'm concerned, you boys are my boys."

That night at the dinner table, Benjamin asked, "Ms. Leah, where did we come from?"

Not sure what Benjamin was getting at, she replied, "What exactly do you mean?"

"You know, how did we get here? Did our mom go out somewhere and get us?"

All four boys were looking at her, waiting for her answer. Not expecting a question like this, Leah thought for a minute and then replied, "Why don't we finish dinner, then while I clean up the kitchen, you boys take your shower and get things ready for tomorrow. Then we will sit down in the den and talk about this."

This seemed to satisfy them for now. Leah needed time to pray and get in her mind what she needed to say and not say. *Oh, if only David were here, he would know exactly how to handle this,* she thought. As soon as Leah went into the den and sat down on the couch, here came the boys.

"Okay, Ms. Leah, where did we come from?" asked Caleb. "Daniel said that mom would go away for a few days and then came home with one of us. He said she had to work hard, for she always came in looking tired, and she was fussy. Do you know where she went to work?"

Leah took a deep breath and said, "Let's see what the Bible says."

Taking her Bible, she turned to the first chapter of Genesis. "Here in the first chapter of the Bible it tells how God created everything," she said. "I will read several verses, and then we will talk about it."

As Leah read the first chapter, the boys sat still taking in everything she read. Daniel said, "You mean God can do all that?"

"Yes, Daniel, God can do anything. Remember in verse 26, it says, "Then God said, 'Let us make man in our image, in our likeness,' then on down in verse 27, it says, 'So God created man in his own image, in the image of God He created him; male and female He created them.' So, God created all of us, He made us the way He wanted us to look. We are all made special and made with love because God is love."

Stephen asked, "You mean God made all those things by himself? How did He know how to do that?"

"If you boys will notice, each of the verses I read started out by saying, 'And God said.' He spoke everything into existence. That's how great He is. We certainly can't do that."

"Wow, if He can do that, He is really something," Caleb replied. "Can we go visit him sometime? I'd like to see what all He can do."

"No, boys, we can't go for a visit, for God is in heaven. As you read and study the Bible, you will learn more about who God is and how you can let him into your life. The Bible is full of instructions on how we should live. Let's take one thing at a time and every night from now on we will go over things in the Bible. We can stay on chapter one for as long as needed, for I want you to understand what it says."

Knowing this wasn't exactly what Benjamin was asking at the dinner table, Leah thought this would be a much better approach, then she could deal with what Benjamin was asking later in time. Also, she would ask Pastor Harrington about the matter, for Leah felt the boys were too young to know about the birds and the bees, as her mother once said.

The boys said their prayers, and after Leah had gone to bed, she could hear them talking about what all God had made. They thought He must be a real neat guy.

Seven

Two days passed and finally Bo called Diane. "Hey, got a job for you tonight, are you interested?"

"Sure, I was beginning to think you had forgotten about me."

"Sorry, I have been busy taking care of some other things and just haven't had the time. This guy will be in town for a few days, and if tonight goes well, you will be working for the next several days. He will be in meetings through the day and should be back at his hotel around eight at night. That's when you will need to be there. He will let me know if any of his plans change."

"That's good. Will you be picking me up, or do you want me to drive?" Diane asked.

"If you could drive that would be great. I have so many things going right now that I'm burning the candle at both ends. Will tell you this much, this guy is very, very, wealthy. What he has offered to pay for your services is more than I have ever gotten. If you play your cards right, you could end up with a nice tip. I'll get with you later in the week to pay you."

"No pressure, right? Thanks for letting me know. I'll see what I can do for this guy to make him happy."

As Bo had said, the guy needed Diane for the next four nights. He was a nice guy, but he didn't miss a beat to let you know he had money. On the morning of the day Diane was leaving, the man came back in the room and laid an envelope on the table. "Here's a little something extra for you. I'll be back in town in about three months. I expect to see you then." With that he walked out the door. Going over to see how much money was in the envelope, Diane gasped. Oh wow! This was just a little extra as Bo would say. Although the guy was not one of her favorites, for this kind of money, she could tolerate it.

Bo kept her busy for the next several months. Diane was so pleased with her bank account. She had never had this much money. For once in her life, she had a decent place to live, a nice car and wore designer clothes. She had contacted Bo and had asked for some time off. She decided to take a small vacation, since now she could afford one.

When Diane returned home, she messaged Bo that she was back. By that evening, she had heard nothing. The next day, again she sent him a message and even tried calling him. Nothing. On the third day, she decided to go to Henry's to see if he had seen or heard from Bo. When she walked in, Henry was busy waiting on other customers, so Diane found a table till he was finished. When he got a free minute, he walked over to her.

"Hey, Peyton, how are you doing?"

"Henry, I'm doing fine. Was wondering if you had seen Bo lately? I have texted, called him and no reply. I know he has been super busy, so was hoping you had seen him."

"Ms. Peyton, I take it you haven't heard."

"Heard what, Henry?"

"Bo had a massive heart attack two days ago. He just fell over and that was it. He was a picture of health. There is a big write-up in the paper about him. He was a real nice guy, and everyone liked him."

Trying to take in what Henry had just said, Diane sat there in shock.

"Are you alright, Peyton? Can I get you anything? Would you like a glass of water?" Henry asked.

"I had no idea," she replied. "What am I going to do? I really need Bo."

"Peyton, I know this is a shock to you, and I am so sorry. Bo's wife found out about a month ago she is expecting. They were both so happy. I can't imagine what she is going through."

"You mean Bo is married?"

"Yes, he was a happily married man. His wife lost their first child about two years ago, and they both were crushed. Bo worked in real estate and has done well. Bo is not his real name. He was showing some homes to a guy, and the man wanted to know if he could hook him up with a decent lady for the weekend. He offered Bo a good amount of money, so Bo honored his wishes. The gentleman passed the word around to others that when they were in town to give Bo a call. These men were well-to-do businessmen that wanted to keep things hush-hush. To keep this separate from his real estate business he took on an assumed name. He had two phones, one for real estate and one for his side job. To my knowledge, his wife never knew. Bo loved his wife very much, and although he had this side business, as far as I know he was never unfaithful to her. She was his world."

"How do you know all this?" Peyton asked.

"Bo would sometimes meet a client here for coffee. He would have a notebook of homes, and they would go over what they liked and didn't like, then he took them to the homes that seemed of interest to them. When he was first approached about hooking women up with men, he didn't want to do anything behind closed doors, so he asked if he could use my place as a meeting place. He promised there would be no trouble. So, I gave it a try and it turned out to be okay. They would meet here, then Bo always took them to where they needed to go. I wouldn't see them again till the next time. He was careful not to destroy my restaurant's reputation, and I earned a little extra income on the side. For Bo, it was a business meeting place."

"So do you know Bo's real name?" Diane asked, still somewhat shocked by all Henry was telling her.

"Yes, if you look in the paper, you will see a nice article about him. His real name is George Mitchell. Just like you, I am sure Peyton is not your real name, but that is all I know you by. Bo tried to keep everyone's real identity quiet. He didn't want any trouble."

Diane sat there trying to take in all Henry had told her. Bo had always treated her well. Never had he gotten out of line with her or been pushy. He told her what job was available and that it was up to her whether she took the job. Looking at Henry she said, "What am I going to do? I relied on Bo for work. He always made sure I was going to be safe when he hooked me up with a guy."

"Have you thought about going back to school to study a

trade or whatever you like? It would be much better for you, and you could find something with benefits since that's what you are going to need."

"Henry, I have no desire to go back to school. I don't want to work in a factory, I really like what I have been doing. I have some money saved up, so I will be alright for a few months. Do you know anyone who does what Bo did?"

"No, Peyton, that's something I don't keep up with. Bo has been a customer here for years, I knew him and knew he wouldn't bring any bad business here to my café. Give some thought to what I said about going to school. If you are not careful, without someone to screen the guys you go out with, you could end up with some serious problems. Do you have any family that you could turn to?"

"No, no family. Just me. Thanks, Henry, for letting me know about Bo. I really do appreciate it. See you around."

"Peyton, take care of yourself, and do be careful. Stop in sometime and let me know how you are doing."

Diane walked out to her car, feeling numb. What was she going to do without Bo? Diane saw a newspaper stand across the street and walked over to purchase a paper. There on the front page was a picture of Bo and a lengthy article. As she read it, she cried. She wondered if she should attend his funeral, but if someone recognized her, what would she say to his wife? So many things went through her mind. The funeral wasn't until the next day. She decided to go by the funeral home, and if no one was there, she would go in to pay respects. The funeral home was only six blocks away from where she was, so she could be there in a few minutes. Diane felt nauseated as she entered the parking lot. Her palms began to sweat for she had never been inside a funeral home. She took a deep breath and walked to the door. A man opened it and asked who she was there to see. As Diane hesitated, trying to remember Bo's real name, the man asked, "Are you here for Mr. Latham or Mr. Mitchell?"

"Oh, I'm here to see Mr. Mitchell."

Just go around the corner and you will see his name on the

door. You may go right on in."

Walking down the hall to where Bo was, Diane thought, by the way the man at the door was talking, you would think Bo was still alive. It all seemed strange to her.

No one was in the room, for which she was grateful. Walking up to the casket, tears ran down her cheeks. Bo was a handsome guy and one she had always felt so comfortable around. He was more like a close brother. She reached over to lay her hand on his and when she did, she jerked her hand back quickly. He was so cold. Were dead people supposed to be cold?

Diane heard some voices coming toward the room, so she walked away to the back of the chapel. An attractive lady and the man she had met at the door came in. Slowly, Diane made her way around to the doorway and slipped out without being seen. As she walked to her car, part of her wished she had not stopped to see Bo and part of her was glad.

Back at her apartment, she felt so lost. How was she going to make it without Bo? Then she remembered the guy from out West that told her she needed to find other work. But what kind of work could she do? Henry suggested she should go back to school, but that wasn't something she wanted to do. She felt like she did the day Jake walked out on her, so lonely and with no idea what to do with her life.

She curled up on her couch and cried herself to sleep.

Eight

The boys each had his own laptop with programs downloaded for the subjects they needed. After breakfast, they were all eager to start their studies. Leah was afraid they would want to go out to play, but they were happy to do the work assigned them.

That Saturday, Nick stopped by early in the morning and asked the boys if they would like to go fishing. Having never gone fishing, the boys had lots of questions. They decided to give it a try.

That evening when Nick and the boys came home, they had to show Leah all the fish they had caught. Nick showed the boys how to clean them to get them ready to fry. This was a job the boys did not enjoy, but they were happy once Leah and Nora had the fish cooked and ready to eat.

"Boys, how would you like to go to a baseball game next Saturday?" Nick asked.

They had never been to a ball game before, and like fishing, they decided to give it a try. Leah reminded them that their studies came first and had to be completed before Saturday morning.

Sunday morning, Leah was preparing breakfast and opened what she thought was a container of butter. She carried it over to the stove to dip out the butter when she realized it was a container of worms. The thoughts of those worms in her refrigerator all night didn't set well with Leah. It was a closed container, but still other food was in the refrigerator. Knowing it was probably left over from fishing, she would have thought they would have thrown them away. Daniel came in and asked if he could help her.

Leah showed him the worms. "Why did you boys put these worms in the refrigerator?"

"Mr. Nick said they needed to be kept in a cool place, and that's the only place we could think of."

"Daniel, why don't you take these worms over to Nick and let him store them. I'm sure Nora would be so pleased," Leah said, smiling.

Daniel took the container of worms and out the door he went. Soon he came back in. "Mr. Nick thanked me for bringing them over. He has a place to keep them."

Leah only shook her head. David had gone fishing with friends many times, but never brought home any worms. She wondered where Nick had put the worms, for knowing Nora, they certainly wouldn't go in the refrigerator.

Just as church was dismissed, it started raining. Leah and the boys went straight home. After lunch, the boys were in their rooms, and Leah was still reading up on being a foster parent. Then Leah heard someone pecking on the piano keys. She got up to see who it was. There, sat Stephen at the piano. He was doing pretty good.

Leah asked, "Stephen, have you ever had piano lessons?"

"No, but I would like to. Over at Cody's shop, he has all kinds of musical instruments. I like the piano. He showed me some things on one of the pianos, and I thought I would see if I could remember it."

"You are doing quite well. If you want, we can see about starting you on piano lessons. Since we have the piano here, we might as well make good use of it."

Stephen smiled, "That would be so cool. How soon can I start?"

"Let me talk to Cody and see what he recommends, and then we will go from there. Okay?"

Stephen was so excited. Leah went back to her reading and Stephen kept on working on what Cody had shown him.

On Monday, they went by where Cody worked and found out he also gave music lessons. While Leah and Stephen were talking to Cody, Daniel picked up a guitar and started strumming on it. Caleb picked up a mandolin and Benjamin a banjo. The boys seem to be in their own world.

Cody said, "Ms. Leah, looks like the boys have found the instruments they like. We can make you a good deal on each and get the boys started on music lessons."

Not expecting this, Leah wasn't sure what to say. She hated

to deny the boys the opportunity to take lessons.

"Cody, do you have any instruments that we could rent to see if the boys really want to play or if this is because Stephen wants to take piano lessons?" Leah asked.

"Ms. Leah, every time I bring the boys here to the shop, that's the first thing they go to. They each know what they want to play. I think we are past the renting stage. They are ready for their own," replied Cody.

"Well, just how much are we looking at?" Leah asked.

"Let me do some figuring, and I'll get back with you. Leave the boys here for now. My next student is not due for several hours. Let me work with them and I'll figure out which one is best. Do you have any errands to take care of? If not, I'll give you a call when we are finished."

Leah decided to go home and take care of a few things around the house. When she pulled in her driveway, Nora was outside working in the flowers. Leah walked over to Nora and said with a smile, "When you are finished here, come on over and we can freshen up my flower beds."

Looking around, Nora asked, "Where are the boys?"

"They are with Cody at his music store. Stephen was trying to pick out a song on the piano yesterday. Seems Cody has been showing him a few things on the piano. When I took the boys to Cody's this morning, it seems each one is interested in a different instrument. Remember when our girls first took piano lessons? We would sit out back while they practiced. Then when they got to where they could play, it wasn't so bad to stay in the house."

They both laughed at the memory. "Seems like a short time ago, and now here they are married with children of their own. Leah, if the boys each get a different instrument, you are welcome to come over while they practice. By the way, what instruments are they interested in?"

"Stephen the piano, Daniel went for the guitar, Caleb likes the mandolin and believe it or not, Benjamin likes the banjo."

"Benjamin, playing a banjo? That boy is too small. Maybe they come in different sizes. Leah, you definitely need to either come over when they start practicing or wear ear plugs." At that, they both laughed again.

"Leah, I will have to admit that when you first brought the boys in, I thought you had lost your mind. But now, I can't imagine not having them around. They are so well-behaved, and Nick thinks the world of them. He thinks those boys need to be around when he is doing things. Oh, did I tell you about the other day? This was before school was out. Nick was in the garage working on his truck. He was lying on one of those things that roll around when he is working under a vehicle. He looked over, and there was Chester. He had gotten out of his fence. He said Chester just sat there looking at him while he worked. When Nick finished, he put Chester back inside his fence and sealed off another place he had dug out. I am so surprised Chester is still around. Thought for sure he would have gotten away by now."

"Oh, Nora. Benjamin checks on him every morning and as soon as he comes home from school. As long as he stays outside, I'm okay. You know, Nora, you and Nick should become foster parents. Nick loves kids so much."

"No, Leah, we will help you with those four boys. Besides, our chances of getting well-behaved kids would be unlikely. You just got blessed."

"No, Nora, I was where God wanted me. I will admit, I have learned a few things listening to them. Sometimes I'm a little shocked."

Before long Leah's phone rang, and it was Cody. The boys were ready to be picked up. When Leah walked in the music store, there stood four boys smiling from ear to ear: Daniel, Caleb, and Benjamin with their new instruments and Stephen with his piano music. Benjamin was struggling with the banjo, so Stephen reached over to carry it for him and asked him to carry his piano music.

"Well, looks like you boys are ready. Put your things in the car and I'll be right out. I need to talk to Cody for a minute."

When the boys were out, Leah asked Cody. "Okay, how much do I owe you?"

Cody smiled and said, "The instruments are already paid for. All you will be paying for is their lessons."

"No, Cody, I will not let you buy them those instruments. I know they can't be cheap, so how much are they?"

"Ms. Leah, I called Pastor Harrington. He made a few phone calls, and the money has already been delivered. I'm not at liberty to say anything more."

Leah blinked back tears, once again touched by the kindness of people around her. "Cody, I don't know what to say. Thank you doesn't seem enough."

"Ms. Leah, did you see the smiles on those boys' faces? That said it all. Before long, those boys are going to be playing in church. They have natural talent. They need a little help getting started, but they are going to be fine."

"What about Benjamin? He chose a banjo, and he is so little."

"I wouldn't worry about him. I think he is going to surprise you. In fact, I believe all four will surprise you. Each one is special in their own way."

As soon as they got home, the boys wanted to show Nick and Nora what they had. Then in the house they went, each working on their own instrument as Cody had shown them.

By Saturday, the boys had their school lessons done, ready to go with Nick to the ball game. When the boys got excited, they all four wanted to talk at the same time.

Soon Nick was at the door ready to pick the boys up. As they started out, they came back to Leah and gave her a hug. She remembered when she first met them, they wouldn't say a word. She was so happy with the progress they had made and now they truly felt like they were hers. Their little hugs meant everything to Leah.

Taking a moment, she gave thanks for the boys and how well everything was going. She was no longer lonely, and her home was filled with love and laughter again.

Nine

It had been three months since Bo had passed away. Looking at her bank statement, Diane knew she was going to have to find work, and possibly move into a cheaper apartment. After getting dressed, she drove to one of the hotels where Bo had dropped her off many times. Diane was hoping to see a familiar face, but nothing. She even went inside the restaurant, hoping by some chance she would see someone familiar. Nothing. The lady at the front counter asked her, "Can I help you? Are you looking for someone?"

Turning to the lady, Diane said, "By any chance, has a guy by the name of John checked in here?"

"Miss, do you have a last name, or is John the last name?"

Diane realized she didn't know any of the men's first or last names. She always referred to them as John. Not wanting to admit this to the lady, she said, "I need to go to my car and check on the name. I'll be back."

Once outside the hotel, Diane wanted to cry. What was she going to do? She didn't want to go back to doing factory work. She had to find work, but where? Getting in her car, she drove for a while trying to see something that she might want to do, and nothing seemed to appeal to her. Finally, she stopped at a small restaurant to grab a bite to eat. Nothing on the menu looked good, but she knew she needed to eat something. She managed to eat about half of her meal; she wanted to go home and try to think. On her way to her car, a man she had never seen before came up to her. "Excuse me, I notice you were sitting alone at the table, you looked so sad. Can I help you in anyway?"

"Thank you, but I'm fine." Getting in her car, the guy took hold of the car door and asked, "Would you mind if I call you sometime?"

Diane looked at him and replied, "I don't think so," and closed her car door. He stood there and watched her drive off, then got in his car to follow her. He was able to stay far enough back so she could not see him. When he saw her pull into the Ivy-Rose Apartments, he knew the lady had money. Driving a Porsche Panamera was another clue, and he wondered if she was a widow or had come into a big inheritance. Either way, this lady had money and he had to figure out a way to make an impression on her. He also noticed she wasn't wearing a wedding band, which was a good sign for him.

The next morning, Diane decided to try the employment office and see what jobs might be available. When she walked in, the lady at the counter asked if she could help her.

"Yes, I am looking for a job and wondered what might be available," Diane replied.

"Have you looked online?" the lady asked.

"No, I haven't. You see I don't have a computer and I only know how to call and text on my phone, that's why I came here."

The lady looked at Diane a little surprised and said, "Follow me."

She took Diane over to a table where several computers were. "Take a seat, and here is a paper to show you how to log in on what kind of work you are looking for. It's easy and if you see something you are interested in, follow the directions and it will print the information up for you. Any questions?"

Feeling so embarrassed, Diane looked at the lady and said, "I have never used a computer. I know nothing about them."

Taking a deep breath, the lady looked around and had one of the other workers to cover the front desk for her. Turning to Diane, she said, "Come with me."

She took Diane into a room and closed the door. "My name is Faye, and I will try to help you the best I can. Here is a form that I need you to fill out. This will help me in finding what kind of work you are best suited for."

While Diane was filling out the forms, the lady wondered if Diane had ever worked, and why she didn't know anything about computers. She looked to be in her late twenties or early thirties, and all young people knew about computers. She noticed Diane was well-dressed. Something just didn't seem right. When Diane finished with the forms, she handed them back to Faye.

"So, your name is Diane Baker. You haven't listed any previous jobs or anything. What type of skills do you have? You have nothing listed here."

Not wanting the lady to know what kind of work she had been doing, she said, "My husband passed away a few months ago. I have never had to work until now. He took care of everything. You could say I have been a lady of leisure. Since my husband passed, my lifestyle has changed, and now I am at a loss of what kind of work to do."

"I'm so sorry. Did your husband not leave you anything to live on? Again, I'm sorry, I have no right to ask that. Let me see what I can find that might work for you."

Turning to the computer, Faye looked at job after job. With Diane having no experience, she didn't qualify for any job that paid well.

Finally, she asked Diane, "Do you think you can do factory work?"

Diane said, "I would rather stay away from factory work. Do you have anything else?"

"The only other things I have, and I'm not sure they would interest you, is an opening at the hospital for a housekeeper. Then I have an opening in a school as a custodian. One of our finer hotels is looking for a waitress and cook. All the other jobs are for factory workers. The pay is not good, but you will have benefits."

"If I took one of those jobs, then if later something better comes open, could you call me?" Diane asked.

"We deal with so many people, the best thing that you can do is stop by every so often and check. Have you ever worked? Do you have any experience at all?"

"No," Diane replied.

"Do you think you would like to work in a restaurant?"

"The housekeeping job I think I would like. How do I go about applying for it?"

"Wait here, let me make a phone call." Faye walked into

another room and was gone for several minutes. When she came back to Diane, she said, "Ms. Baker, take this paper to Memorial Hospital. I have already called and spoken to a Mrs. Hamilton. She is waiting for you, and she will go over the job description. Then you can decide if this job is for you."

Diane thanked Faye for her help and left. Back in her car, she knew she would have to sell her car and move into a more reasonably priced apartment. First, she would see what Mrs. Hamilton had to say.

Memorial Hospital was a large hospital. How would she ever learn her way around? Finding the information desk was a task within itself. An older man at the desk looked at her papers and tried to give her directions to Mrs. Hamilton's office. Thanking him, Diane went down the hall and stopped a nurse, hoping her directions would make more sense. The nurse was super nice. She told her she would take her to where she needed to go. Having never been in a hospital, Diane was taken aback at all the people and workers. The nurse turned to Diane and said, "Here, this is Mrs. Hamilton's office. You have a good day," then turned, and she was gone.

Opening the door, Diane walked in to find other office rooms. A lady came out of one of the rooms and asked, "May I help you?"

"Yes, I am Diane Baker." Before she could say anything else, the lady said, "Yes, Mrs. Hamilton is expecting you. Follow me."

Mrs. Hamilton was smiling as Diane walked in.

"Hello, you must be Ms. Baker? I'm Helen Hamilton. Please have a seat. Faye from the employment office has called and filled me in on your situation. I understand you would like the position in our housekeeping department."

"Yes. I don't have any training, and this seemed like something I could do," Diane replied.

"Did Faye mention what the pay was?"

"Yes, she said starting out was twelve-fifty an hour. She said I would have some benefits also."

"I have some paperwork for you to fill out, and when that's

completed, I'll show you around and let you meet the housekeeper supervisor. If you are still interested in the position, we will go over the benefits you are entitled to, your schedule, uniforms, and other things. Here are the forms you need to complete. Take these in the next room, and when you are finished, bring them back to me."

Diane took the papers and went into the next room. Pondering over all this, she wasn't sure if this was what she wanted to do. Yet, she needed money coming in, needed to downsize her apartment, and as badly as she hated the thoughts of it, she would need to trade her car. With the paperwork finished, Diane went back to Mrs. Hamilton's office.

"Good, now if you will follow me. I have notified Ms. Moss, our housekeeping supervisor, that we would be coming up to see her. She has offered to take you around the hospital so you can familiarize yourself with where things are and also speak with you about your uniforms, clocking in and out, breaks, where to park for work and so forth. Oh, here is Ms. Moss now."

Ms. Moss was an older lady, but when she spoke, you knew she meant business.

"Ms. Moss, this is Diane Baker, the lady I spoke to you about. Ms. Baker, this is Ms. Moss. You will report to her every day and if a problem arises, she is the one you will need to see. Okay, ladies, I'll leave you two to get acquainted, and I'll be in my office if you need me."

"Ms. Baker, if I may, I will call you Diane. My understanding is you have never worked before. Is that correct?"

"Yes, my husband always took care of me financially, and I never had a need to work. I am willing to try and will do my best to do what I'm told," replied Diane.

"I'm afraid this may be a bit difficult for you at times. Do you have a strong or weak stomach?" ask Ms. Moss.

"I think I can handle whatever I am up against. I am quite strong."

"Good, for some days are more challenging than others. Now, let's get started. We have a lot to cover, and I want you to meet one of the girls you will be working closely with."

After the tour of the hospital, Ms. Moss gave a list of what clothing Diane would need, where she would need to park, when and where to take breaks, and her lunch time. It seemed the list went on and on.

A lady about Diane's age was coming down the hall when Ms. Moss said, "Megan, this is the new hire. She will be working with you. Her name is Diane Baker. Diane, this is Megan Adams. Diane will be starting work on Monday, so she will follow you around for a few days till she is able to go out on her own. I'll leave you two to get acquainted, and Diane, we will see you Monday morning at six o'clock."

Turning to Diane, Megan said, "So, you are the new girl. Have you ever worked in a hospital before?"

"No" replied Diane. "This is my first time."

"Well, it's not so bad. Some things you get a little used to. Do you have any questions for me, or would you rather wait till Monday and ask as we go along?"

"Why don't we wait till Monday. When I clock in, where do I meet you?"

"If you are here on time, I'll be at the computer where we clock in. Did Ms. Moss or Mrs. Hamilton give you a number or a card to clock in with?"

Diane had so many papers in her hands, she wasn't sure what all she had. There were instructions for so many things. "I may have it somewhere in all these papers," she said to Meagan, "I'm not really sure what, I have."

"Go home and sort through what you have, after you have looked over all your paperwork, if it's not there, call Mrs. Hamilton and she will take care of it for you. Make sure you have that number or card, and use it clocking in and out, otherwise, you won't get paid."

"Thanks, Megan, appreciate the advice. I may become your shadow for a good while."

"Don't worry, Diane, you will get the hang of all this. It seems overwhelming at first, but soon it will be so routine. See you on

Monday, bright and early."

When Diane got back to her apartment, she looked over all the papers she had. Sure enough, highlighted in bright yellow was the clock number she would need but no card was in the packet. She remembered Ms. Moss showing her something on a computer, but for the life of her, she couldn't remember. Poor Megan, she had no idea how much she was going to need her. She seemed nice, and hopefully, she would be patient also. Looking through the papers, Diane realized she had to furnish her own uniforms and shoes. On the list were places to purchase the items needed. Purple. Her uniform was to be purple. Diane never wore purple. Come to think of it, Ms. Moss and Megan both had on purple. Diane wondered what she could do to spruce up her uniform, for it certainly needed something.

Ten

Sitting outside in the swing, Leah was listening to the boys practice their music. It was amazing how well they were doing. Even Nick and Nora had commented on their progress. Closing her eyes, she was saying a little prayer when Daniel said, "Ms. Leah, can I talk to you?"

Opening her eyes, Leah said, "Why yes, Daniel. What can I do for you?"

Taking a seat by Leah, Daniel looked up at her. "Ms. Leah, we haven't heard from our mom in a long time. I don't think she wants us."

"Oh Daniel, we can't say that. Your mom might be sick and can't come for you. We don't know what your mom is going through right now. I'm sure when she can, she will try to find you boys."

"Ms. Leah, me, Stephen, Caleb, and Benjamin have been talking. We want to stay here with you. We don't want to go back to our mom. She never was there for us. We were always in the way, especially when she had some guy around. Here, it's different. We like it here and don't want to ever leave."

Taking Daniel in her arms to give him a hug, Leah said, "Oh, Daniel, I would like nothing better than to keep you four boys. But if your mom comes, I'm afraid I'll have to give you boys back. She is your birth mother."

"Can't you adopt us and make us yours? We love you, Ms. Leah."

Holding Daniel close, Leah knew deep down inside, she wanted to keep the boys forever and never let them go. But what if their birth mother showed up and wanted the boys back? What would she do?

"Ms. Leah, remember you said that when we pray, we should pray from our heart and not just say words. We have been trying to do that. Every night, after you turn out the lights, we get up, get down on our knees, and ask God to let us stay here with you forever. We ask God to let you be our mom. Please, Ms. Leah, don't ever let us go."

Daniel was crying, and Leah could not hold back her own tears. Oh, how she loved these boys. Finally able to speak, Leah looked at Daniel.

"It's not up to us to make that decision. It's God. I truly believe He will work things out for the best for all of us. We must live each day to the fullest and always thank him for it. We must have faith and wait to see what wonderful things God has planned for us. God loves you boys, and so do I."

Ms. Leah, can we call you mom instead of Ms. Leah?"

Taking Daniel in her arms, tears flowing, Leah said, "Oh, Daniel, I would be so honored. In my heart, you four are already my boys."

About twenty minutes later, the other three boys came out to see what Daniel and Ms. Leah were doing.

Daniel smiled and said, "Guess what, we can call her mom. She is okay with it."

The four boys climbed in her lap, hugging, and kissing her on the cheek. What joy! Leah wished all days could be like this for these boys, for they surely deserved it.

Nora went outside to water her flowers when she saw Leah and the boys. "My goodness, you all look so happy and having a great time."

Caleb went over to Nora, "We don't have to say Ms. Leah anymore. We get to call her MOM!"

Nora looked at Leah, not sure what to say. Then Leah spoke up and said, "I'll explain later."

The summer was going by so fast. The boys were doing exceptionally well with their schoolwork and of course, practicing their music. They enjoyed going over to Cody's for music lessons. In fact, they always stayed longer than they were supposed to.

Then one Sunday at church, Cody got up to say they were having some special music that day. Each of the boys went up on stage with their instruments and began to play. They played, "Amazing Grace." Leah was so shocked. Nora and Nick were sitting behind her, and both reached up to pat her on the shoulders. Everyone in the church knew the situation with the boys, and not a dry eye could be found. When the boys finished, they received a standing ovation.

After church, everyone went to the boys to let them know what a wonderful job they had done, and they expected to hear more from them soon. Leah waited till the boys were ready to leave then she gathered them close to her. With tears in her eyes, she said, "You boys are such a blessing. I had no idea you could play so well. I am so proud of you."

With smiles beyond words, the boys returned Leah's hug. Nick and Nora came over, "You guys were outstanding. This calls for a celebration. You pick the place you would like to go eat and that's where we will go."

With this, the boys were trying to decide. They finally decided on a restaurant in town that had a buffet. You could eat all you wanted, plus they had all kinds of desserts. Nick and Nora laughed because they thought the boys would want pizza.

On Monday, the boys turned in all their homework and computers. They were finished with school for a few weeks. They would receive a report on Tuesday on how well they had done. Since they had no more computer classes, they headed outside to see if Nick needed any help working on his car. As Leah went to the kitchen to see what she could prepare for dinner that night, the doorbell rang. When she opened the door, there stood Julie Knight.

"Ms. Knight, I wasn't expecting you, did we have a meeting?" Leah asked.

"No, Mrs. Conner, I came by because we need to talk. I hope this is not a bad time?"

Leah's heart began to sink. She was thinking about the talk she and Daniel had had regarding them not wanting to go back to their mom.

"May I come in, Mrs. Conner?" Julie Knight asked.

"Yes, yes, I'm so sorry. Please come on into the living room. The boys are next door right now. Is everything alright?"

Julie Knight looked at Leah and said, "That's good, for I would like to talk to you alone. We have been working hard trying to track down their mom. With what little information Daniel was able to give us, we still have nothing. Although we don't know for certain if they are the ages, they say they are, we feel that the ages Daniel gave us are correct. What month or day is anybody's guess. Whoever their mother is has gone to great lengths to keep this all hidden."

"So, do we pick a month and day so they can say this is their birthday? What about getting a Social Security card? Since I have had the boys, they have been given all the shots they can take for now. The ladies at the doctor's office had to assume they had never had any vaccines, so we started out from the beginning. This is so unfair for the boys. Ms. Knight, my main concern is whether the boys will be able to stay here with me."

"Mrs. Conner, that's one of the reasons I'm here. How are you doing with the boys? Having them here, has it been hard for you?"

"Oh no, Ms. Knight. I couldn't ask for better boys. They are a gift from God."

"I spoke to the teachers that have been working with them this summer, and the reports are good. I was afraid that they wouldn't want to do schoolwork through the summer, but they have surprised me. They have not missed a day. Was it hard for you to get them to do schoolwork this summer?" Ms. Knight asked.

"No, the boys looked forward to it. In fact, besides schoolwork, they each have a musical instrument and are taking lessons. This past Sunday in church, they surprised everyone by playing 'Amazing Grace.' They did a wonderful job. Pastor Harrington's sermons are online, you need to watch it. Your heart will be blessed."

"Well, I had no idea. Mrs. Conner, I must say, you have

amazed me at how well you have handled all this. Most young couples will take only two children, mostly just one, but you took all four, and you are a widow. How have you done it?"

"Ms. Knight. I prayed about what to do with my home. It needed to be filled with love, laughter, and happiness. I had the room, and those boys needed a home, and God brought us together. The Bible says in Proverbs 24:3-4, 'By wisdom a house is built, and through understanding it is established; through knowledge its rooms are filled with rare and beautiful treasures.' Those boys are my rare and beautiful treasures. The Bible also says in Romans 8:28, 'And we know that in all things God works for the good of those who love him, who have been called according to his purpose.' This is God's home. I am here to do God's will. He loves us, and we are to love each other. God is love and that is what I'm trying to teach the boys, that whether they are here or somewhere else, they should always look to God for guidance."

"Mrs. Conner, I wish we had a dozen or more foster parents like you right here in our town. Those boys have no idea how fortunate they are."

"Ms. Knight, those boys do realize it. They have told me so. May I ask you a question? Since neither parent has been found, how long do I have to wait before I can adopt them and make them fully mine?"

Julie looked at Leah. "You want to adopt the boys? Why? You are their foster parent and a good one. Why not leave things as they are?"

"You see, Ms. Knight, if I adopt the boys, they will have a name they can relate to, a date of birth, a home that is truly theirs, a parent they can say 'This is my mom.' They will be like other children with parents. Those boys deserve this and want this. Now, how long do I have to wait to make those boys officially mine?"

"Mrs. Conner, I was not expecting this. I'm sure you have prayed about it. With my experience from other cases, it will take as much as six to eight months no matter if the mother says she wants nothing to do with the child and the father can't be determined. The state also always tries to locate a blood relative rather than allowing the foster family to go ahead and adopt. When I get back to the office, I'll get started on the paperwork for this will be a long process."

"Ms. Knight, I want to wait until everything is official before we say anything to the boys. Then, I want the boys to pick a month and a day they would like to observe as their birthdays, and I want to have a surprise party for them when we can present the papers to them saying they are officially the Conners."

"Mrs. Conner, this case has been a difficult one, trying to find answers regarding the boys. Now, those boys have so much happiness thanks to you. I certainly am glad I stopped by today. If all my days could turn out like this one! You will be hearing from me in a few days. Again, Mrs. Conner, thank you so much. Not only have you been a blessing to the boys, but to me also."

Leah leaned over and gave Julie Knight a hug. "Talk to God and listen. It's amazing the journey He will take you on if you will let him."

Julie left, and when she got in her car, she bowed her head and thanked God for giving her this case and meeting Leah Conner. She needed that lady almost as much as those boys did.

Stephen saw Ms. Knight get in her car. He ran to the others, "Hey, I just saw Ms. Knight get in her car. She came from the house. Do you think she plans to take us away?"

Not sure what to do, they went to find Leah.

"Well, boys, did you help Nick with his car?" Leah asked.

Benjamin looked at her and asked, "Is everything alright?"

Smiling, Leah went over to the boys to give them a hug. "Everything is fine. Now let's see how much grease you boys have on you. Are you sure Nick's car got greased?"

Laughing, she took them outside to find Nick and to see about getting some of the grease off the boys.

That night as the boys were getting ready for bed and ready to do their devotions, Benjamin climbed up in Leah's lap and gave her a big hug.

"Are we going to have to leave here?" he asked.

Leah gave him an extra hug, "Why no, Benjamin, whatever gave you that idea?"

"Stephen saw Ms. Knight leaving here this afternoon. We know they can't find our mom, and we are afraid they will take us away."

"Oh, boys, come sit close to me. No one is going to take you away from me if I have any say so. I plan to do whatever I can to keep you four here with me. This is your home, and you have all filled it with so much love. You guys have stolen my heart."

Caleb spoke up, "Then why was Ms. Knight here?"

"She stopped by to check and see how things were going. Since you boys are in my care, they can make random stops whenever they want to make sure you are in a good home and being properly taken care of. They do this at all foster homes. It's for your protection. Ms. Knight wants only the best for you boys and so do I." Leah reached out and gave each one a hug.

"Now for devotions tonight. While I get my Bible, be thinking of what prayer requests you might have."

When Leah returned, she decided to start out in prayer, then have their Bible reading. The boys sat around her holding one another's hands. Then Leah began praying.

"Heavenly Father, move our hearts with the peace of your Spirit as we care for ourselves and each other. Lift our minds with your wisdom to act responsibly and effectively for everyone's benefit. Bring us together in your Holy Spirit to work as one in protecting each other. As it says in John 14:27, 'Peace, I leave with you; my peace I give to you. Not as the world gives do I give to you. Do not let your hearts be troubled and do not be afraid.' Then in Romans 5:1, it says, 'Therefore, since we have been justified through faith, we have peace with God through our Lord Jesus Christ.' Father, I pray that your peace will fill each one of my boys' hearts, souls, and minds. Amen."

They each opened their Bibles for the next reading in Joshua 1:1. Daniel asked, "Can I read first tonight?"

"Yes, Daniel, you can read three verses, and then the others can read two verses. Let's break chapter one into two nights. Okay, Daniel."

Stephen was the last to read. "Mom, I like that verse. I think I will memorize it."

"Why don't you read it again, Stephen? That is one of many to carry in your heart."

Stephen read, "Have I not commanded you? Be strong and courageous. Do not be afraid; do not be discouraged, for the Lord your God will be with you wherever you go. (Joshua 1:9)"

"Mom, I think that God was with us when our other mom would go off and leave us. Daniel always watched out for us, but now I think God was watching over him. He helped Daniel. I had never thought about it till now," Stephen said with a smile.

Leah's heart was so blessed by what Stephen had said. She could see God working in each of their lives.

"Any prayer requests tonight?" Leah asked. They each had something they wanted to pray about, and Caleb asked that he could close in prayer.

Eleven

Monday morning came early. Thankfully, Diane had laid out everything she would need. It was about a thirty-minute drive and at this time of morning, traffic was not bad. Pulling into the assigned area, Diane was hoping to be there before Megan so she could take notes on what she did, especially with the computer.

When Diane walked up, Ms. Moss was standing there. "Good morning, Diane. Are you ready for your first day?"

"Yes, I purchased everything on my list and am ready to start."

"Good, but first let me show you where your locker is. You will need to keep your things locked up and only bring to work what you really need. For example, the scarf you have on is pretty and you can wear it to work, but it must go in your locker before you go out on the floor. Your bracelets are nice also, but they, too, must stay in your locker till you leave to go home. If you want to wear a necklace, that is fine, but it must not be on a long chain, a short one. As for earrings, I would suggest nothing dangling."

Diane felt like she had been stripped of everything. All that was left was the drab purple uniform.

"Here is your card that will let you clock in and enter certain areas of the hospital. You must keep this with you always. It has a clip that you can clip onto your uniform, or you can carry it in one of your pockets. If you need supplies, Megan will show you how to use your card to pick them up. Any questions?"

"I'm not sure. Will Megan be working close by so if I need help, she can help me?" Diane asked.

"For the next week, you will be following Megan around and she will have you doing things. She will be able to answer all your questions. By the way, did you bring your lunch?"

"Was that on my list of things, Ms. Moss? No, I didn't bring anything."

"You can go to the cafeteria or pick out something from one

of the snack machines. We don't furnish you a meal, that's up to you."

"I'm sorry, Ms. Moss, I didn't think about that. I'll be more prepared tomorrow."

Ms. Moss turned just as Megan walked up. "Megan, you are just in time. I will turn Diane over to you. I wish you both the best of luck."

With that Ms. Moss was gone.

"Well, are you ready to start your new day?" Megan asked.

"I'm not sure," replied, Diane. "I came in a little overdressed and she let me know it."

Megan laughed. "Oh, around here, dressing up is the last thing you want to do. You may come in looking nice and fresh, but you'll go home some days, and the first thing you want to do is take a shower. Now let's get you clocked in. Did Ms. Moss assign you a locker?"

"Yes, she did. That's where the rest of my things I had on are."

"Be sure to bring you a lock for it. Now here is how your card works on clocking in."

The morning went rather fast. Before long, Megan said to Diane, "It is time for lunch."

"I didn't bring a lunch. How is the cafeteria food?" Diane asked.

"Depends on the day. We have a machine that has sandwiches in it, and some of those are not bad. Are you picky about what you eat?"

Diane said, "No, I can eat most anything."

"Good, follow me. The snack machine will be a better choice. We have a refrigerator in our break room so tomorrow bring a drink, but make sure your name is on it, for if no name can be found, it's up for grabs."

Diane didn't realize when she signed up for housekeeping, she would be cleaning patient rooms and bathrooms. She thought she would be cleaning offices. So far, it hadn't been bad. Megan was easy to work with, and she took the time to explain things as they went. When the shift was over, Megan asked Diane, "So how was it? Coming back tomorrow?"

"It wasn't so bad. Yes, I'll be here in the morning. Hope I didn't get in your way. I don't know how you remember all that you do."

"Like I told you, after a while it becomes routine. Don't forget your lunch tomorrow and whatever you want to drink. Oh, also no alcohol. That will get you fired quick."

"Thanks for everything, Megan. See you in the morning."

On the way home, Diane stopped to pick up a paper and a brochure for rental homes. On her pay, she would have to move.

After dinner, she sat down to look at what was available. Nothing close to her work was in her price range. Some seem promising, but it would mean a longer drive to work. She called a few places but could only leave a voice mail. Deciding to get things ready for work the next day, she looked at her drab uniform. This was going to take some getting used to. Megan and the others that wore this color didn't seem to mind at all, so drab purple it would have to be. Now what to take for lunch? Diane did not cook much, so fixing a sandwich was about her only choice unless she wanted to buy those frozen meals. At the moment, that didn't seem appealing.

The next morning, Diane was getting ready to clock in when Megan walked up. She wasn't smiling or her peppy self.

"Is everything okay, Megan?" Diane asked.

"Yes and no. I received a letter in the mail yesterday, where I live, they are going up on the rent. I do well to pay the rent now. When I was looking for a place all they had was a two-bedroom, so I took it. It's close to work and in a good area. With what I make, I have only the bare necessities in it. I may have to get a part-time job, which I don't want to do."

Diane asked Megan "Have you thought about a roommate? Someone to help share expenses?"

"No, not really. I wouldn't want just anyone moving in with me. I don't know what to do. I prayed about this last night and this morning. God will get me through this. I must be patient."

"Megan, I am looking for an apartment. I need to downsize, and I have plenty of furniture. Would you mind sharing your place with me? I know we have not known each other long, but this could benefit both of us."

"It might work," Megan replied, "Why don't you come over to my place after work and you can look at what I have. If you like it, then we can look at what you have and see if it will fit in the apartment. We could give it a few months and see how it goes."

"Megan, this sounds great."

After work, Megan met Diane in the parking lot and told her to follow her to her apartment. When Diane went to get in her car, Megan said, "That's your car?"

"For now, it is, but I need to sell it and get something that I can afford on my income. Getting an apartment is first on my agenda and then trading cars next."

"Just exactly where do you live, Diane?" Megan asked.

"At Ivy-Rose Apartments. It's not far from here."

Megan looked at Diane, "You live at Ivy-Rose? I can assure you my apartment is nothing like that. To live there must cost a fortune."

"Why do you think I need to move? I don't have the income coming in that I once had."

"If you don't mind me asking, what happen?" Megan asked.

Using the same story, she had used before, Diane said, "My husband passed away, he had a heart attack, and unfortunately, he left me with little money in the bank. He has been gone for a few months, and I realized the money was going down fast, so I am having to change my lifestyle."

Megan looked shocked. "Did he not have any life insurance or provide some means of income for you in case something happened to him?"

"No, with what money was available, funeral expense and other bills had to be paid, and after all that, I was left with little."

Megan reached over and patted Diane on the arm. "I'm so sorry to hear all this. What was your husband's name and where did he work?"

"Megan, if you don't mind, I really don't want to talk about this. I need to move on with my life and do the best I can. Now, let's go to your apartment and hopefully we can make this all work out for the two of us."

Two parking spaces were available directly in front of the building where Megan's apartment was located. Diane saw that the outside was well-manicured. As Megan led the way, Diane was so relieved to find out Megan's place was downstairs and not upstairs. As Diane entered, she realized Megan was right. There was plenty of room, and she had little furniture in it.

"Megan, I have more than enough furniture to furnish your apartment. Which room will be mine?" Diane asked.

As they walked toward the bedrooms, Diane saw one room was completely empty while the other had only a bed and small table.

"You can have this room. I didn't realize when I took the apartment it had two full bathrooms in it. This one has never been used. I did clean it once," laughed Megan. "I will need to take some things from the closet. I put my winter jackets in it to save space in my closet. Well, what do you think? Still interested?"

Smiling, Diane replied, "Yes, this is perfect. Let's go over to my place and decide what we want to bring here, and then I'll try to sell the rest."

"Have you ever thought about selling it on Facebook Marketplace?" Megan asked. "That's where I bought my bed. Oh, let me show you out back. I went to a garage sale about a week ago. When I got there this guy was selling a grill. Looked brand new. When I ask the price, I told him not on my salary. I told him where I worked and what I did, then right out of the blue he said, 'Give me ten dollars and its yours.' I nearly fell over. No one else was at his sale. I don't know if he was thinking no one else would show up or what, but he made me one fantastic offer. Then I asked him if he delivered, and he just shook his head and asked for my address. That afternoon, he showed up with the grill."

"Wow, you only paid ten dollars for this?" Diane said in surprise. "This thing is family size. You certainly did get a deal."

"Diane, you would be amazed at what you can find at garage sales and Facebook Marketplace. Those places are for poor people like me. But I love them. God bless the person that started them."

"I have never put anything on that marketplace you were talking about. Could you do that for me?"

"Of course, I can. I live at that site. You name it, it's there. So, want to head over to your place?"

"Sure," replied Diane. "Remember, anything you want to have brought over here is fine with me. By the way, want to ride with me? When we finish, we can grab a bite to eat, and I'll bring you back home."

Megan was speechless when she saw Diane's apartment. She couldn't imagine this furniture in her apartment. But it was free, so who was she to complain? Never had she ever had furniture so nice.

"Have you ever sat on the couch or chairs in here, Diane? Wish we could move in here instead of at my place."

"Remember our salary, Megan. By any chance would you like to have the curtains? They go with the couch and chairs. Rugs too. Like I said earlier, go through and pick out all you want and then sell the rest."

As Megan walked from one room to the next, she was in complete awe. She thought, "This must be hard for Diane to walk away from this lifestyle." What kind of man would leave his wife in such a financial situation? Diane had said he had a heart attack, but still, you would think he would have thought of her future at some point.

"Well, Megan, have you decided what we need for your place?"

"Yes, I think so. Some things we need to measure to make sure it will fit. Have you thought how we are going to get this over to my place?"

"Don't worry Megan, once we decide what to take, I'll call a moving company and have them bring it over. Would it be alright if I moved in this weekend?"

"Saturday will be fine. Sunday would be good also if it's after church, and we could be finished by six o'clock. I go on Sunday nights also. Where do you go to church, Diane?"

"I don't. I'm busy taking care of things that don't get done through the week. So, you go to church twice in one day? Why?"

"To hear God's Word and to learn about Him, also to fellowship with other Christians. I go on Wednesday nights, too. Not going to church is like a day without sunshine. It lifts you up. Helps you to strive to live the life God wants us to live."

"Megan, if you want to go to church, that's fine, but don't be upset with me for not going. That's just not my thing, especially going that often. Do you not have any kind of a life?"

"Living for God is my life. He is my everything. I can't imagine not going and worshipping him. Besides, I believe God brought us together. It wasn't by accident this was His plan."

Diane was beginning to have second thoughts about moving in with Megan. She didn't want any of this church or God stuff, but she did need a new place to live. Taking a deep breath, she knew living with Megan was better than living on the street.

Saturday morning early, the moving van pulled up in front of Diane's apartment. In no time the things that went to Megan's place were loaded up. Diane called Megan to let her know they were on their way. When they arrived, two young men were carrying out Megan's things from the apartment.

"Megan, what are these guys doing with your things?" Diane asked.

"Well, since you had so much and yours was so much nicer than mine, I sold my things to make room for yours. This way the whole apartment will have all nice things in it."

"You mean you sold them in just a few days?"

"Diane, remember I told you Facebook Marketplace was an area I was familiar with. Posted it and in the hour, it was sold. So don't worry about the furniture at your place that we don't bring here. I'll have it sold in no time," Megan replied with a smile.

Diane couldn't believe Megan had sold her things so quickly. "You will have to show me how you do that. I can talk and text on my phone, take pictures, that's about it. It's too much like a computer, and I don't do computers."

Laughing, Megan looked at Diane, "In the evenings, I will give you classes on how to use your phone. You will be surprised at all that you can do. There is a world of information you can find out on your phone. You can order things, look up information, even find out about your ancestors. You name it, you can find it."

Looking at her phone, Diane asked, "Does it have a tracking device on it? Can people find out where you are?"

"Sure, you just have to know what you are doing."

Diane wondered if Jake or anyone else would be able to find her. Her phone was listed as Peyton Myers. Bo had said it would be best not to use her real name.

The movers unloaded the truck and got everything in its place in no time. Megan and Diane were in awe at how it changed the looks of the apartment.

"Diane, I can't believe how different this place looks. I never wanted anyone to come here, for it looked so drab, but now, it looks like a show place. I can't thank you enough. I even feel better."

"Glad I could help. Besides, you have helped me by letting me move in here. I think this is going to work. Being able to save some money is going to be the big plus. Do you have any wine or champagne to celebrate our big day?" Diane asked.

Megan looked at Diane and replied, "I don't drink, and I know this is going to be your home, too, but I don't want any alcohol in here. It's against my beliefs."

"You mean you don't have a nightcap or anything? What about when you come home from work, and you need a little something to take the edge off the way you are feeling? What do you do?"

"Diane, I read my Bible. God's word is relaxing, a blessing.

There is scripture for whatever you need. Praying also helps. You just pour your heart out to God, and He will take care of it. Just like when I received the notice about the rent going up. I prayed right then. That night before bed I prayed and the next morning before going to work. By the time I arrived at work, God had my problems worked out. I don't need alcohol; all I need is my God. He's fat-free, leaves no hangover, no headaches, and He is with you, twenty-four seven. As for the cost, just turn your life over to him. No alcohol can do that."

Again, Diane wondered if moving in with Megan was a good idea.

Twelve

Soon it was time for school to start. When Leah took the boys in to find where they would be for the year, she was hoping the work they had done during the summer had brought them up to the level they needed. They stopped at the office to find the list posted with the child's name and teacher they would have for the year. Sure enough, each child had been promoted. At this point, the boys let her know they knew which classroom to go to and they would see her that afternoon. Headed to her car, Leah lifted a prayer of thanks.

As Leah was pulling into her driveway, Nora came running out to find out about the boys. "Well, how did they do? Were they able to move up a grade?"

Smiling, Leah said, "Yes. They were so excited and didn't need my assistance after that."

"Oh, Leah, Nick and I have been praying for them. To have lived the life they have, those boys are exceptional boys. They were so undernourished when they came here, dirty, and yet well-mannered. As I have said before, I really had my doubts about them when I first saw them, but Leah, you saw them through different eyes. You taught me a valuable lesson. We need to see people for who they are on the inside and not on outward appearance. Nick and I can't imagine not having them as our neighbors. Mark my word, those boys are going to grow up and be a blessing for so many. I don't know how, but it's a gut feeling, and I feel it when I pray for them."

"Nora, I know exactly what you are saying. If nothing else, they have been a blessing to me. Don't mean to cut our talk short, but I have a meeting with Ms. Julie Knight. Don't want to be late because this is an important meeting."

"Leah, do you think things will go your way?" Nora asked. "Nick and I have been praying about this also."

"I really believe it will. I have prayed and prayed. I don't think my age will be a factor in this, but if it should come up, I'm confident that God will make a way."

As Leah walked up to the courthouse, she saw Julie Knight coming from the other direction.

"Good morning, Ms. Knight. How are you this fine morning?"

"Good morning, Mrs. Conner. I'm doing well. You seem in the best of spirits. You do realize this could or could not go the way you want."

"Ms. Knight, I have prayed and prayed about this and asked my church and neighbors to pray with me also. It's in God's hands so it will go the way He knows best."

"Mrs. Conner, you are such an inspiration to me. I have never been one to go to church. I might go on special occasions, and as for praying, if a need arises, I will lift a few words up. But you, you talk like God is your best friend, and He is with you all the time. I don't think anything gets you down."

"Ms. Knight, I would love for you to come and visit my church. Don't just come one time, come for several Sundays for a while. Give God a chance. You just might find out what you are missing out on in life."

"Mrs. Conner, I don't know. I wasn't brought up in church. My grandparents went all the time, and sometimes they took me, but not often. You quote scripture from the Bible, and it makes good sense, but when it comes to learning and understanding all that, I'm afraid I wouldn't be good at it. It takes someone who is wise and understands what's written."

"Ms. Knight, I didn't learn what the Bible talks about overnight. It has taken years of reading and studying. Do you have a Bible?"

"No. Like I said, I have never had a need for one."

"I will get you a Bible, but you must promise that you will come to church and give God a try. In Proverbs 2:1-11 it says, 'My child, if you accept my words and store up my commands within you, turning your ear to wisdom and applying your heart to understanding – indeed, if you call out for insight and cry aloud for understanding, and if you look for it as for silver and search for it as for hidden treasure, then you will understand the fear of the Lord and find the knowledge of God. For the Lord gives wisdom, from his mouth comes knowledge and understanding. He holds success in store for the upright, He is a shield to those whose walk is blameless, for He guards the course of the just and protects the way of his faithful ones. Then you will understand what is right and just and fair – every good path. For wisdom will enter your heart, and knowledge will be pleasant to your soul. Discretion will protect you and understanding will guard you.'"

"That's in the Bible? I love it. How did you ever memorize all that?" Julie replied in amazement.

Leah smiled at Julie. "Years of reading and studying. I also had a strong desire to learn about God's Word. God blessed me with a godly husband who had the same desire for the Lord. We grew together in learning about our heavenly Father."

"I'm not married, but I am living with my boyfriend. Maybe someday we will get married, and hopefully he will want to go to church, and we can study the Bible together. We had better go in, we don't want to be late. Do you think we can talk again sometime?"

"Yes, we do need to talk and soon," replied Leah. "Look at your schedule and let me know when you can come over. Don't forget about Sunday, I will be looking for you at church."

"But I don't have a Bible."

Leah said, with a twinkle in her eye, "It's not Sunday yet."

Together the two walked into the courthouse and found what courtroom they were to meet in. Leah had been praying for a judge with a heart for children. She was not going to give her boys up without a fight. They walked into the courtroom and found a seat. There were several other people in the room, and Leah had no idea who they were or why they were there. It didn't really matter as long as she was able to keep the boys. When the judge walked in, everyone had to rise till the judge was seated. Leah focused her thoughts on Philippians 4:13: "I can do all things through Christ my Lord who strengths me."

Leah soon realized that the other people were there for different situations. As your name was called, your case was read. Soon a man in a police uniform called out "case for Conner." As Leah and Julie walked forward, a calmness came over Leah, and she knew God was with her. With a sigh of relief, Leah was at peace. When the judge heard the case and all questions were answered, he finally looked at Leah and Julie with his reply.

"I will review this case in my chambers, and when I have made my decision, you will receive a letter in the mail with my findings. This case is dismissed. Next case."

Julie and Leah walked outside. "Mrs. Conner, I hope you didn't become discouraged by the judge's decision. He does this quite often. He is a thorough judge. It may take several weeks to receive a reply from him."

"Ms. Knight, he can take all the time he needs. I already know the outcome. You see, God gave me a peace while in the courtroom."

"How can you be so sure? Do you have that much faith in God?"

"Yes, Ms. Knight, I do. There is scripture for that also. In fact, the Bible is filled with scripture on faith. No matter what is before you, the Bible has scripture for it. Are you busy Saturday morning? The boys usually go somewhere with my neighbor. That would be a good time for us to talk. I don't have any plans, so what time would be good for you?"

"Don't make it too early, Saturday is our time to sleep in," answered Julie.

"Is ten o'clock too early for you?" Leah asked.

"No, that should be about right. See you Saturday."

As Julie walked away, Leah walked to her car with one thing on her mind. She was going to a Christian store and buy a Bible for Julie.

At ten o'clock on Saturday, Julie rang the doorbell at Leah's home. Leah answered the door, and said, "Hello, Ms. Knight, please come in."

"Mrs. Conner, every time I see you, you have a smile on your face. I remember the first time we met you; you were smiling with four unknown little boys by your side. Even in the court room the other day, you had a smile. How do you do that? And please call me Julie.”

“Julie, that’s why I wanted you to come over this morning. You, too, can have a smile on your face. Even in tough times and if tears may fall, you can still smile and give thanks to God.”

“I don’t think so, Mrs. Conner. When I’m sad, I have nothing to smile about.”

“Julie, when my husband passed away, it was a shock, and my heart was broken for I loved him dearly. But through my tears and broken heart I had something to smile about. My David was with our dear Lord. That was something to smile about. Come on in and sit down. Would you like a cup of coffee or a glass of tea?”

“No, thanks, I have had my quota on coffee today, and I don’t drink tea. So how could you smile about your husband’s passing? If you loved him like you said, I would think you would have a sad expression on your face.”

“You see, Julie, that’s where God comes in. Don’t get me wrong. I have missed David much and at times felt alone. But that would pass for God gave me scripture that would lift me up. Reading his Word was such a comfort; such peace would come over me. If you looked around, you would think I was all alone, but I wasn’t. God was right by my side. When I went to bed at night, some nights I read my Bible and some nights I sang. God always gave me what I needed to put me to sleep.”

“Oh my, God can do that? When I have trouble sleeping, I have a big night cap, then I go right to sleep.”

“How do you feel the next morning? Do you have a headache, maybe a bad taste in your mouth?”

Julie looked at Leah, “Yes, but with some Tylenol the headache goes away. Is that the way you feel when you have a little too much to drink?”

“Julie, I have never had a drop of alcohol in my life. My husband, David, would go to the jail to witness to the inmates, and that’s what they told him they felt like the next morning. You see, when you read God's Word or sing his songs before going to bed, the next morning the only after effect you have is rejoicing. When I wake up every morning, the first thing I do is give God thanks for watching over me through the night. I do have my share of aches and pains, but I look to God to get me through every day."

"You have never had a drink of alcohol?" Julie looked amazed.

"Were you never curious about what it tasted like or felt like to get a buzz?"

"No, you see, in my parent's home, alcohol was not allowed. I saw some of my school friends go out and party with the wrong crowd, and that just didn't appeal to me. My parents had taught me about worldly things and reminded me over and over again of what the repercussions would be. I also witnessed a cousin who was older than me turn to the things of the world and all she went through. I had a choice. We all do, but I didn't want to be like her. I'm so grateful for what my parents taught me. Also marrying a godly man was a big plus."

"So how long did you and David live together before you two got married?" Julie asked.

Leah opened her Bible. "Julie, it displeases God when a man and a woman live together and not married. Hebrews 13:4 says, 'Marriage should be honored by all, and the marriage bed kept pure, for God will judge the adulterer and all the sexually immoral.' You see, the Bible promotes abstinence before marriage as the standard of godliness. Sex before marriage is just as wrong as adultery. Living with your boyfriend could be the reason you are unhappy."

Julie looked down. "I was not brought up in church, and my parents were not happy when I moved in with my boyfriend. They don't like him. In fact, when I go visit them, he stays home."

"Do you and he get along or do you fuss and argue a lot?" Leah asked.

"No, we fuss and argue all the time. Some mornings, by the

time I get to work, I'm so upset my whole day is a wreck."

Reaching over to pat Julie's hand, Leah said, "Why don't you try doing things God's way for a while? It can't hurt."

"I don't know, Mrs. Conner, I have nowhere to go."

"Why don't you ask your parents if you can move back in with them? Explain why, and who knows, it might encourage your parents to get into church. God does have a way of working things out and his way is always right."

Rubbing her forehead, Julie said, "It would please my parents if I left Leo, but I don't know about me moving in with them."

"Julie, go and talk to them. They are your parents, but before you do pray, and ask God for guidance. You see, if you seek God's help beforehand, He can make your situation with your parents much easier. Ask God to prepare not only you but your parents also. Oh, I have something for you."

Leah handed Julie a beautifully wrapped package. Julie was so surprised she didn't know what to say at first.

"You bought me a gift, Mrs. Conner? Why?" asked Julie.

"Open it, and then we will talk," replied Leah.

Julie carefully unwrapped the gift and lifted the lid of the box. She just stared at what she saw. Then tears filled her eyes. Taking the Bible from the box, there in gold letters was her name with praying hands under her name.

"Mrs. Conner, I don't know what to say."

"Julie, my dear. You can thank me by reading God's Word and reaching out to him. He is right here now, waiting for you to let him in your heart. If you ask, He will show you the scripture you need to read. Please, all I'm asking is to give it a try. All your problems will not go completely away, but with our dear Lord, they are so much easier."

"Mrs. Conner, you make it sound so easy. I'm afraid I don't have your faith."

"Julie, it will come. Look at my four boys. I have been working with them ever since the first day they came here. With what they have told us about the life they have had, don't you think God intervened? Like I have told you before, I needed someone here in my home, and those boys needed a home. This wasn't about luck—God had a plan. We were right where we needed to be that morning. When a child starts out praying, the prayers are simple yet sincere. Let your prayers be sincere and reach out to God the best you can. He is listening. The boys have found that out, and their prayers are already so much stronger. I can't tell you how proud I am of them. In my heart, they are my sons and always will be."

"Mrs. Conner, you are truly an inspiration. Those boys are so lucky to have you."

"No, Julie, I am the one who is blessed to have them. Remember, it's not luck, it's a blessing. When something good happens, remind yourself it's not luck but God's blessings on you."

"Mrs. Conner, I have enjoyed our talk this morning. I feel better already just listening to you."

"Then, my dear child, read your Bible and pray. You will be so surprised at how you are going to feel. You are welcome to come to our church Sunday. Church starts at ten-fifteen. We have plenty of people your age and single, I might add. If you feel this church isn't for you, there are plenty around here for you to try."

Getting up from the table, Julie picked up her Bible and said, "Mrs. Conner, you have given me a lot to think about. I appreciate your time, and I really do appreciate the Bible. Who knows, I may show up at your church tomorrow."

Walking Julie to the door, Leah said, "So happy you came over. Be sure to talk to your parents. They might surprise you and want to go to church with you."

As Julie walked to her car, she wondered if she could ever be half the woman that Leah Conner was. What would Leo say when she walked in with a Bible and refused to drink alcohol anymore and take the verbal abuse she received from him daily? What would her parents say if she asked to move back home and that she wanted to change her life around? So many things were going through her mind. Was she strong enough to do this? What was it Mrs. Conner said, "Pray believing?" Getting in her car, Julie looked back at the Conner home. It was neat, clean, and beautiful not only on the outside but on the inside. That was the way Mrs. Conner was. Julie wanted to change, and the change was going to start now. She knew Mrs. Conner would be there for her, and for the first time, she felt God would be there for her also. With a smile on her face and tears in her eyes, Julie was excited about her future, and she had Leah Conner to thank. She was also thankful that when Officer Kelly called about the four boys, she took the call and witnessed firsthand the love that this special lady had. Not only had Mrs. Connor reached out with love to four little strangers, Julie knew she was blessed also. Mrs. Conner said, "God was working things out for his glory," and now Julie could see this.

On Sunday morning, as the choir was singing, Julie Knight walked into the church looking for Leah Conner. Benjamin saw her and turned to Daniel.

"Look, there is the lady that comes to the house about us. Is she coming to take us away?"

Daniel turned and saw her walking toward them. When Caleb and Stephen saw her, they froze. She walked up to the pew where they were and sat down beside them. All four boys just stared at her. When the song was over, Leah happened to look down at the end of the bench and saw Julie. With a smile on her face, Leah winked at her.

For the special music that morning, the boys got up to go on stage. As they crossed over Julie, they gave her a look as to say, "What are you doing here?" They had practiced a song to sing as well as to play. They wanted to surprise Leah. She thought it was to be musical only.

As they sang, everyone was so surprised. Their voices blended so smoothly. They sang, "It Is Well with My Soul."

Everyone had tears as the boys sang, Julie included. Leah turned and slipped down to the end of the pew and put her arm around Julie and thought the boys couldn't have sung a more perfect song.

After church, everyone gathered around the boys telling them how much they enjoyed their singing. Some shook their hands, and nearly all the women gave them hugs. Julie even went over to them.

"I can't believe how well you boys sing and play. How do you do this?"

Caleb replied, "It comes natural, we each were able to pick out the instrument we wanted to play, and then we tried singing, and that was easy."

Stephen looked at Julie and asked, "Why are you here?"

Leah said, "Stephen, this is church. Everyone is welcome at God's house."

"But is she going to take us away?" he asked.

Julie spoke up, "No, I came to church because I need God in my life. Mrs. Conner has not only helped you boys, but she has helped me." She held up the Bible Leah had given her.

"Yesterday, I made some changes in my life. I am now living at home with my parents, and I'm going to try to live the life that is pleasing to God. Like you, I have this wonderful lady to thank."

Julie walked over to Leah and gave her a big hug. "Thank you. Yesterday was a rough day, but I made it through, and I'm going to press on."

Benjamin said, "Then we should have prayer. Mom always says we should always give thanks when things go well."

In the parking lot of the church, Leah, the boys, and Julie held hands and prayed.

Thirteen

Megan came home from church all excited only to find Diane wasn't there. She started preparing lunch for them and just as she had it ready, Diane came in.

"Hey, where have you been?" Megan said. "I have some great news for you. A man at church is interested in your car. He gave me his number, and you are to call him to set up a time for him to stop by and look at it."

"Really, you found a buyer for my car? Don't tell me, you put it on that marketplace you were telling me about," replied Diane.

"No, this man is my Sunday School teacher. He overheard me telling one of my friends about your car, and he came over to inquire about it. Go ahead and call him. I have already been praying he would give you a good offer on it. I explained your situation to him."

"Megan, please don't be telling people about me. I like to keep things private. Where's his number?"

Handing Diane the number, Megan continued putting the meal on the table. Diane called the number and set up a time for the man to stop by. As soon as lunch was over, the girls cleaned up the kitchen, and the doorbell rang. Megan opened the door to find Mr. O'Riley and another young man with him.

"Hello, Megan, hope you don't mind, I brought my nephew with me. He knows all about cars, and I wanted his expert advice. Megan, this is Keith Newcomb. Keith this is Megan Adams."

As soon as Megan saw Keith, her heart took an extra beat. He looked to be about her age and had the most beautiful green eyes. Trying to regain her composure, she said, "Please, won't you both come in? It's nice to meet you, Keith."

Diane walked in and introduced herself. "Hello, I'm Diane, the one with the car for sale. So, which one of you is looking for a Porsche?"

Mr. O'Riley spoke up, "I'm the one who's interested. My name is Luther O'Riley. This is my nephew, Keith Newcomb.

Keith knows a lot about cars, so I brought him along for advice. I take it the Porsche out front is yours since that's the only one out there?"

"Yes, it is, and I have the keys right here. Let's go out and let you guys look it over." Diane led the way outside.

Megan, on the other hand, couldn't take her eyes off Keith. Since she didn't see a wedding band, was he dating someone? She began wondering if he was in church, and if so, where?

The men looked the car over thoroughly and even took it for a drive. When they came back, Mr. O'Riley made Diane a cash offer on the car. It was way more than her payoff, so she took it. When they left, Diane couldn't believe she had emptied her apartment and sold her car all so quickly. She would be meeting Mr. O'Riley on Monday to finalize the transfer.

"Megan, how can I ever thank you? You don't know what this means to me to be free from those payments. Now I need to find a car I can afford. Is it possible that I can ride to work with you till I get my own set of wheels?" Diane inquired.

"Diane, you can repay me by going to church with me. You saw what a nice man Mr. O'Riley is. The church is full of wonderful people. Did you notice his nephew?" Megan smiled.

"Yes, I saw him, and no, I won't go to church with you. Sorry, I told you I don't do church." With that, Diane turned and went to her room. Looking at her watch, Megan knew she needed to change and get ready for church.

On Thursday of the next week, Keith stopped by the apartment. When Megan opened the door, her heart skipped a beat.

"Hello, Keith, what a nice surprise. How can we help you?"

"Hey, Megan, is Diane here?"

Hearing him ask for Diane broke her heart. "Yes, come in, I'll go get her."

Coming from her room, Diane smiled and said to Keith, "Megan said you needed to see me?"

"Yes, I found a car that you might be interested in. It has low miles, easy on gas and I think would serve your needs. I have it out front if you would like to look it over."

Diane said, "Sure, I have nothing to lose by looking."

As she walked out the door, Keith turned to Megan, "Would you like to see it too?"

Megan was disappointed at the thought that Keith had simply made an excuse to see Diane again. She did not want to appear ungracious, though, and walked out to see the car.

It was a Nissan Versa, 2012, black and in good shape for a used car. When Keith told Diane the price, she knew she would be able to pay it off and not have a car payment. She was so excited to be having her own set of wheels again. He told her where to go the next day and get everything all taken care of. She thanked him and went back inside the apartment.

Megan turned to Keith. "This was a kind thing that you have done. How can we ever thank you?"

Looking at Megan, Keith said, "I knew if I found her a car, it would give me a reason to come back over here and see you."

With that comment, Megan's face lit up. "I'm sorry, I thought when you ask for Diane you were wanting to see her."

"Well, I was hoping she hadn't found a car, and this was the best reason I could think of. By the way, do you have any plans Sunday after church?" Keith asked.

Smiling from ear to ear, Megan replied, "No, I don't."

"Good, after church we can go somewhere and grab some lunch. You can leave your car at the church till that night."

With that, Keith turned to get in the car that was for Diane.

"You know, I'm glad I found this car for your roommate."

Still on cloud nine, Megan replied, "Me, too."

Megan couldn't wait for Sunday to come, but she couldn't remember ever seeing Keith at her church. Maybe Mr. O'Riley had something to do with Keith going to be at church.

Sunday arrived at last. As Megan walked into her Sunday School class, she looked around but didn't see Keith. Maybe he was planning on coming for church only. As soon as class was over, she went straight to the sanctuary. Looking around, still no Keith. Although disappointed, she tried not to let it show. She hardly heard the songs, and when the preacher got up, still Megan did not hear what was being said. Then she heard Keith's voice. Looking up, she saw that he was bringing the message that morning, and the pastor had introduced him. Megan became attentive to what Keith had to say.

After church, Keith and the pastor were at the door to speak to everyone as they were leaving. When Megan walked up, both men greeted her and Keith said, "Pastor Cook, here is the lady who agreed to have lunch with me today."

"Megan, it's so good to see you today. When Keith mentioned you, I had only good things to brag to him about you."

"Thank you, sir. Any words for me about him?" she smiled.

"Well, I will say this, you have a nice lunch partner for today," he replied, patting Megan on the back.

Keith spoke up, "Megan, if you want to wait inside until everyone has come through, then we can go for lunch. It's a little warm outside today."

"Sure, I'll slip around everyone and be inside when you're ready," Megan replied.

Once seated, Megan wondered what Keith had said to Pastor Cook about her and what exactly had Pastor Cook stated about her. She was lost in thought and unaware that Keith had come in.

"Are you ready?" he asked, surprising Megan, and causing her to jump.

"I'm so sorry," said Keith. "I didn't mean to startle you."

"Oh no, you're fine. I was just doing some thinking and didn't hear you walk up. So, are we ready?" Megan asked.

"Yes, I have picked a place I hope you will enjoy. Hopefully, it won't be crowded."

It was a small restaurant more out toward the country. The scenery was so relaxing, something Megan enjoyed.

"Keith, I have never been in this area. The drive alone is breathtaking. How did you ever find it?" she asked.

"I was raised in this area. My parents own the restaurant we are going to for lunch."

With that statement Megan felt a large lump come up in her

throat.

"Your parents own the restaurant we are going to?"

"Yes, it's okay, don't get upset. I haven't been home in several weeks. With my studies, I stay in town and drive in about once a month if possible. My mom is a great cook, so I thought I would invite you to lunch to get to know you better and get to eat my mom's cooking."

Megan said, "I see! Like, they say, kill two birds with one stone."

"Don't say it like that. Once you have tasted my mom's cooking, you will be glad we came. Plus, afterwards, we can walk around. There's a stream of water not far from the restaurant and a gazebo close by in the shade. We can walk there and sit for a while if you like."

Taking a deep breathe, Megan said, "It does sound nice."

The restaurant was busy, but a table had been reserved for Keith and Megan. Keith explained that he had called ahead to let his parents know he was coming and bringing a friend.

As they entered the door, a beautiful older lady walked up to give Keith a hug.

"Keith, it's so good to see you, and you must be Megan," she said reaching out her hand to shake Megan's hand.

"I'm Keith's mom, Holly. Welcome to our restaurant. I have you two a table by the window. At this time of year, it's the best seat in here."

Taking a seat, Megan looked around for the menu. She was just getting ready to ask Keith about the menu when Holly brought out enough food for five or six people. It all looked good, and Megan wasn't sure what to try first.

"Now if you need anything let Keith know. He knows where everything is." With that, she was gone back to the kitchen.

Before they had had a chance to take a bite, Keith's dad appeared.

"Hey, Son, it's so good to see you."

Keith stood up to give his dad a big hug.

"It's good to see you, too. Dad, this is Megan, the lady I was telling you and Mom about."

"Well, hello, young lady. So nice to meet you and we hope you enjoy your meal. Don't mean to be so short, but as you can see, we are packed today, and I'm needed in the kitchen. Maybe things will slow down to where we can all talk later. If you need anything let us know or tell Keith. He knows where everything is, so help yourself. Megan, it's our pleasure to meet you."

As Keith's father walked away, Megan said, "Keith, your parents are so nice, and they have a wonderful business here."

"Yes, they are both happy here, and if a stranger comes in, they know it. They know everybody. Shall we pray before our food gets cold?"

After they had eaten, Keith and Megan walked up to the gazebo. It was all so beautiful.

"So, what are you studying in school?" Megan asked.

"I'm going to seminary. It's a dream I have had for a while. I am truly enjoying it, and it involves a lot of reading. Seems like all I do is read," Keith said.

Laughing, Megan said, "I thought you worked at a car lot, selling cars. You came over with your uncle that night to look at Diane's car, and then you brought that car over for her to look at."

"Let me explain," said Keith, "My brothers and I were raised here, and when something broke, we had to fix it. I became a pretty good mechanic, but that's not what I wanted to do for the rest of my life. That's why my uncle asked me to come along to check the car out. As for the other car, one of the guys in my class was selling his car, and I thought of your roommate. I knew this would be the perfect excuse to get to see you again. End of story."

"I like your story, your mother's cooking, and this place. You did good today, Mr. Keith Newcomb. Oh, might I add, your message was wonderful this morning. I was a bit surprised when I realized you were bringing the message. Are you preaching tonight?"

"No, studying for a message I enjoy, but it takes weeks for me to get it down to where I feel it is ready for a congregation."

"Well, you were relaxed and never stumbled at all. Was this your first time?" Megan asked.

"No, I have spoken two other times. I would say it gets easier and in time I'm sure it will, but for now, the knots in the stomach and sweaty palms are still present."

"Have you always gone to Highland Church?" asked Megan. "I don't recall ever seeing you. I have only been going about ten months myself."

"No, I go some because it is not too far of a drive from the school. Sometimes I go to church with some of the guys in school. It's good to see how others worship. Gives you something to think about. When I go to one that's a different denomination, I come back and do some serious studying. It's good for me, for then I search for what God's Word really says. I want to make sure I understand and stand for what is correct. I don't want to take man's word on anything about the Bible. What I believe and preach about comes from my Heavenly Father."

With that, Megan smiled at Keith. She had prayed that someday God would send her a godly man and deep down inside, she believed that sitting in front of her was just that man. What a blessing! But for now, she would keep this to herself. What did God have in store for her and Keith? Would it only be friendship or something more? To herself, she said, "Thank You, Lord, for this special day. I love You so much and am so grateful You love me, too!"

Keith interrupted her pleasant thoughts saying, "We need to head back to be on time for church. Ready?"

"I'm sorry, what were you saying?" she asked.

"I was saying, we needed to head back, for soon it will be time for church."

"Yes, I'm ready. Thank you for this day. This has been the best Sunday I have had in such a long time."

Looking pleased, Keith said, "So glad you have enjoyed today. Hopefully, we can get together again. I can't promise when since I devote most of my time to my studies. Maybe I can call you, and we could talk if that's alright with you?"

With a glow on her face she said, "Oh, that would be perfect. Maybe we could FaceTime, that way, we could see each other."

"That's right, I hadn't thought of that. What a great idea. When we get back to the car, I have a pad and pen, and we can exchange phone numbers."

The ride back to church was as enjoyable as the ride that afternoon. Soon church was over and time to part ways.

"Hope you have a great week, Megan, and if I have a spare minute, I'll give you a call. If I do, it will be in the evening between eight and nine o'clock."

"I'm always home in the evenings so call anytime, Keith. Hope you have a wonderful week as well."

He waited till she was in her car and had driven off before he got in his car. Once inside, he saw the cup she had been drinking her tea from. On the side of the cup was the print of her lipstick. Picking it up he held it to his lips, then smiled as he thought about their day and what their future might hold.

When Megan walked in the door, Diane looked at her and said, "Are you alright?"

"Oh, Diane, this has been the best day. God is so good. He has answered so many prayers for me. I can't thank him enough. How has your day been?"

"Well, apparently not as good as yours. Went for a long walk at the park. It was so crowded that all I did was dodge kids. Came home, showered then went to the grocery store. I did a little laundry, you know, those colorful uniforms we wear at work? That's about it. Oh, I did watch 'The Titanic,' or nearly all of it."

"Diane, you really need to go to church with me. Do you remember the guy that was here when you were selling your car, and then he came back with a car for you to buy?"

"Yeah, I remember him. What about him?"

"He asked me out to lunch today. We spent the entire day together, and it was wonderful. We started with church this morning and ended with church tonight. I am so happy. God has blessed me so much. I'm telling you; God has something in store for you. I just know it."

"Megan, I am happy for you. If this church stuff makes you happy, then go for it. But please, leave me out of it. I have no use for God, his so-called churches, or all that praying you do. What happens, happens. It's just luck, that's all."

"Oh, Diane, what happens is not being lucky. It's blessings from God. Someday, you will know what I'm trying to tell you. I'm going to bed. It will soon be time to go to work. Good night."

For the life of her, Diane could not understand Megan at all. She wondered if she was getting involved in some kind of cult. As long as she didn't move out and leave her stuck with the rent she didn't care. It was her life; she could do whatever she wanted with it.

Fourteen

After getting the boys off to school, Leah went next door to visit with Nora. Nora was making a fresh pot of coffee when Leah knocked at the door.

"Morning, Leah, you are just in time to have a cup of coffee with me. Have a seat, and I'll grab an extra cup."

Leah took a seat at the table, but just stared out the window. Her mind was not on what Nora was saying or doing.

"Hello, Leah. Are you with me?" Nora asked as she placed a cup of coffee in front of Leah and sat down.

"I'm sorry, Nora, I have a lot on my mind this morning. That's why I came over, thought maybe you could help."

"Sure, Leah, what's on your mind? You have a concerned looked. Is everything alright with the boys?"

"Nora next month will be Thanksgiving. I was hoping I would have custody of the boys by now so we could decide on birthday dates, and we could celebrate who they are. They have never had a birthday to celebrate. I wanted Thanksgiving to be special, but it's been several months, and the way I felt leaving the courthouse, I just knew things would be settled quickly. When I left, it was like the weight of the world had been lifted off my shoulders."

"Leah, didn't you tell me, Ms. Knight said it would take some time, that the judge reviews each case thoroughly?"

"Yes, she did, Nora, but I thought we would have heard something by now."

"Leah, you also know God never rushes through anything. We are talking about four boys here, not one. How many times have I heard you say this? When the time is right, it will happen. By the way, are the boys going to the church 'trunk or treat,' and have they said what they wanted to dress up as?"

Rubbing her fingers around the cup, Leah said, "They have been talking to Cody about it. Since they have never been trick-or-treating, they are all excited. He said he would help them with what they would wear. They get to choose who they want to be."

"Can you imagine being a child and never have gone out on Halloween?" replied Nora.

"Oh, those boys have missed out on so much. I have tried to explain all the holidays to them. You should have seen their faces when I told them about Thanksgiving and Christmas. They were so excited on the Fourth of July and Labor Day."

"Oh, I know. When Nick took them to buy fireworks, he said just watching them was a joy. That night at the church festival, they had so much fun. Can't wait to see their faces when they see all the cars lined up, trunks opened, filled with candy they can collect in their plastic pumpkins. Nick and I have already made a small bag of goodies for them to get them started."

"Nora, you and Nick spoil those boys. If I was guessing, the goody bag you have for them is not a small one."

"Now, Leah, with our girls gone, like you, those boys are a little blessing, and they are so appreciative of what we do for them. You can't help but want to do things for them. Look at you. Are you going to sit there and tell me you don't spoil them?"

"Well, maybe in the beginning, but not so much now. I don't have to. You and Nick do that for me, plus Cody is always doing things with them too. Speaking of Cody, he is really working hard with the boys on their music. When they practice, it is enjoyable to listen to them."

"We can hear them over here, and yes, they are doing remarkably well. I have sung along here in the kitchen while they practice. Nick said my singing was improving," laughed Nora.

"Don't tell him I told you," Leah said, "but he was working in his garage one day while the boys were practicing, and I could hear him singing. They were playing 'Amazing Grace,' and Nick was really into it. He was certainly getting a blessing from it."

Both Leah and Nora laughed. Then Nora said, "I think our cup of coffee did us both some good this morning. Care for another cup?"

"Sure, not only was the coffee good, but the company I shared it with was better. Thanks, Nora, I feel so much better now, even if we don't know what the judge is going to do and when."

"Maybe you will hear before Thanksgiving. That would be a big blessing for all of us. Say, are the girls coming in for Thanksgiving or Christmas this year?"

"I'm not sure. They would have to fly in order to spend any time with us and since I have the boys, I'm not able to go to their house like I did last year. I do miss them and want them to meet the boys. We have FaceTimed each other but that's not the same as being together. How about you? Are your girls coming in?"

"Unfortunately, they can't this year. Nick and I hope to fly out to see them for Christmas. I'm so thankful that Sharon and Karen live only an hour from each other. It doesn't seem like Christmas when we go see them, going to the beach in December with the weather all sunny. Then go back to their house and it all decorated for Christmas, just doesn't seem right. But they love Florida, so we make the best of it."

"I think I would take Florida over Indiana. It is so odd that both my girls married men that their jobs took them to the same place. Anna and Abigail both are not happy where they live and keep asking me to pray with them that they will be sent to a better place. My prayer is they will move back to Virginia so they can be close to me. Nora, I know what you are going to say, I should not pray a selfish prayer, but until the boys came along, they were all I had."

"Oh, Leah, I don't think that's a selfish prayer, for I have prayed our sons-in-law could find work closer to us. Florida is nice in the summer but for Thanksgiving and Christmas, it just isn't cold enough and doesn't seem right. At least it's cold in Indiana in the winter."

"That is true, Nora, but if they could move closer here, then my grandchildren would get to know the boys and they could grow up together. Guess we will just have to keep on praying."

"Leah, it seems we never run out of anything to pray about. If it's not for our family, it's for other families or our country. Wouldn't it be nice if we could see a screen that shows all the prayers going up to our Heavenly Father? That would be a blessing.”

“Nora, I had never thought of it like that. That would be a sight to behold. That reminds me, one of the prisoners one day at the jail told David that God was too busy for him, that when he prayed, he felt like he was on a party line. David told him he needed to find another line, that he had a direct line to God, and he used it all the time. He had never received a busy signal, and he didn’t have to leave a message for God to call him back. You know how David was. Those prisoners could come up with all kinds of excuses, and it didn’t faze David at all. He had a biblical answer for anything they threw at him.”

“David was a godly man, and everyone loved him. I know you miss him greatly for I know Nick and I do.”

“I do, but having the boys has helped so much. God’s hand was in this and what a blessing He has given me. Well, I must go and get some things done, the boys will be home from school soon, and all I have gotten accomplished today is drinking coffee and chatting with my precious neighbor. Nora, thank you. I don’t know what I would do without you and Nick.”

“Leah, we feel the same way. God brought us together years ago for a reason. You are more like a sister to me than a neighbor. Come to think of it, we are sisters. We are sisters in Christ, and I love you so much.”

The two stood and hugged one another with tears in their eyes. It had been a good morning.

Leah and Nora had made cookies for the boys to take to school for their Halloween party. They made chocolate chip cookies, sugar cookies, and peanut butter cookies. They put one of each in a bag so they wouldn’t be handled by everyone. If they counted correctly, they had made over three hundred cookies.

The next morning, Nora stopped in after Nick had taken the boys to school. “Leah, did the boys take the cookies to school?”

“Oh, Nora, they were so excited. Having a party at school today and then going trunk or treating tonight, you can only imagine what it was like here this morning. I know they talked poor Nick’s ear off going to school. Cody called before they left for school, and he will be picking them up around five tonight. This only added to their excitement.”

“Oh, don’t worry about Nick. He enjoys it. Why do you think he offers to take them to school and pick them up? Having girls, which he loved ours, and did things with them, I never realized how much men enjoyed boys being around. Nick is different now that you have the boys. It’s hard to explain, I wouldn’t say he is happier, but the change is a good change.”

“Nora, those boys will keep you active, and maybe that’s what Nick needed, some activity in his life. He understands things about boys that we can’t. With our girls, we understood things they went through. Having Nick around has been a blessing, just like Cody is a blessing. That’s why God made man and woman, for when you have children, you need both parents.”

“You are so right, Leah. Some things a boy needs his mother for and some things he needs a dad, same for girls. Like I said, having the boys around has helped Nick so much. It’s been a big blessing for me.”

Nick picked the boys up for Leah, and as soon as they came through the kitchen door, they were all four talking and wanting her to see what all they had gotten at school. They finally settled down to eat because they knew Cody would be by to pick them up soon.

“Boys, you have yet to say what you are dressing up as tonight. Can you give me a hint so I will know who you are?”

Daniel smiled, “No, you will just have to wait. We want to surprise you.”

At that time, the doorbell rang. Benjamin said, “It’s Cody, let’s go.”

They all turned to Leah to give her a hug and kiss, then took off. When Leah walked to the door, Cody said, “I’ll take good care of them and see you at church later tonight. I hope you will be pleased by their costumes. They choose what to wear themselves.”

“Well, they haven’t said a word about what they are wearing.

I'm looking forward to seeing them. Thanks, Cody."

Leah waved goodbye and went to the kitchen to clean it up and get ready for church. She wanted to get there early to get a good spot to park her car.

Several cars were already at the church when Leah arrived. It didn't take her long to get her trunk set up. Soon Nick and Nora came. As the trick or treaters came by, Leah studied them carefully and was unable to pick out her boys. When it was almost time to leave, Cody walked up with four people. "I believe these guys are yours."

Studying them carefully, Leah asked, "So who are you supposed to be?"

Daniel said, "I'm Peter."

Stephen said, "I'm Andrew."

Caleb said, "I'm John."

Benjamin said, "I'm James. We are the first four that Jesus picked to be his disciples."

Leah put her hands up to her face, so touched by their choice. They had beards, wigs with long hair, and the robes she should have recognized from the Christmas plays at church. Trying hard not to cry, she reached out to hug them.

"You boys have picked out the best costumes, and I am so touched by your choice. Go over to Nick and Nora to see what they say."

Turning to Cody, Leah asked, "Did you help them decide in any way who to dress up as?"

Shaking his head, Cody said, "No, not at all. We had discussed the disciples a few months ago, and they came to me with the idea when I announced about the trunk or treating here at church. They had never heard of it, so as I explained it to them, they got together, and this is what they wanted. We went through the costumes we wear here at church for Christmas, and here we are. God laid it all out for us. Those boys were willing, and God supplied what they needed. Leah, God has something special in mind for those boys. I can't say what, but I just know they will be serving God in a special way."

"Cody, I agree. They are a blessing, and I feel so blessed to have them. Thank you so much for all you do for them. They look up to you as a big brother. God's hand is everywhere; we need to open our eyes and see the glory He showers on us."

As Leah made out a list for her Thanksgiving meal, she took special care because she wanted everything to be special for the boys. It was Saturday, and she could hear them outside with Nick. Caleb came through the door with the mail in his hand. "Mom, here's the mail." Then back outside he went. Going over to look at the mail, there on top was a letter from the court. Before opening it, Leah took the time to pray.

"Dear Lord, You, know I have been waiting so long for this. I pray that the court has ruled in my favor, and that I will be able to adopt these boys as mine. But if for some reason it's not the news I want, please help me to be strong, for I know you know what's best, and your plans are for them are the right plans. They are your precious children that I love so much. I do thank You for them."

Feeling the tears roll down her cheeks, Leah slowly opened the letter. With hands shaking, as she read, the tears began to pour. Then she fell to her knees and cried, "Oh, Father thank You, thank You, thank You. I promise to do my best for these boys. Each day, Lord, please guide me in making the right decisions for them. I lift them up to You and pray they will always look to You in all things. May they have a serving heart for You. Dear Lord, I love You so much. Forgive me for ever doubting You. Amen."

Nora knocked on the door and stepped in as usual and saw Leah on her knees.

"Leah, are you alright? What's wrong, why are you crying?"

Leah handed the letter to Nora. As Nora read the letter, she threw her hands up in the air and said, "Praise the Lord! Oh, Leah, you have something to be happy about. I need to go tell Nick."

"No, Nora, don't tell Nick in front of the boys. I want to have a celebration party for them. At that time, I will let the boys decide what month and day they want to pick out for their birthday. It must be a special day for them, and in the meantime, I need to go fill out the papers for adoption. According to that paper, everything has been approved, and all it needs is my signature and a few other legal things to do. Nora, it's going to happen. The boys will soon be legally mine."

"Let me know what I can do for the party," Nora said, "This can't be just any party. This must be the party of all times. I'll start on a list of people to invite and things we will need. Oh, what a blessed day this is!"

As Nora went out the door, she was saying "Thank You, Lord. What a day of rejoicing this is."

The party for the boys was held on the Sunday before Thanksgiving at the church fellowship hall. This way decorations could be put up and everything would be a total surprise for them.

The boys had no idea what was going to take place that afternoon. After church, they went out to eat with Cody, but thought it strange he wanted to go back to the church instead of taking them home. When they pulled up in the church parking lot, Stephen said, "Why are all these cars here?"

Cody replied, "Sometimes they have meetings in the afternoon, or someone maybe having a baby or bridal shower. Things are always going on around here."

Getting out of the car, the boys followed Cody inside. When he opened the door to the fellowship hall and walked in, with the boys behind him, the boys stood in awe. They had no idea what was going on. Leah walked up to them, smiling, and said, "The court not only awarded you to me but the paperwork for the adoption has been finalized, and you four belong to me. You are officially my sons!"

All four hugged Leah as hard as they could. Leah was officially their mom. It seemed everyone in the room was crying. A large cake on a table had writing on it that said, "The Conner Boys" with each one's name on it. They looked at each other smiling and crying. Everyone gathered around to congratulate the boys and Leah.

After things began to settle down, Leah told the boys, "I need you to be thinking of a month and day that you would like to have for your birthday. With no records to be found, you can decide and choose for yourself. When you decide, I'll send it in, and you will officially receive a birth certificate stating who you are, and your birth date will be on it."

The boys didn't fully understand why they needed a birth certificate, but they were happy that they would have a day to call their own.

That night as they were getting ready to say their prayers, Daniel spoke up and said, "Mom, I have decided on a day that I want to use. I want my birthday to be in April. Easter is usually in April and that is when Christ arose. I know it won't always fall on the same day but at least it will be in that month. So, I am choosing April ninth.

Stephen spoke up. "I'm choosing May because that's when Mother's Day is, and a lot of flowers are blooming. My day is May fourteenth."

Caleb smiled and said, "I chose November, for that's the day I found out that I am your son, that we belong to a special lady who loves us as much as Christ does. My day is November twenty-second."

Benjamin climbed up in Leah's lap. "Mom, I chose October, for that's when the leaves on the tree changes color and everything is so pretty. You once said that God paints the leaves in pretty colors for us to enjoy. So, I picked October sixteenth."

"Well, I am so pleased with your decisions. I had no idea you would choose so quickly. I feel you boys have given this some serious thought, and your reasons are good ones. I'll put this down and turn it in tomorrow. Now, let's bow our heads in prayer for we have so much to be thankful for."

With hearts full of joy, Leah and her sons huddled together for prayer, just as a family should.

Fifteen

Monday morning at the hospital seemed long to Diane and she felt it would never end. She was relieved when lunchtime came, and she already had her food spread out on the table when Megan joined her. Megan bowed her head for a silent prayer. Not saying a word, Diane only shook her head, thinking Megan was getting entirely too involved with the churchiness.

As Megan unwrapped her sandwich, she said, "Keith will be coming in this weekend. It will be so good to see him in person and not have to FaceTime him. He is going to bring one of his friends from school, and at church this Saturday they are going to have a car wash to raise money for the youth. Later we will probably go out for pizza. Would you like to join us?"

"Is his friend studying to be a preacher?" asked Diane.

"Of course. They are good friends and Keith says he is a godly man. You should come! You might find him not only attractive but someone you would want to become good friends with."

"Megan, like I have said over and over to you, and I don't know why you can't understand, but I am not interested in your church, your God, your religion, your so-called godly people, your praycrs, or your Biblc. All that makcs mc sick. I don't want to hear about Keith or any friend he has. I have had enough, so please refrain from bringing any of that up. Please." Diane then got up, threw her sandwich in the trash, and walked out the door.

Megan bowed her head to say another prayer for Diane. If only God could give her the right scripture or words to say to help her. She knew Diane was lost and wanted so much to see her saved and turn her life around. Megan and Keith had been seeing each other for about six months now, and Diane seemed to grow more bitter each day. Was Diane jealous of Keith, was it because she focused more time on him than her? Keith had won Megan's heart and wanted the same things in life that she did. Even after six months, Keith showed her respect and treated her like she was someone special. Why wouldn't Diane want someone like that? Megan knew that Diane would probably avoid her the rest of the day at work, and after work would only speak to her if she had to. It seems her good intentions for Diane backfired big time.

As Megan left for church Saturday morning, she turned to Diane and said, "I hope you have a good day. Not sure what time I'll be home." Then she closed the door behind her.

Diane was glad to see Megan go. This way she had the apartment all to herself and didn't have to listen to Megan sing along with her gospel music. In fact, with Megan gone all day she could jam the place up with her music. About an hour later, she heard a knock on the door. When she opened it, a police officer was standing there.

"Hello, I'm Officer Bradley Kirk. Could you possibly turn your music down so I can talk to you without shouting?"

Diane went to her room to turn the music off and went back to the door.

"What's the problem, officer?" she asked.

"Several complaints have come in about the loud music. Some said they tried knocking on your door, but no one answered. I had to bang hard before you came to the door. According to your lease, no loud music is acceptable. Your landlord will be by tomorrow to talk to you. He is out of town at the present and that's why I was sent here. Appreciate it if you could keep your music down. Have a good day."

As Diane closed the door, she said, "Oh, what a jerk. My name is not on the lease, so I'll do what I want. If anyone gets into trouble it will be our precious holier-than-thou little Ms. Megan. Then she can pray to her God to get her out of trouble."

Diane was getting a little hungry, so she decided she would go and pick something up, then come back and irritate the neighbors some more before Megan came home. As she took off down the road, she came upon a traffic light that turned red, but she kept on going. The next thing she knew, blue lights were flashing behind her. Pulling over, Diane was furious for she knew he was going to give her a ticket. She lowered her window down only to find Officer Kirk standing there.

"Well, hello again, Ms. Adams. Seems we have already met once today. So, you have gone from playing loud music to running red lights. May I see your driver's license, please."

Diane reached for her purse, but she had left it on her bed. Just her luck.

"Sir, you know where I live, which is just a block away. It seems I left my purse on the bed. Would you mind following me back to the apartment? My licenses are in my purse."

Office Kirk looked at Diane and wondered if she was up to something. "Sure, I'll follow you back to your apartment, but if you try to get away, I will catch you and you're off to jail. Understand!"

Not at all happy with him, Diane turned her car around and drove back to her apartment. By the time she got to the apartment door, Officer Kirk was right by her side and then followed her as she walked into the apartment. She retrieved her wallet and handed her driver's license to the officer. He looked at it and said, "This is your picture, but you're not Megan Adams, are you? What are you doing in her apartment and where is she?"

"Oh, I can explain," replied Diane. "Megan and I are roommates, and we work together at the hospital. We share this apartment because we don't make enough money to go out on our own."

Officer Kirk took out his phone and made a call. When he finished, he looked at Diane.

"I spoke to the landlord, and your name is not on the lease. He said he rented the place to a Megan Adams. He has never heard of you before. Care to explain?"

"Yes, I can. I needed a place because where I lived the rent was too high. Like I said, Megan and I work together. She had received a letter stating her rent was going to go up, and she was going to have to get a second job. If I moved in here with her, we could split the cost, and we would both benefit from it."

"A good story. Do you know how to reach Ms. Adams? I need to verify that what you're saying is true, Ms. Baker."

"Yes, I can," said Diane. "I'll call her, and she can back up all I told you." Diane pressed speed dial for Megan. The phone rang and rang and finally went to her voice mail. Officer Kirk stood waiting patiently for what Diane would come up with next.

Not getting an answer, Diane said, "She went to Highland Church this morning. They are having a car wash. If we could go there, I know she can answer all your questions."

Part of Officer Kirk wanted to believe her, and part didn't. "Okay, I'll follow you to the church, but that's all. You had better hope this Megan Adams is there."

Getting back in her car, Diane was fuming over how her day was going. Then she realized she didn't know where Highland Church was. Sitting at another red light she reached for her phone to use the GPS to find the church. "This is just great," she said. Her phone was at home because she had picked up her wallet but left her phone. About that time, she heard a noise, and the car jerked making steering difficult. Pulling over, she got out and went to the other side of the car and found she had blown a tire.

Officer Kirk walked up, looked at her and said, "This just isn't your day, is it? Do you have a spare tire in the trunk?"

Diane had no idea, nor did she know how to change a tire. "I don't know. I have never looked."

Thinking to himself, leave it to me to take this call and get stuck with an idiot, he said, "Could you pop the trunk so we can look to see if you have a spare?"

Diane opened the trunk, and it was full of everything.

Taking a deep breath, Officer Kirk shook his head. "If you would please, I need you to remove all this so I can get to your spare."

"Where do you want me to put this stuff? I can't dump it out on the sidewalk. What will people think?" Diane replied.

"You could put it in your back seat. That way no one will see all the junk you have here." By this time, Officer Kirk's patience was wearing thin.

"I really don't want all this in my back seat. It would look junky if anyone looked in my car!"

"Let me put it to you this way," he said, "Either remove this junk so I can see if you have a spare tire, or I can call a tow truck and have your car towed away and then take you to jail."

As Diane started gathering up the things in her trunk, she mumbled under her breathe the whole time about him being the worst police officer around. Finally, the trunk was empty and sure enough, she had a spare tire.

Officer Kirk worked to replace the tire and hoped they would find a Megan Adams at the church, for he was over this lady.

Looking at the tire he put on her car, Diane said to the officer, "You don't expect me to drive my car with that ugly thing on it, do you?"

"That ugly thing will do till you can buy a new tire to replace it. It's up to you how long that will be. I only made it possible for you to drive your car. Now, let's go find your friend."

As he turned to go to his cruiser, Diane asked, "Do you know where Highland Church is? I left my phone at home, and my car doesn't have a GPS."

Officer Kirk's took a deep breath, again wondering at his luck in coming in contact with such a woman. He said, "I have an idea. Leave your car here in this parking lot, get in the cruiser, and I'll drive you to the church where hopefully we will find your roommate."

"I don't want to ride in your car. People will think I am a criminal."

Officer Kirk said, "Now, that's not my problem," and opened the door of his cruiser for her to get in. They were about two miles from the church. When they pulled up at the church, a man came up to the cruiser and asked if he wanted his cruiser washed. Officer Kirk told him, "No. I am looking for a Megan Adams. Do you know if she is here?"

"I don't think so," he replied. "Let me check." He walked over to a group of people to see if they knew Megan Adams before telling Officer Kirk, "Sorry, we don't know a Megan Adams, but then we have several people here and she might be on the other side."

Officer Kirk turned to look at Diane with disgust in his eyes. Seeing his anger she said, "Can't you drive around to the other side to see if she is there?"

Gripping the steering wheel, he headed to the other side of the church where another group of people was vacuuming cars. He pulled over to the side, and Diane yelled, "There she is. That's Megan next to the blue car."

Getting out, Officer Kirk opened the back door for Diane to get out. About that time, Megan saw Diane. Stopping what she was doing, she walked over to Diane. "Are you alright? What are you doing in a police car?"

Before Diane could answer, Officer Kirk asked. "Do you know this lady, and if so, how?"

Megan began to explain how she knew Diane and answered all of Officer Kirk's questions. Turning to his car, he pulled out his ticket book and wrote Diane a ticket for running the red light. Handing it to her, he said, "Ms. Baker, for what I have gone through with you today, you deserve more than a ticket for running a red light. Please go home, stay quiet and try to enjoy the rest of this day." Getting into his cruiser he drove off, hoping never to see Diane Baker again.

Turning to Megan, Diane asked, "Can you take me to my car? I want to go home."

"Since you are here, would you like to stay and help? It's for a good cause," Megan said.

"No, I don't want to stay. I have been to you know where and back today. Just take me to my car," Diane angrily replied.

Other people turned to look at Diane for she had raised her voice while speaking to Megan.

Keith walked over and said, "Megan and I will be happy to take you to your car."

When Megan got home that night, Diane was in her room with the door shut. She decided she would wait till tomorrow to try to talk to her.

It was Monday before Megan saw Diane, and she soon realized Diane was still in a foul mood. They drove separately to work, which was alright with Megan. It was lunch time when Pearl Moss walked into the employee lounge and told Megan she had a visitor. When Megan went down to the visitor's lounge, there was her landlord. Surprised to see him, Megan's first thoughts were had someone broke into the apartment or had it burned down.

"Mr. Niles, is everything okay at the apartment?"

"Megan, the apartment is fine. What I want to talk to you about is your roommate. I wasn't aware you had someone living with you."

"Mr. Niles, when I received your notice about the rent going up, it put me in a real bind. My co-worker, Diane Baker, was in the same position as I was, so she moved in with me so we could share expenses. I didn't think it would be a problem."

"Megan, I understand, and I don't have a problem with that if your roommate takes into consideration that she is not the only tenant around. Saturday was unacceptable. If she carries on like that another time, I will be forced to have you both evicted."

Unaware of all that had occurred on Saturday, Megan asked. "What exactly happened? I was at church at a car wash and was gone most of the day."

Mr. Niles explained about the music, how Diane wouldn't come to the door when the neighbors knocked and how they had no choice but to call him. He was out of town, and the only thing he could do was call the police. He knew some of the men on the force and had asked if one of them could check it out.

Megan couldn't believe all he was saying. Finally, she said, "Mr. Niles, I am so sorry. I had no idea all this went on. I'll talk to my roommate. Please don't evict me."

"Megan, we have never had anything like this go on before, and it won't start now. If your roommate can't consider others around her, you might want to look for a new roommate before she gets you both evicted. This is your warning." With that, Mr. Niles left.

Furious with Diane, Megan went into a small bathroom to be alone and pray. Remembering Palms 25: 1-5 she repeated, "In you, Lord my God, I put my trust. I trust in you: do not let me be put to shame, nor let my enemies triumph over me. No one who hopes in you will ever be put to shame, but shame will come on those who are treacherous without cause. Show me your ways, Lord, teach me your paths. Guide me in your truth and teach me, for you are God my Savior, and my hope is in you all day long."

That night after dinner, Megan turned to Diane. "I understand there were some problems here Saturday. Would you mind sharing what happen?"

Not wanting to rehash Saturday's turn of events, Diane replied, "Nothing I couldn't handle."

"Diane, my landlord came to see me today at work. He told me about the music. If it happens again, we will be evicted. Neither one of us can afford to move."

"I never hear anyone complain about the music you play. So, what's wrong with mine?"

"Diane, I don't play the music so loud that we can't hear someone knock on the door."

"Megan, don't you ever get tired of being so perfect? Do you not ever do anything wrong?" With that Diane stormed off to her room and slammed the door.

Not use to this kind of behavior, Megan called Keith. When she heard his voice, she broke down and cried. Being the man he was, he prayed with Megan over the phone and gave her some scripture. By the time they hung up, Megan felt better.

The rest of the week, Megan and Diane kept to themselves. Megan hated this but thought it best to let whatever was eating at Diane work itself out. Keith came in again on Sunday so he could spend the day with Megan. He knew she was going through a rough time with Diane, plus some things had happened at school, and he needed to discuss it with her.

After church, they drove up to his parents' restaurant. Megan loved it there and Keith knew it was one of her favorite spots. After lunch, they walked up to the gazebo. Sitting looking out over the creek, Keith took Megan's hands in his.

"I have something I want to share with you. I didn't want to talk about it over the phone, and that's why I came in this weekend. I have been offered a full-time job at a church that I have preached at several times. It's about a three-hour drive from here. They have made me a good offer, and I like the area and the people."

"Oh, Keith, this is wonderful. I am so happy for you. Those people made an excellent choice in picking you."

"Well, I have one problem. I don't want to make this move alone."

Getting down on one knee, Keith pulled out a ring and held it up to Megan.

"Megan, would you do me the honor of being my wife? I know no one else I would want by my side as I travel down this new journey in my life."

With tears in her eyes, Megan could hardly speak. Finally, she said, "Yes. I would love to share this journey with you."

"There is one more thing," he said. "They want me to come in two months, by then all my schooling will be behind me. They have a parsonage close to the church for us to live in. Can you plan a wedding in two months?"

With a look of shock, Megan said, "Two months? I don't know. I'm not sure where to start."

Smiling, Keith looked at Megan, "I have thought about it, and I realize we don't have much time, but what if we got married at the church I'm taking. I'm sure my Uncle O'Riley, Pastor Cook at Highland and some others from Highland would be happy to help. I think it could be done."

Megan's mind was in overload. There were so many things to think about, and she wasn't sure where to start. Taking her hand again, Keith said, "Let's go down and tell my parents. I'm sure my mom can be of help. She loves planning things."

The restaurant was not busy when they walked in. Keith and Megan went to the kitchen where his parents were. Keith held up Megan's hand to show off the ring, and his parents were so thrilled. Keith's mom, Holly, hugged Megan and said, "Let me know whatever I can do to help. Do your parents live close by, Megan?"

"My parents are both deceased. They were killed in a boating accident a few years ago."

"Oh, honey, I'm so sorry. If you want, I'll help you with shopping for a dress or whatever you need. I'm here for you, for soon you will be our daughter, not a daughter-in-law. I must say, Keith has made a good choice. Welcome to our family."

Megan was so delighted with the way things were going. It wasn't until Keith took her back to her apartment that the thought of facing Diane with the news was upsetting. Turning to Keith, she said, "I dread so much telling Diane. Her temper is getting worse, and today has been such a beautiful day that I hate for her to ruin it."

"You will not have to face her alone. I'm going in with you. Remember we do everything together. We face nothing separately. I saw how she reacted at the car wash, and you don't need that. She has a problem, and she shouldn't take it out on you."

As Megan and Keith walked in, Diane was in the kitchen making a sandwich. When she saw Keith she said, "Give me a minute, and I'll be out of here."

"Actually, Diane, we would like to talk to you," replied Keith.

"I don't know of anything you need to talk to me about, so if you'll excuse me, I'm going to my room."

"What we have to say has to do with your future here at this apartment. I think you might want to listen to what Megan, and I have to say."

Diane stopped dead in her tracks. Looking at Keith with darts in her eyes, she said, "What do you mean? This apartment is Megan's in case you have forgotten. We pay half on everything, and I do pay my part."

"Yes, you do, but soon IF the landlord agrees, you will be paying all the bills, unless you can find a roommate. You see, Megan and I are getting married soon, and we will be moving away.”

“You’re what? Getting married? Megan, have you lost your mind? Why would you want to marry someone like him? He has you so messed up that you’re not thinking straight. He calls himself a preacher. What kind of life will you have? Go to church all the time, pray, read that Bible that is supposed to be so holy. Come on, girl, wake up before he totally destroys you.”

“No, Diane, you are the one who is destroying me. Keith is my solid rock; he is someone I can trust and lean on. You don’t have any of that. I love Keith, and he loves me. We haven’t set a date yet, but it will be soon. I’ll talk to the landlord, Mr. Niles, and see if he will let you stay here after I move out.”

“Well, you are not going to take any of this furniture. It’s mine. I was good enough to let you use it in your poor pitiful apartment. This place was as drab as drab could be. Look at it now. If it wasn’t for me this place would still be the pits, and this is the thanks I get for being kind to you?”

“Diane, I do appreciate what you have done, the place looks so good. But Keith and I will be getting our own furniture for our home.” Swallowing hard, Megan added, “We would like for you to come to our wedding. I don’t think it will be big since we have only a short time to prepare for it.”

“Don’t tell me. He got you pregnant and you need to get married before you start showing! Right?”

Keith put his arm around Megan, “Sorry to disappoint you, Diane, but Megan is not pregnant, I can assure you. A true gentleman will never touch a woman until they are married. That is God’s Word, and I will stand on it.”

Diane laughed. “Oh, here we go again. God says this, and God says that. I can’t believe you went to school to study a Bible. What kind of job is that? Do you think it will pay your bills? Megan will have to work to support you while you sit around and read your little Bible. What kind of man does that? Is that in your little book also?”

“Diane, if you would stop being so harsh and listen to God and His Word, you would find yourself so much happier. This is your choice to be so unhappy," replied Keith.

"You think I'm unhappy? Look at what I have to put up with. You guys make me sick. I would take the life I have any day than to have to live like you two do. There is so much to do, and you waste your time reading a book that was written millions of years ago. Did those people even exist or are they fictional characters someone made up? You don't know because you were not there. I don't know how to make it any simpler than that. That school took your money and then fed you garbage. Now you want to stand here and defend it? I'm going to bed." Throwing her sandwich in the trash, she said, "I lost my appetite," and went to her room.

Turning to Megan, Keith took her in his arms and said, "I'm going to talk to Pastor Cook and see if we can find someone who will let you stay with them until we can get married. I don't want you around her any more than possible."

"Keith, Diane wasn't like this when I first met her. I don't understand her at all. I knew from the beginning church was not her thing, but I was hoping that would change."

"Still, Megan, you shouldn't have to live with this, and I don't want you to. What kind of a man would I be if I didn't do all I could to protect you?"

Megan looked at Keith with a smile on her face and stars in her eyes.

"Keith, I know for sure, marrying you is the right thing. I'm so glad God brought us together."

Keith gave Megan a hug and whispered, "I love you and always will."

Tuesday evening Megan had just gotten home when her cell phone rang. Not recognizing the number, she started not to answer it, but then for some reason she did. "Hello."

"Megan? This is Betsy O'Riley from church, how are you dear?"

"Mrs. O'Riley, I'm fine. I just got home from work."

"Have I called at a bad time? If so, I can call back later."

"No, this is perfect. After being on my feet all day, I like to come home and rest for a minute."

"I totally understand, my dear. What I am calling about, Keith called us yesterday and explained the situation you are in and asked if we knew anyone who could help. Luther and I both looked at each other when Keith asked this, for we have a studio apartment above our garage that is not in use right now and would be perfect for you. It is furnished and ready for you to move in today if you like."

"Mrs. Riley, this is wonderful. How much is the rent a month?"

"My dear, you are getting ready to marry our wonderful nephew, and the apartment is yours rent free for as long as you need it. Luther and I wouldn't dream of charging you. Also, I enjoy cooking and I expect you for dinner every night."

"Mrs. O'Riley, you are an angel, an answer to a prayer. I don't know what to say!"

"Megan, when Keith told us you needed a place, Luther and I both knew God had this all worked out. The Bible says pray believing, and I truly believe that. Now, when do you think you would be able to move in? The apartment is clean, ready for you."

"I don't have furniture to move, just clothes and some personal things. Why don't I move this Saturday? That will give me time to sort through things."

"Megan, my dear, that is perfect. Luther and our son, Jeremy, will be there around nine o'clock Saturday morning. Do you think a pick-up truck will be big enough to put your things in?"

"The biggest thing I can think of right now is my grill. I don't want to leave it behind. Keith and I can use it after we are married."

"I may have them both drive their trucks, and that way you will have plenty of room for your things. I'm going to let you call Keith and tell him the good news. We didn't say anything to him last night. Luther and I talked it over after we got off the phone and thought you should be the one to let him know. I'm not going to keep you. I'm sure you have plenty to do. If you need anything before Saturday, give me a call. Till then, see you Saturday, my dear."

Megan was so thrilled that God again had come through for her. Her tears were tears of joy as she prayed thanks. Diane had been avoiding her since Sunday night. They no longer drove to work together. Diane took her breaks at a different time at work, and at lunch she was nowhere in sight. Megan hoped Diane would come in at a decent hour so they could talk. She prayed it would go well.

Sixteen

Thanksgiving and Christmas were so special for the boys. Never had they ever had anything like it. Anna and Abigail had sent the boys gifts for Christmas and signed them, "your big sister." When they got to FaceTime, the boys said they had never had a sister and couldn't wait to see them. Cody had gotten each one an ornament with their names on it that said, "First Christmas" and had it dated.

Benjamin found Chester on New Year's Day, dead. He was so heartbroken. Nick had tried to explain that he had kept the turtle much longer than he had expected and that Chester had had a good life. Everyone else was glad that Chester was gone for they had all gone looking for him so many times but never said so to Benjamin.

Soon it was April ninth, Daniel's birthday. Although he was turning eleven, he now had a date to celebrate, and he called it his first birthday. Stephen, Caleb, and Benjamin played their instruments and sang happy birthday to him that morning. He had a skating party which the boys all thought was fun, even though they all fell a lot while trying to skate.

At the end of the day, Leah asked Daniel, "How did you enjoy your birthday today?"

"It was awesome. I looked at the calendar for next year, and my birthday will fall on Easter. That will be extra special."

Leah put her arms around the boys, and said, "You need to remember one thing. When you wake up every morning, be sure to give thanks for each day is special also. Birthdays are special, but every day that God gives us is special."

May fourteenth came, and Stephen's birthday fell on Mother's Day. At church that morning, the boys played and sang a song, dedicating it to Leah. The song they sang was, "The Perfect Fan." Leah had never heard it before, yet it touched her heart greatly. What a blessing those boys were.

Stephen had chosen to go play putt-putt at a new place in town that had just opened. So, after church, they headed for Mini Golf. What a fun day they had. That night after church, Nora had planned to have a surprise birthday party at her house for Stephen. When they told him to make a wish and blow out his candles, he said, "My wish has already come true. I prayed my birthday would fall on Mother's Day, and it did, because I have the best mom in the whole world. God picked her out for me and my brothers."

All four boys looked at Leah and smiled, then said, "Happy Mother's Day to the best mom ever. We love you."

Soon, it was October. Summer had passed and school had started again. Benjamin wanted to have a hayride for his birthday, which was good, since the leaves were changing colors and the weather was much cooler. On the night before Benjamin's birthday, while they were doing their evening devotions, the boys asked a lot of questions about their salvation. They had prayer and when the boys were off to bed, Leah knelt to pray for them. She knew God was speaking to their hearts.

Saturday morning as they were getting ready for the hayride, the boys came into the kitchen.

"Mom, can we talk to you for a minute?"

Always taking time for them, Leah turned to them, to find them with tears in their eyes. "What's wrong, why are you boys crying?" she asked.

Caleb spoke up, "Mom we were in our room, and we asked God to come into our lives. We think He did because we all felt something. It's hard to explain, but it's like something came over us!"

Gathering the boys in her arms, Leah's tears began to flow. "Oh, what a beautiful day this is!" she cried.

The kitchen door opened, and Nick walked in. "Is everything alright?"

Caleb spoke up, "We asked God into our lives this morning."

"Well, hallelujah! I thought we were going to celebrate

Benjamin's birthday today, and here we are celebrating a day that God saved four of his little children. What a fine day this really is."

Nora walked in and looking at everyone she said, "Okay, what have I missed? I can see in everyone's face there is something going on."

Nick replied, "We have more to celebrate than Benjamin's birthday. These boys asked God into their hearts, and we have four saved little souls right here. The day can't get any better than this."

Nora went to the boys to hug them. "I'm so proud of you guys. This is not only a prayer answered, but a blessing."

Daniel looked at Leah, "Can we see a calendar?"

Taking one from a drawer, the boys went to the table to look it over. Then in a few minutes they handed it back.

Daniel said, "We have agreed that we want to be baptized on November twenty-second. That is Caleb's birthday. Since we got saved on Benjamin's birthday, we will have our sins washed away on Caleb's."

Nora shook her head. "You boys are so thoughtful of each other. I couldn't love you more than if you were my own. Come here, I need another hug."

The day turned out to be a perfect day for a hayride. The leaves were all glowing with such beautiful colors and everyone's heart was filled with joy.

That night Benjamin said, "I think for my birthday, God really came through. I'm so glad I chose October sixteenth for my day. It is really special to me now."

Everyone agreed that so far, they had chosen the right day to celebrate their birthday.

November twenty-second was a Sunday and Caleb's birthday. The boys were so excited for they would be baptized, and Cody was going to baptize them. Before the baptism service, the boys sang the special for the morning. They sang, "What can Wash Away my Sins," then, "Sweet Hour of Prayer."

Cody then took the boys back to get ready to be baptized. Daniel was first and Cody asked if he had anything to say. Clearing his throat he said, "Before we met our mom, Leah, we knew nothing about God, praying or church. We really didn't know much about anything. I'm so thankful that God placed us in the home of Leah Conner who is now our mom. She showed us what life with Christ is about. My brothers and I want to live the rest of our life serving God." Then Cody baptized Daniel.

Next was Stephen. Cody asked him if he had anything to say. Smiling, he replied, "We came from a terrible life, a sinful life. We saw things that we should never have seen. Thanks to our mom, Leah Conner, we have a better life now. God knew we needed help and led us to her, and she in turn led us to know God." As Cody baptized Stephen, Leah was praying for each of the boys.

Caleb walked down into the water, and he looked at Cody and said, "My brothers and I hope to help others that don't know God. We don't have an earthly father, but we certainly do have a Heavenly Father, and mom says He will always be with us wherever we go, and I believe that." By this time Cody couldn't control his tears. These boys had become so special to him.

Stepping down into the water, Benjamin started singing, "Thank you Lord, for your blessings on me." In the background you could hear his brothers singing also. When they finished the song, Benjamin said, "I want to grow up to be like my mom, Leah Conner. She always loves the Lord, and I want to be just like her." Trying hard to pull himself together, Cody was finally able to baptize Benjamin. As the boys left to go change clothes, leaning forward, Cody said, "I have met a lot of people but never have I seen the hand of God on anyone like these four boys. They have been a blessing to me from the day I met them, and I can honestly say they have helped me to be a better person. When they asked me to baptize them, it was such a great honor. John baptized Jesus, and God sent a dove. When I baptized these boys, there were angels all around. I wish you could have seen what I was seeing." Then he held up both hands and said, "Oh, thank you,

Jesus."

At the close of the service, as soon as the pastor said, "Amen," Benjamin turned to Leah, "Mom, do I look any cleaner?" he asked.

"Benjamin, remember what we talked about. It's the sins on the inside that we change. We are to try to think good thoughts, watch what we say and refrain from doing things that are not pleasing to God. Do you still have that bracelet that Nora gave you? It says, 'What Would Jesus Do?' You should wear it, so when something comes up and you're not sure what to do, look at the bracelet and ask yourself, 'What would Jesus do?' After a while, your mind will automatically think, 'What Would Jesus Do?'"

"Okay, Mom, as soon as we get home, I'm putting on my bracelet, for I want to be like Jesus."

When they turned to walk out, there stood Anna, her family, and Abigail and her family. What a surprise. Leah walked up to the girls, so happy to see them. "I had no idea you girls were coming in. Why didn't you tell me?"

Anna said, "We wanted to surprise you, and after all this is a special day. When you told us the boys were being baptized, we decided to come in for them, and be here for Thanksgiving."

When the boys saw their big sisters, they were so excited. The pastor finally came up to them and said, "I know this is like a reunion, but everyone has left. We need to lock up."

Not realizing they were the only ones there at the church, they headed for Leah's house. When they arrived, Nora knew the girls and their families were coming in, so she had lunch prepared for everyone at her house. It was also decorated for Caleb's birthday with another cake decorated for their baptism. In the middle of that cake was a figurine of a person being baptized, and at each corner were the boys' names. The boys loved meeting in person their new sisters and all the family. Finding out Anna, Abigail and the whole family were staying till after Thanksgiving made the day even more special. Nora kept some at her house, for to her they were family. Leah and Nora both agreed, this was like it used to be years ago. Both homes were full of people. It was so wonderful. This was the best Thanksgiving they had had in a long time. Nora wished so much her girls and grandchildren could have made it in. Laughing to herself, she thought both homes would be overloaded but that would be alright. They had sleeping bags, couches, and a few beds for everyone.

The next Sunday Pastor Harrington talked about the families getting together for Thanksgiving. He talked about when we all get to heaven, what a feast we will have. Then he looked over the congregation and said, "This week I have had some things on my heart. I have prayed, but don't know who I have been praying for. This morning let's bow our heads and pray for the one next to you. If God is speaking to you, I pray you heed his call. Let's all pray."

Finally, Pastor Harrington said, "Amen." Then from the corner of his eye, he saw someone step out and walk down the aisle toward him. With a smile on his face, he held out his hand and Julie Knight fell into his arms. Her tears had consumed her, but finally she was able to speak. She whispered something into the pastor's ear, and Pastor Harrington was smiling and raised his hand, as if to give God the glory.

When Julie had finished talking to Pastor Harrington, he turned to the congregation. "We have here Ms. Julie Knight, who comes to us as a candidate for baptism. But before we except her, she has something to share with everyone."

Clearing her throat, Julie said, "I never gave much thought as to how God works. In fact, I never gave God much thought at all. Then one day I received a call regarding some children that had been abandoned at a store. Taking the call, I had no idea what was in store for me. I was met by a police officer that explained the situation to me and one thing he said to me was, 'The lady who is helping those boys right now is an amazing lady. You would be wise to get to know her.'

"Not putting much thought into what he was saying, I only wanted to get those kids in a foster home that night because I had plans, and I was afraid all this was going to take longer than I wanted. It turned out, the lady wanted to take those boys home with her. She was a widow, had never taken any classes on being a foster parent, but was persistent. Since we needed foster parents and really had nowhere to put the boys, my supervisor agreed to let her keep them for the night. Little did I know, this lady had turned to God for guidance. I soon learned that she prayed about everything, even had her neighbors, the church, anyone who believed to pray. Seemed like things always went her way. One day when we went to court over the boys, I tried to tell her not to expect too much, but she had been praying and let me know God was with her. This lady was calm, but not me. I was so nervous, for I just knew she was going to be disappointed. Then later I met with her in her home. I opened up to her about some things in my life, and she explained to me that if I made some changes, I would be a much happier person. She even gave me a Bible. I followed her advice, and it has taken me a long time, but I read that Bible through. I shared with my parents some things and now they are coming to church with me. By following this lady's advice, I am much happier and much closer to my parents. As I look back, God had a plan and I'm so thankful He included me in that plan. Those boys didn't just happen to be in that store, God put them there. He also placed me on that call. Those boys were touched and given a wonderful chance in life. I was touched and through me, my parents have been touched. God's love just keeps on spilling over on people, even when you don't expect it. I watched last Sunday as those four boys were baptized and I knew then, I needed to make that walk to the front of the church. I need God, and I need Christian friends like you in my life."

As Julie finished speaking, her parents came forward and asked God to come into their lives.

Pastor Harrington turned to the congregation, "Now I know what I have been praying so hard about this week. God is certainly good."

The next Sunday, Julie and her parents were baptized.

Seventeen

On Saturday morning, Mr. O'Riley and Jeremy showed up at nine o'clock. Megan had knocked on Diane's door several times, but Diane would not only open her door, nor would she answer. As they started carrying out boxes, Diane finally opened her door to see what was going on.

"Diane, I'm so glad you finally came out, I didn't want to leave you a note stating what I was doing."

"What's going on here?" Diane said, "Who are those guys and why are they carrying out boxes?"

"This is why I have been trying to talk to you. Did you not listen to any of my phone messages?" Megan asked.

"No, I figured it was more of your church junk you wanted to talk about. So, what's going on here?"

"I'm moving out. I have found a place to move into until Keith and I are married. I talk to Mr. Niles, and he has agreed to let you stay here if you go by the rules. He should be by soon for you to sign a new lease. I went ahead and paid my half of the rent for next month to help you out and not put you in a bind. I called the light and water company and here in this envelope is my half for the bills. You will need to have everything put in your name, because on the first of the month, my name will be taken off."

Diane turned to Megan, "How could you do this to me? That jerk you want to marry has messed your mind up so bad. You know I can't live here on what I make alone. What am I supposed to do?"

"Diane, that's why I paid half of next month's rent. This will give you time to find a roommate. There are several girls at the hospital that are struggling financially. You should have no trouble finding someone to move in here. It's a good location. Also, here is an invitation to my wedding. I would love to have you come."

Diane took the invitation and tore it in two. "I have told you repeatedly. Church is not for me, especially to sit there and watch you make a fool of yourself. I'll sit here at home and have a toast to your misfortune. When you fall flat on your face, don't bother to come back here, for I'll close the door in your face, and tell you where to go."

Jeremy walked up and told Megan, "I think we have all the boxes loaded. If you want to walk around and make sure we haven't left anything, we should be ready to go."

"Oh, Jeremy, did you get my grill out back? I don't want to leave it because this is something Keith and I can use. Besides, that's one of my garage sales bargains that I was blessed with," replied Megan.

Diane turned, "You're taking the grill? I could use that. What am I supposed to use?"

"You could do like I did, hit the garage sales on Saturday morning. You can really find some great deals," Megan said.

"Oh, you make me sick," Diane turned to go to her room. Then before slamming the door, she said, "If any of my stuff comes up missing, I'll report it to the police."

Taking Megan by the arm, Jeremy said, "If this is everything, we need to go. That woman has some serious issues."

Staying with Mr. and Mrs. O'Riley was a blessing. Megan didn't realize the strain she was under living with Diane. True to her word, Holly Newcomb helped Megan with all the wedding preparations. What she couldn't do, Betsy O'Riley did. Megan felt like she had two mothers, and they both were wonderful.

The day of the wedding was beautiful. The church was packed with friends, family, people from Highland Church and people from Cedar Creek, the church where Keith was going to be the pastor. Keith and Megan both were so excited about the new journey they were taking. It wasn't till well after the honeymoon that Megan thought of Diane. She wondered how things were going with her and prayed that one day soon, Diane would allow God into her life. Until she did, her life was going to be so miserable. Megan decided to send Diane a card, knowing she would not respond, but still, hoping to plant one more seed in Diane's life.

Diane had asked around at work if anyone was looking to share an apartment. It seemed everyone was content with where they were living.

Ms. Moss, the housekeeping supervisor, came up to Diane one afternoon. "Diane, I need you to come into my office. We need to talk."

Following Ms. Moss to her office, Diane was wondering why she wanted to see her. Taking a seat, Ms. Moss looked at Diane and asked, "Can you tell me what is going on with you?"

Not sure what Ms. Moss meant, Diane replied, "Nothing is going on. Why do you ask?"

"Well, for the past few months, your attitude has changed drastically. I noticed things between you and Megan were not the same as they once were. Now Megan is gone, and the other girls tell me it's hard to get along with you. What's going on, Diane?"

"The things I am having to deal with are not my fault. Megan is the one who started everything. Always going to church, praying, reading her Bible was bad enough, then she hooked up with this guy that says he is a preacher, and then more church stuff was going on. He has her mind so messed up that she does not realize what is happening to her. She thinks she needs to be doing, I quote, 'her Lord's work' all the time. She does not know how to go out, have some fun and relax."

"Diane, what is wrong with being active in church?"

"Those people, Ms. Moss, are crazy. Do you pray every morning when you get up, before you eat, and before you go to bed? If you see someone going through a hard time, do you stop to pray for them? I mean, Megan has a bad case of church-itis, or religion-itis. It has consumed her. We could be watching a television program, and if something came up that she thought was inappropriate, she would turn it off. Even in a commercial if she felt something was out of line, off it went. She only wanted gospel music played at the apartment. I'm telling you, that church and those people have destroyed her. She doesn't know how to go out and have a life!"

"So, Diane, what does your version of going out and having a good life mean to you?"

"Having friends over, have a few drinks. Play some decent music, not this religious stuff. Maybe go out dancing, just have a good time."

"Diane, have you ever been to church?" Ms. Moss asked.

"No, I don't go for all that. I heard Megan say one day she was going to be working in the nursery at church. Who in their right mind would want to take care of kids? That's not for me."

"Diane, the church nursery is so when people are in the sanctuary listening to the preacher, if the child starts crying, it won't disturb others around them. The workers in a nursery watch over them, and it gives the parents a little break. Nurseries are wonderful and most beneficial. Have you ever been to the nursery here at the hospital?"

"No, I haven't and have no desire to work on that floor. I couldn't handle listening to a squalling kid."

"Maybe if you settled down and had a child of your own you just might change your mind, Diane."

"I have no use for kids in my life. Kids, church all that are not for me."

"I understand, but back to the reason I called you in here, we have received complaints not only from the workers, but from some of the patients. I also understand you have been trying to find a roommate since Megan left. Diane, with your attitude, no one here wants to room with you. They are doing well to work with you. I am giving you a thirty-day written notice, and if things don't change within that time, we will have to let you go. I have already talked to Helen Hamilton. She has received several complaints also, and this is what has been decided. When you first came to work here, you were a wonderful worker. If you should decide to change jobs, I would advise you not to use us as a reference for as it stands right now, we could not give you a good one. Do you have any questions?"

Diane looked at Ms. Moss and replied, "None of this is my fault. Megan brought all this on, and now you want to punish me for what she did?”

“Diane, you are putting the blame on the wrong person.” Opening a drawer, Ms. Moss took out a mirror. “Here, look and tell me what you see?”

“I see myself, who did you think I would see?”

“That’s right, Diane, you see yourself. The person you see is the one at fault. You need to learn to take responsibility and stop trying to put the blame on someone else. Megan has been gone for what, two months and your attitude is worse. If she was at fault, then you should be getting better. Like I said, we are giving you a thirty-day written notice. What happens between now and then is up to you. It’s your choice.” The paper was signed by Helen Hamilton and Pearl Moss. “You need to give this some thought, Diane.”

Taking the paper, Diane walked out the door thinking, “I wish I had never met Megan. What am I going to do?”

When Diane got home, still upset over her written notice, she sat down on the couch to look over her mail. There in the stack was a card. It had no return address. Opening it up, Diane could feel her blood pressure rising. It was a card from Megan, wishing her the best, and as usual she signed it along with some scripture. Diane tossed it aside, thinking this was the last thing she needed. Megan had become a thorn in her side. As Diane opened the rest of her mail, she had a light bill, water bill, cable bill, credit card bill and the rent due in a few days. Her checking account was not looking promising in paying all that was before her, and this just made the day even worse. Laying it all aside, she went to the kitchen to find something for dinner. She had to admit, she missed Megan’s cooking. Not finding anything quick to fix, she grabbed her purse to go to a bar. Hopefully, she would find some guy to take pity on her and buy her dinner and a few drinks.

Eighteen

The school year was ending, and the boys had found odd jobs to do for the summer. Nick was always showing them how to do things, and if they came across a problem, they knew Nick would have the answer. Mrs. Milligan, a neighbor down the street, called Leah and asked if the boys were able to paint her house. Her husband was sick and not able to do any outside work. Leah had the boys go down and visit Mrs. Milligan. This way she could see for herself what she felt the boys could do. About an hour later, the boys came running into the house.

"Mom, we have a job, one that hopefully will last all summer, maybe into the fall. Mrs. Milligan not only wants her house painted, but we get to mow the yard, and she wants the garage cleaned out. Not only will she be paying us, but she likes to make cookies and things like that. She said she would feed us our lunch because it was hard to cook for just her and her husband. We start tomorrow."

"Boys, this is good news. Mr. and Mrs. Milligan are sweet people, and you will enjoy working for them. Make sure you do your best every day and listen to what they say they want done."

Daniel spoke up. "Mrs. Milligan said since I was the oldest, she would put me in charge. I'm to make sure the work is done right."

All four boys were so eager to start work the next day. They had agreed that they would get paid at the end of the week for what they had done.

Early the next morning, the boys took off to the Milligans' home. They were so excited about having a summer job. Mrs. Milligan was outside walking around when they arrived. She had made out a list of things they wanted done and wanted to go over it with the boys. They agreed the list was things they could do, so she took them to the garage where tools were stored. Soon the boys were at work, and while they worked, they sang. Mr. and Mrs. Milligan sat in the house listening to the boys, and what a blessing it was. They had no music, singing acapella, and they never missed a note. At lunchtime, Mrs. Milligan went out to let the boys know she had made them lunch.

Stephen said, "We'd rather eat out here. Our clothes are dirty, and we don't want to mess up your house. We can eat over under that shade tree."

"Oh, no, you boys need to come in where it's cool to eat your lunch. Don't worry about your clothes," Mrs. Milligan said.

"Oh, we can't. Our mom talked to us about respecting other people's things. We are pretty nasty. We just need to wash our hands, and we can do that at the faucet. Do you have any paper towels for us to dry our hands on?" asked Caleb.

Mrs. Milligan fixed a plate for each boy, put it on a tray, then took it outside to them. They thanked her and took the tray over to the tree. She went back in to get them their drinks, and when she went back out, the boys were standing in a circle praying. How this touched her heart. How many children did she know that would take the time to pray without being asked? She couldn't think of a one.

At the end of the week, the boys had accomplished quite a bit. The Milligans were so pleased with what they had done. Before they left on Friday, she handed each boy an envelope containing their pay for the week. They thanked her and took off home. Leah and Nora were grilling outside when the boys walked up.

Daniel held up his envelope, "Look, Mom, we got paid today."

The other three held up theirs also.

"Wonderful, what do you plan to do with your money?" Leah asked.

Benjamin spoke up, "First, we are to give ten percent to God, put ten percent in savings and then we can spend the rest, but I think I will put all of mine in savings except for the ten percent that goes to God."

Nora smiled. "Benjamin, I think that is a wonderful idea. Are you saving for anything special?"

"No, not right now. I'm sure one day I'll think of something."

Nora turned to the other three. "What are your plans with your money, anything special?"

Daniel, Caleb, and Stephen all agreed they would be giving ten percent to God and putting the rest in savings for now. While they were talking, Leah's phone rang. It was a neighbor down from where the Milligans lived wanting to know if the boys were available next week to do some work for them. The Milligans had bragged about what a great job the boys had done for them, and they had some things they wanted the boys to do for them, too.

After going over the list of things they needed to finish for the Milligans, the boys put them down for the week after that. Saturday morning, Leah's phone rang again with another neighbor needing help from the boys. By that afternoon, the boys had six more calls from neighbors wanting to hire them for odd jobs. Leah was so surprised at all the calls that were coming in, yet so pleased that the boys were being called upon.

That night, Nick and the boys took a dry erase board and made a calendar big enough to mark their daily jobs. They put it on the wall in the garage, so every day, they would stop to see whose house they were going to.

One morning, after the boys had left, Nora popped her head in the door and said, "Leah, are you busy?"

"Just picking up and straightening up. What arc you into today?"

"I know why the boys are so popular. Want to go for a little ride?"

"Nora, is something wrong? Are the boys in trouble?"

"Come with me, Leah. I want to show you something."

Going down the road, Nora rolled the windows down in the car. Soon she pulled up in front of the house where the boys were working. People from the houses around it were outside sitting in lawn chairs. You could hear the boys singing while they worked.

"Leah, I was at the hardware store this morning to pick up some things for Nick and overheard some people talking. Everyone loves to hear the boys sing, so they pay them to do work around their home, because they know the boys sing while they work. The boys' work is good; it's nothing shabby. The people get things done around their home, plus they are being serenaded. You could say they are getting two things for the price of one."

"Oh, Nora, I had no idea. I know the boys enjoy singing. They practice with their instruments nearly every night, as I'm sure you know."

"Leah, those boys have talent. When they get older, they can go on the road and sing in other churches or do concerts. This proves it."

"Nora, they are still young. We don't know what they will want in a few years. We can only pray that they will always want to sing for the Lord and serve him. This is my prayer for them every day. Thank you for sharing this with me this morning. It blesses my heart so, especially seeing these people sitting out here listening to them."

"Leah, I thought you would want to know. Those little guys work so hard to please the people. They are known all over town. They are referred to as 'Leah's boys' or 'The Conner boys.' Wouldn't David be happy if he were here?"

"Oh, Nora, you have no idea how many times I have wished David could be here. He would have loved these boys, and they would have loved him."

By the end of the summer, the boys had worked all over town doing odd jobs for people. Each had his own savings account, and the tellers at the bank knew the boys well.

Usually on Saturday mornings, Cody got with the boys to work with them on their music. In the afternoon, they would go somewhere with Nick. School would be starting in a week, and they had not taken a vacation all summer.

Leah asked the boys, "You guys have worked all summer, and we have not been anywhere. Is there somewhere you would like to go for a few days?"

Thinking for a few minutes, Caleb said, "We have never been camping. Could we do that?"

Leah, not sure about camping, said, "Well, we could invite Nick and Nora to come along. I'm sure Nick would know what to do and what we would need."

"Great," Stephen said, "Let's go ask them." Out the door they went.

Leah, still not sure about camping, was hoping Nick would not be able to go, and they would have to choose something else to do.

Daniel came back in and said, "Nick thinks this is a great idea. He has a tent, sleeping bags and all that good stuff. He even knows of a place to go camping. We are going to help him get things ready. Do you know when we can leave?"

"Daniel, I need to talk to Nick. This is all new to me, and I need to speak to Nora also."

"Oh, it will be fine. Nick knows what he is doing. We are going to have a blast." With that he was out the door.

In a few minutes, Nora came in. "Stephen tells me we are going camping. Do you know anything about this? He said we would be sleeping in tents and in sleeping bags!"

"Nora, I ask them if they wanted to do something before school started, and Caleb mentioned camping. I said we should invite you and Nick. They asked, and Nick agreed."

"Leah, we have done a lot together, but camping, out in the open? Have you lost your mind? At night I need a bed to sleep in, not a sleeping bag on the ground."

"I understand, Nora, but it might not be so bad. We could give it a try for the boys!"

"I think Nick and Cody should take the boys camping, we could stay home and go shopping. That I can handle. Leah, sleeping on the ground, I don't think I can do that."

"We could do it for one night. Surely, it's not that bad. Plenty of people camp all the time."

"Leah, if we had a motor home, I would be fine. What about going to the bathroom? For guys it's no problem, but we are made differently. I have issues with that."

"Nora, I'm sure they have those port-a-potties around for us to use."

"Leah, you're not thinking straight. What is wrong with you? What about taking a shower? They don't have port-a-showers around, I'm sure."

Nick and the boys came in, talking all at once. Finally, Nick said, "I know the perfect place to go camping. I have a friend that will let me use his place. We can stay three or four days at least. If we start now, we should have everything ready by tonight and can leave out in the morning. Nora, you and Leah go to the store and pick up things for us to eat, and the boys and I will take care of the rest."

Out the door they went. Nora turned to Leah, "Three or four days camping? I'm going to die."

"Nora, we are going to be fine. We can do this for the boys. You never know, we might actually enjoy it."

"Don't hold your breath, Leah."

The next morning, both vehicles were packed, and Nick had a trailer hooked to his truck to carry the bigger items. Nora and Leah were in one vehicle, Nick and the boys in the truck.

"Leah, I didn't sleep hardly any last night thinking about this trip. Nick laughed at me for bringing my makeup. He also told me to bring plenty of extension cords for my curling iron."

Smiling, Leah reached over and patted Nora's hand. "We will survive this. It's a new adventure for us, something to tell the girls the next time they call."

"Those girls won't believe we went camping. I can just hear them now. 'Mom, you did what?' They know me. What will your girls think?"

"I called them last night and told them. They both thought it was great, and we should have done this a long time ago. Why don't you call your girls, Nora, and see what they say?"

"No, I'll wait till we get back. Then I will be able to tell them what I think about camping."

Arriving at the camp area, the boys and Nick were all pumped up. They immediately started setting up the tents and putting everything in place. Nora went down to the river to look it over. She decided to step out onto some big rocks to get a better look. Benjamin quietly came up behind her and growled loudly. Nora was so startled as she turned to see the source of the growls that she lost her balance and ended up in the water. Benjamin thought it was funny, but Nora was not at all amused. He offered to help her, but Nora assured him that she could get up on her own.

When Nora made it back to camp, everyone looked at her. Caleb asked, "Why did you get in the water with your clothes on? Didn't you bring a swimsuit?"

Not wanting to get Benjamin in trouble, she said, "My foot slipped on the rocks. I lost my balance and fell in."

Everyone laughed and Nick said, "Oh, I wish I had been there with my camera. That would have been a prize picture for this trip."

Smiling the best she could, Nora went to the car to find some dry clothes. Looking around, Nora asked, "Where do I go to change?"

Nick informed her of a bathhouse about halfway down from where they came in. Gathering up her things, Nora went to find the so-called bathhouse. When she found it, what a shock. It was not what she was expecting. The showers were small with only a curtain to pull around you, and the bathroom stalls were also small. No outlets anywhere to use a hair dryer or curling iron. The lighting was poor, making it hard to see how to put your makeup on. A feeling of defeat came over her as she did her best to make herself presentable. As she walked back to camp, Nick was the first to see her.

"How was the bathhouse?"

"Nick, you knew what I was going find. That place needs to be updated. We are women, not men."

Smiling at her, Nick put his arm around her. "Nora, when you go camping, you don't need makeup and all that hair stuff you use. You need to relax and just be yourself. You're not here to impress anyone, and believe me, you look good. I'm proud of you and love you with or without make-up. I married you for who you are on the inside, your beauty is an extra bonus that God gave me."

"Oh, Nick, I do love you. It's that I have always wanted to look my best for you. Without fixing myself up, I feel like I'm not making myself presentable. I don't want you to be ashamed of how I look."

"Nora, like I said, to me you look wonderful, with or without makeup. The makeup you use is more for your benefit than mine. Whatever makes you happy, makes me happy. These next few days, why don't you forget your makeup and see how you do? If it bothers you, then go back to wearing it."

"I might try, but no promises. I'm so used to getting up in the morning and fixing myself up for the day that it's hard to break a routine. It's like getting up and going without coffee."

"Nora, going without coffee is totally different. I hardly see the comparison."

Going on into the camp, the others were working setting things up. No one said a word about Nora not having makeup on or her hair not dry and fixed. Soon the camp was all set up and everyone was having a good time. Even Nora.

The next day, they went hiking, and when they got back to camp, the guys went fishing. What they caught was plenty for dinner that night. Later they made s'mores, sang, and had a wonderful time. By bedtime, no one had any trouble going to sleep, for they were all exhausted. The next day, they rented some bicycles, and took off on a bicycle trail. By evening, Leah, Nora, and Nick were feeling the effects of the two days' activities. The boys, on the other hand, were going strong. As soon as they were back at camp, they took their fishing poles and headed to the water while the adults stayed at camp and rested. Soon, the boys came back with a string of fish to be fried.

Stephen spoke up and asked, "Is it possible we could stay an extra day or two? We are having so much fun."

Daniel said, "We saw some people out water rafting. That looked like fun, could we do that?"

Caleb and Benjamin wanted to go water rafting also.

"Well, guys, let's see how we feel tomorrow. That is something we haven't done," explained Leah.

Excited, the boys sat around the campfire discussing the next day's activities. Soon it was bedtime.

The next morning, they drove down the road to the raft rental shop. Leah and Nora decided to drive down to where they would be stopping to wait for them. The boys had so much fun, and Nick enjoyed himself, too. As usual, the boys chatted at the same time about what all had happened. When they pulled into camp, they all had a big surprise awaiting them. The food was gone, the tents were torn down and ripped in places and the coolers were overturned. Nothing was left untouched.

"From the looks of all this, I think our visitor was a bear, maybe a mama bear and her cubs," said Nick.

Nora and Leah just stood there looking at the mess. Nora said, "Nick, you never mentioned bears to me."

"Nora, I have used this fishing place for years, and never have I come across a bear before. They must have wandered down from somewhere. Come on, we will separate what is trash, and what we possibly can use again. Might as well get started."

Hungry and tired, they started cleaning up. It was obvious that their camping trip had come to an end. On their way home, they stopped in town to grab a bite to eat since the bears had left nothing behind. By the time they got home, they were all worn out. Nora was especially happy to be home. She had no problem falling back into her old routine.

Nineteen

Work was not getting any better for Diane. In fact, she hated going to work, for she knew Ms. Moss was always watching her. She did try to be more pleasant to the patients but at times that became difficult. The bills were piling up, which made Diane more irritable. She did manage to make it through her month of probation without getting fired.

As she walked up to her apartment, she saw a paper on the door. It was a notice that if the rent was not paid in full by the end of the month she would be evicted. Knowing she did not have the money, Diane could feel her blood pressure going up. Did Mr. Niles not realize she had enough going on in her life without him joining in?

The end of the month came, and Diane was no better off financially. Thinking she could out smart Mr. Niles, Diane left a window cracked opened at the back of her apartment. Every morning, she left for work through the window, closed it almost shut and walked two doors down to her car, thinking this way, she could avoid Mr. Niles.

This went on for a month. Not bothering to go through the front door, Diane had not seen any notices left there for her, and the mail in her mailbox was piling up. She was afraid if she stopped to pick up her mail, Mr. Niles would see her.

One morning, Diane crawled out her window and walked down to where she had been parking her car. When she walked up, her car was gone. Looking around, it was nowhere in sight. A lady came walking out to get in her car when Diane said, "Excuse me. I left my car here last night, and now it is gone."

Before Diane could say anything else, the lady replied, "Yes, a tow truck came last night and towed it away. That spot belongs to someone here at these apartments, and they couldn't figure out whose car it was. Since it was taking up someone else's spot, the landlord had it towed. Do you live here?"

"How dare they take my car away! They could have at least

left me a note that this spot belongs to someone else. Now, how am I going to get to work?" Diane asked in a rage.

Feeling sorry for Diane, the lady said, "I'm on my way to work, I could give you a ride if it's not too far away."

"I work at the hospital. Are you going in that direction?" asked Diane.

"Yes, I am. My name is Christine Pierce. I work a few blocks from the hospital and would be happy to give you a ride to work."

Getting in the car, Diane was grateful for the ride but still upset over her car being towed. Where was she going to get the money to get her car back? Turning to Christine, Diane asked, "Do you know where my car was taken? I really need it."

"There are several towing companies here in town, I would call around and see who has it. Why did you park your car in that spot to begin with? Did you not see the numbers in each spot? Those numbers go with the apartments."

Not wanting to say too much, Diane said, "Where I live, they have been working on repaving our parking area, and I thought it would be safe to park here so I wouldn't have so far to walk."

Christine thought for a moment and said, "When the landlords do something like that, they provide the renters a place to park without the fear of being towed. Who is your landlord?"

Again, not wanting to say too much, Diane decided to change the subject. "Where did you say you worked?"

"I'm going to law school to become an attorney. My uncle has a practice right down from the hospital, and I work for him. He has been such a blessing to me. I don't know what I would do without him. Plus, God has really been good to me. He has opened so many doors and made a way for me to go to school. I certainly don't know what I would do without him. Just pray and ask God for help. He will get you through this little problem with your car. Well, here we are, hope you have a blessed day."

Thanking Christine for the ride, Diane turned and thought, just my luck, another Christian. Those people are everywhere.

As soon as Diane clocked in, she went straight to the break room and started calling towing companies. She was on her third call when Mrs. Moss walked in.

"Excuse me, Diane, but I believe you are supposed to be out on the floor working, not sitting here in the break room on your phone."

"Oh, Mrs. Moss, this is an emergency. You see, my car got towed last night, and I had to bum a ride to work this morning. I'm trying to figure out who has my car!"

"Diane, you can do that on your break. I suggest you get back to work now."

Putting her phone in her pocket, Diane got up and walked out the door. She could feel Mrs. Moss watching her as she walked down the hall.

When break time came, Diane decided to go to the bathroom where others could not hear her phone conversation. Time had gotten away from her as she called one tow company after another. No one had her car. Feeling frustrated, Diane didn't hear Mrs. Moss walk in.

"Diane, I believe your break was over twenty minutes ago. You are behind on your work, and here you are on your phone again."

"Mrs. Moss, I'm trying to locate my car. It seems every tow company I have called doesn't have my car, and I need it."

"Diane, since your car is so important to you, and your job is at the bottom of your priority list, I suggest you go home and make your phone calls from there. Before you do, you will need to stop by my office, I have some papers for you."

"What kind of papers do you have for me?" asked Diane.

Looking firmly at Diane, Mrs. Moss said, "Your termination papers."

"You're firing me? You can't do that. I was only on the phone because my car was towed, and now you want to fire me over that? This is wrong. It's not my fault that someone towed my car. At least I came on in to work this morning, I even had to hitch a ride with a total strange to get here. Doesn't that count for something?"

"I'm sorry, Diane. Your heart is not in your work here, and it shows. If you will clean out your locker, I will have security walk you to the door.”

“Now you are going to treat me like a criminal and have security walk me out? You know what, I don’t need people like you in my life.” With that Diane turned to go get her things.

As soon as she had gathered her belongings from her locker, she walked out into the hall and there stood a security guard.

Diane said, “Well it certainly didn’t take you long to get here. I’m sure ole eagle eyes sent you to walk me to the door. She must be afraid I would take something that wasn’t mine, but let me reassure you, there is nothing in this place I want except my paycheck.”

The security guard handed her an envelope. “I believe this is what you are talking about. Mrs. Hamilton had it ready for you.”

Taking the envelope and opening it, Diane saw that it was her paycheck. “Looks like they want rid of me for sure. When you see her and ole eagle eyes, tell them I said thanks.”

The security guard walked Diane to the door and said, “Wish you the best, lady,” then turned and went back inside.

Standing there looking around, Diane wasn’t sure what to do. At least she had her paycheck. She tried to figure how far the bank was from the hospital, for she needed to cash her check, so if she could find her car, she could pay the tow bill.

Diane finally realized the bank was not close to the hospital, especially on foot. Also, it was in the opposite direction from where she lived. Diane started walking in the direction of the bank. She walked a good four miles and was exhausted when she arrived. Going inside to cash her check, while standing in line, she realized how hungry she was. Once her check was cashed, Diane went back outside to look for a fast-food place. Across the street was a little diner. Upon entering, a man was placing a sign, “Now Hiring.”

“Excuse me, what is the position you are hiring for?” Diane asked.

“I need a cook. You need a job?” he replied.

“As a matter of fact, I do.”

The man smiled at Diane and asked, "When can you start? Can you start now?"

"Well, yes, I just got laid off from my job and need one badly."

Taking the sign down, the man said, "Great, follow me."

They walked to the back of the café and the man said, "By the way, my name is Zack, and your name is?"

"Oh, I'm Diane."

"Good to meet you, Diane. We will worry about filling out the paperwork later. Right now, you are needed in the kitchen. Follow me."

Diane followed Zack to the kitchen, where he handed her an apron and started explaining how things worked.

"First the orders will come through on a screen above where you will be cooking, then you are to prepare the order and send it out through a side window. Right now, things are slow because we just finished the lunch hour rush. Soon it will be the five o'clock rush. Any questions?" he asked.

Looking around, Diane said, "No, I think I can do this."

Zack turned and walked away leaving Diane alone. In her mind she was wondering how this was going to go. Cooking was something she did not enjoy. Then an order popped up on the screen. Taking her time to read the order carefully, she started trying to prepare the order. A lady came around the corner and saw Diane at the grill.

"You must be the new cook. Zack wasted no time in hiring one. Have you been doing this kind of work for a while?"

"No, this is my first day at this line of work. Shouldn't be too hard," Diane replied.

"Well, honey, let me say this, Zack expects perfection in the meals, and he doesn't like his customers to wait long. From where I'm standing, you need to shake a leg. At the rate you're going you won't make it here an hour." Turning, the lady walked out.

Out of nowhere Zack walked up behind her. "Here, let me show you how I want this done."

Taking over, he had the order prepared and out the side window in no time. He wiped down the area to keep it clean. Looking at Diane, he asked, "Have you ever been a cook before?"

"No, I worked in a hospital before this, but I need a job, and I'm willing to learn. Please give me a chance. I'm sure I can catch on."

Taking a deep breath, Zack told her, "I'll work here beside you for the next little while. When the rush hour starts, you are on your own. I will be busy somewhere else."

True to his word, he worked with Diane showing her how to do things, then the rush hour hit. Patting her on the back, he said, "You're on your own. Don't let me down."

Then on the screen popped up two orders and before she could get started on them two more orders popped up. The lady that had talked to her earlier came around and started helping her. Finally, the rush hour was over. Diane was so exhausted and felt like a blob of grease.

Turning to the lady who helped her, she said, "My name is Diane, and I'm so grateful for your help."

"My name is Tina. If I hadn't helped you, we would still be on the second order. I can't do this every day, and besides, Zack will let you go if you don't pick up some speed. Believe it or not, today wasn't a bad day. Otherwise, I would not have been able to come back here to help you. You owe Jan a big thank you. She had to waitress all by herself so I could be back here with you."

"I do appreciate everyone's help. By the way, when do we take a break and are meals included?" Diane asked.

"When things are slow, we grab a bite to eat, but usually we only get a five-to-ten-minute break. Sometimes, you just grab a bite when you can. May take you two hours to eat a burger on some days."

"You must be kidding? What about going to the bathroom?"

"Again, honey, you do it when time allows. Some days are slow, and some days you wish there was two of you." Laughing, Tina told her, "You will get used to it, if you survive the next few days."

Turning, Tina walked back out front. Diane was already dissatisfied with this job, but she needed the money to get her car and to make her cell phone payment. On top of that, she was not sure how much longer she was going to be able to avoid Mr. Niles, for she was way behind on the rent.

Finally, it was closing time, and Diane was so glad.

"Well, Diane, do you plan on coming back tomorrow?" Zack asked.

"Sure, why wouldn't I?"

"Well, you struggled today, and if Tina hadn't helped you, we would have probably lost some customers, and I can't have that. Come in early tomorrow, say around eleven, to fill out your paperwork and I want you to watch our morning cook. She is good, but unfortunately, she can only work the morning shift and must leave around two. Maybe she can help you out."

"Sure, no problem, see you tomorrow." Diane walked out in the fresh night air, and it hit her. She was going to have to walk to her apartment and that was on the other side of the hospital. She was probably looking at about an eight-mile walk, for she had walked four miles from the hospital to the bank. Already worn out, Diane headed for her apartment.

When she arrived, the window she had been using to get in and out of was shut all the way and locked. Going around trying all the other windows, Diane had no other choice but to use the front door. When she got to the door, there she found notices of eviction, and when she tried her key, it didn't work. What was she going to do? She was so exhausted, and needed a shower, a change of clothes and somewhere to sleep. Going over to the next apartment, she knocked on the door. Finally, a little lady came to the door.

"I'm sorry to bother you, but I live next door and for some reason my key is not working."

"Are you aware that Mr. Niles has been trying to get in touch with you?" the little lady replied.

Not wanting her neighbor to know she was indeed trying to avoid Mr. Niles, Diane said, "I have been working a lot, and when

I come home, I haven't paid any attention to what was on the door. I thought it was someone soliciting and leaving flyers on the door."

The lady looked at Diane with doubt in her eyes and said, "Did you need something?"

Swallowing hard, Diane said, "Yes, may I ask a favor of you. Since it's late, and my key is not working, could I possibly sleep on your couch tonight? Tomorrow I will get things fixed to where I can get into my apartment. My clothes are in there, and I have to go to work in the morning at eleven."

Hesitating the little lady finally said, "You can stay here tonight, but never again. I have a feeling you are not being up front with me."

Opening the door for Diane to come in, the little lady went and got a blanket and pillow, then pointed to the couch. "I have an appointment early in the morning, my ride will be here at seven to pick me up. You need to be up and gone by then."

Turning to go to her bedroom, Diane asked, "Do you mind if I take a shower before I turn in?"

The little lady turned to Diane, looked at her clothes and said, "I guess you would like to wash your clothes also?"

"Oh, that would be wonderful. Thank you for suggesting that. Do you by any chance have a robe or something I can put on till my clothes are done?"

Taking a deep breath, the little lady went and got a robe for Diane to use. "The washer and dryer are in that closet. You do know how to operate them don't you?"

Not in any position to get smart with the little lady, Diane smiled and replied, "Yes, I do. I really do appreciate you helping me out."

With that the little lady turned to go to her bedroom and shut the door.

The next thing Diane knew, the little lady was standing over her saying, "Its six-thirty, and my ride will be here soon. You need to leave."

For a minute, Diane forgot where she was, then she

remembered. If only the little lady would let her sleep till seven. Walking home from the café last night, bumming a place to sleep, then having to do laundry, Diane was so exhausted. Another thirty minutes would be wonderful, but then the little lady started nudging her.

"Okay, okay, I'm getting up," Diane replied.

"Don't forget you are wearing my robe. You need to get dressed in your own clothes."

"I'm going. You have no idea what kind of day and night I had yesterday," Diane said.

When Diane came out of the bathroom, the little lady was standing with the door open for her to leave.

"Again, thank you for letting me use your couch last night. I'll get my key fixed today for my apartment."

Diane had just made it out the door when the little lady shut the door behind her. Going over to her apartment, now that it was daylight, she was hoping to see what the problem was. As she was working with the key, a voice from behind her said, "Having trouble getting in?"

Turning, Diane saw that it was Mr. Niles.

"Yes, for some reason, my key is not working."

Walking over to the door, Mr. Niles pointed to all the envelopes on the door. "Have you bothered to look at any of these notices?"

"I have been busy working, and to be honest I really hadn't paid any attention to them. When did you put them up?"

Looking at Diane, he said, "You are nearly four months behind on the rent. You refuse to answer my calls or return any texts I have sent you. These notices have been here for a good while. If you had been using this door, you would have known they were here, but instead you chose to go in and out of the back window of this apartment. You even went to great lengths to park your car in the next apartment complex so I wouldn't see your car out front. When they ran your tags, I was called, and they said they were going to have your car towed for parking in the wrong complex. I told them to go ahead."

Furious, Diane looked at Mr. Niles, "You, told them to go ahead and tow my car. How could you? What kind of creep are you?"

Smiling, Mr. Niles nodded his head, "Oh, it gets better. I know the attorney that lives next door, and she helped me fix the papers up to have you evicted. When you didn't respond, a truck came yesterday and removed everything from the apartment. We found a small suitcase that we put some of your clothes in, and there's a small box with some toiletries in it. "I wasn't sure when you'd show up, so those items are just inside the door. The apartment has been rented and the new renters will be moving in soon."

Diane was ready to explode. "What nerve you have. Just who do you think you are to go into my apartment and remove my things? I'm going to report this to the police and have you thrown in jail."

"Ms. Baker, would you like for me to dial the number for the police? I have my phone here. I'm sure they would like to talk to you about your car and possibly your furniture, even the fact that you are way behind on your rent. You see, I had an officer here yesterday to oversee all that took place. I'm sure you will find them more on my side than yours. I have all the paperwork to back me up."

Realizing she wasn't going to get anywhere, she asked, "May I have what things you left me?"

Opening the door, Mr. Niles stepped into the empty apartment. Diane looked inside and felt sick to her stomach. All the beautiful furniture she had bought when she worked for Bo was gone. How could this be happening to her? She didn't deserve to be treated this way.

"Here you go, Ms. Baker. Here are your things. Believe it or not, I do wish you the best. I didn't want to have to do this, but you left me no choice. Things can get better for you, but you must first take responsibility for your actions. You can't go around blaming others for your mistakes. I noticed you don't have a Bible. You should consider getting one, take the time to read it and study it.”

“I have better things to do with my time than read a Bible.”

“Ms. Baker, in Proverbs 28:13-14, it says, ‘He who conceals his sins does not prosper, but whoever confesses and renounces them finds mercy. Blessed is the man who always fears the Lord, but he who hardens his heart falls into trouble.’ Do you have any idea what this means?”

“No, nor do I care. All you, holy rollers have a messed-up mind, and I want no part of it. Right now, I just want to know where my things are so I can get them back and get on with my life.”

Shaking his head, Mr. Niles realized nothing he said was going to help Diane. “Go to the police station, and they should be able to help you. I don’t know where they took your things. I do know that if the items are not claimed in a certain amount of time, they will be auctioned off.”

“You had better hope my things are there and have not been damaged. If they are, you will pay for the damage, understand?”

Picking up her things, Diane walked off. When she got to the street corner, she had no idea what to do. Her car had been towed, she lost her job and now her home. Standing there, she decided to head to the café. At least she could get something to eat. As she started down the sidewalk, she heard someone say, “Hey, need a ride again.”

Looking, it was Christine Pierce, the lady who gave her a ride yesterday morning. So grateful, Diane said, “That would be great.”

Walking over to get in the car, it just dawned on Diane, something that Mr. Niles had said. There was an attorney at the next apartment complex that had helped him draw up the eviction papers. Getting in the car, Diane thanked her for the lift.

Christine asked, “No luck in getting your car yesterday?”

“No, some other things came up, and hopefully today I’ll be able to pick it up. Did you tell me you are an attorney?”

“Yes and no. I’m studying to be an attorney. When some cases come up my uncle lets me handle them, but he oversees it all. I go before the bar next year. I'm so excited. I will be working in my uncle's firm. I already have an office."

"Do you handle eviction notices and things like that?"

"As a matter of fact, I do. It's sad to have to evict people from their home, but it's wrong for them to refuse to pay the rent. They bring it on themselves. Sorry, I need to run in here and pick up something up for the office. I'll be right back."

While Christine was gone, Diane got out of the car and hid. She decided she would rather walk to work than ride with the person who helped get her evicted. She could see the hospital, so she knew she only had four blocks to walk to the diner.

When Christine came out and saw that Diane was gone. She looked around and even went back in to see if she had gone to the bathroom. Diane was nowhere in sight, so Christine got in her car and drove on to work.

Diane walked on to the café and saw it was packed. Hoping to get some breakfast, she went into the kitchen. When Zack saw her, a smile broke out on his face.

"Am I ever glad to see you. We are swamped this morning. Grab an apron and start cooking."

Diane was so tired and hungry that reading the orders was frustrating to her. It seemed she was messing up more orders than she was getting right. Zack came over, "Hey, Diane, what's wrong? The customers are complaining about the food. You must stay focused on what the screen says."

Irritation began to set in, and Diane thought the customers should be grateful they had food. The day had gotten off to a bad start, and the last thing she needed was people complaining about what they were eating. It was, after all, cooked and not raw.

Finally, Zack came back over. "I don't know what is going on in your mind, but if you don't pay attention, you will find yourself out the door. I have a whole dining room full of customers complaining about their order."

Unable to control her temper, Diane looked at him and snapped, "I'm doing my best. I wasn't supposed to start till eleven, I have had no breakfast, and this whole morning has been a wreck. Now get off my back."

With that Zack went to his office. In a few minutes, he came back and handed Diane some money. "Here is what I owe you for yesterday and a little extra for this morning. Grab you something to eat, and then get out of my café and don't ever come back."

"You mean you are firing me? Just because you have a dining room full of idiots that feel like complaining over their food? It's not like we served it uncooked. So now, you want to take it out on me? Why don't you let them come back here and see how well they can do?"

With that, Zack picked up a biscuit, put a fried egg and a few slices of bacon in it. He wrapped it up, filled a Styrofoam cup with coffee, handed it to Diane and led her to the door.

"Don't ever come back here. You're not welcomed in my café."

Diane's things were in a corner in the kitchen. She knew she had to have them for that's all she had. Finally, getting a waitress's attention, she asked her if she could bring them out to her because she was afraid to go back in. In a few minutes, the waitress came out with Diane's things.

"I'm not sure what you did to tick Zack off, but if I were you, I wouldn't hang around here. He's pretty mad right now."

Taking her things, Diane walked off, having no idea where to go or what to do. Finding a shady area, Diane walked over and sat on the grass to eat her food. While eating, a cop came up and said, "Can't you read?"

Diane thinking, he was just being a smarty, said, "Only if it's in English. What language do you read?"

The officer asked her to come over to him. When Diane did, he pointed to a sign that said, "Keep off the grass."

Looking at the officer, Diane said, "I'm sorry I didn't see the sign. Let me get my things and I'll leave."

When Diane went to pick up her things, she left her biscuit wrapper and coffee cup lying near the tree. The officer pointed to the tree, "I believe those are your things also?"

"Sorry, I can't get them for the sign says keep off the grass."

As Diane started to walk away, the officer came up behind her and told her she was under arrest. First for not paying attention to the sign and second for littering. Putting up a fight, Diane was determined she was not going to jail. The next thing she knew, four more officers were there, and they had her pinned to the ground and handcuffed. Then they put her in a police car. After spending the night in jail, Diane was released the next day around noon. Walking out of the police station, she had no idea where to go or what to do. She was to appear in court before a judge in four weeks. She hated life and she hated this town. She had a little money but not enough to rent an apartment. She spent the rest of the day walking around trying to figure out what she should do.

That night, she found a park bench and that was to be her bed for the night. When morning came, someone had taken her bag of clothes but left her box of toiletries. The one thing she didn't want to do but knew could give her a new start away from everyone who knew her in this town, was to call her brother. He lived out West, hopefully he would let her come stay with him for a while.

Looking at her phone, her battery was getting low, and she didn't even know where her charger was. Her brother was her only hope, and the last time they had spoken was about sixteen or seventeen years ago. Searching for his number in her contacts, Diane hoped he would answer.

Twenty

On Saturday, Daniel woke up early, and while the others were sleeping, he laid there thinking that soon he would be turning fifteen. Nick had been taking him to the church parking lot to let him practice driving. When he first came to the Conner home, he was only nine, now he would soon be fifteen. At nine, his life had been so unstable. He didn't know from one day to the next where they would be, if they would have any food to eat or a place to sleep at night. Six years later, he had been introduced to God, given a new mother, a home, family, he was in school, had decent clothes, food, the list could go on. Tears began to form in his eyes as he laid there so thankful for the life he now had. He wondered what ever happen to his birth mother. Was she alright or had she passed away? If she was alive, he wondered if she ever thought about them or if she had ever tried to find them? He wondered what he would do if she did come back into his life! Looking around the room, he knew he would never leave Leah. She was his true mother in his heart and always would be. Leah Conner had shown them what love really was, she was always the same, day after day. So happy, she had a godly spirit about her that drew everyone close to her. Daniel closed his eyes and said, "Lord, thank you so much for bringing me and my brothers into this home. We now truly know and experience what love and happiness are. You have given us the best mother in the whole world. I pray we will always do what You would want us to do. To live the life that is pleasing to You. You have given us the ability to play instruments and sing. May we always serve You and lift others up with the talent You have given us. I don't know what we have done to deserve all this, but I want You to know, I thank You. I love You God, and I love our mom, Leah."

Turning over in bed, Daniel wept. Not tears of sadness, but tears of love and joy.

Leah was in the kitchen cooking breakfast when the boys finally came in. Then the doorbell rang, and Caleb said he would answer it. It was Cody, wondering if they had plans for the day.

"Mom is making breakfast. Want to eat with us? Then maybe we can spend the day with you if Mom says it's okay," replied Caleb.

Cody laughed, "You know I can't pass up any of your mom's cooking."

Walking into the kitchen, Caleb said, "Hey, it's just Cody. Mom, do you have any plans for us today? Could we possibly spend the day with Cody after we eat?"

Leah turned to Caleb, "Don't you think you could have said, 'Cody is here,' instead, 'It's just Cody?' I'm sure Cody didn't appreciate being announced that way."

"Sorry, Mom, I wasn't thinking."

Turning to Cody, Caleb said, "I'm sorry. I didn't mean for it to sound the way it did."

"You're fine, Caleb. I knew what you meant. No hard feelings. But I do think I'll sit over here next to Benjamin and Stephen."

Laughing, they all gathered around the table to pray and then eat.

Soon the guys were gone, and Leah was trying to clean the kitchen. The doorbell rang and she wondered who it could be. When she opened the door, there was Julie Knight.

"Oh Julie, it's so good to see you. I haven't seen you in a long time. Come in."

"I hope this isn't a bad time for you. I should have called first, but I happened to be out this way and wanted to stop in."

"You know, Julie, you are welcome to stop in any time. How are you doing? We haven't seen you in church for some time."

"I got a job offer in West Virginia, which has turned out to be a good move for me. My parents moved to West Virginia also."

"That is wonderful, Julie. I must say, you look so good. I take it you are happy?"

"Oh, Mrs. Conner, I am happy. I have you to thank for that. You showed me what I needed to do to clean up my life. In moving, my parents and I have found a wonderful church, and I have met a super nice guy. He treats me like I am somebody. He won't let me lift anything heavy, he doesn't refer to me as his ole lady, and if I make a mistake, he doesn't go around telling others, 'Oh you won't believe what stupid thing she did.' He brags on me, always lifting me up. We have been dating for over a year and he has never done anything inappropriate. He lives at his house, and I am at mine. Living together is out of the question."

"Oh, Julie, this is wonderful. I am so happy for you. A godly man will treat you the way you should be treated. The way they talk, and their actions are signs of what kind of man they are."

"He has asked me to marry him, and I said, 'Yes,'" Julie said, holding out her hand for Leah to see her ring.

"That is beautiful."

"The reason I wanted to stop by, I would like for you to be my matron of honor at our wedding. Also, I would like the boys to play the music."

"Julie, are you sure you want me to be your matron of honor? Wouldn't you rather have someone closer to your age?"

"Absolutely not. You helped me to get my life in order. I can't think of anyone else I would want to be standing by me on this special day. I have told Jared, my fiancé, all about you, and how you help me so much. He agreed that you would be the perfect one. I also told him about the boys. By any chance are they here?"

"No, they left a few minutes ago with Cody Lay, a young man from the church."

"I remember him. He is a remarkable young man and I remember how he helped the boys when you first took them in."

"Well, Julie, you will be surprised when you see the boys. Daniel is nearly as tall as I am. The others are not far behind. They are turning into handsome young men. In fact, Daniel will soon be fifteen."

"I can't believe that. My, how the time flies. I must say, the day we first met, I didn't think you would be able to handle all four boys. You saw more than what was on the outside. They were hungry, dirty, smelly, pitiful looking boys. You looked at what was on the inside and what they could be. If everyone would take the time to do what you did, this world would be a much better place. We need more Leah Conners.”

“Thank you, Julie, for your kind words, but you must remember. God’s hand was in this. If we would just listen to him and let him guide us, things would be a lot better. Sometimes, you think God is asking more of you than you think you can do, but with him by your side, you can do it. Even the impossible things.”

“Mrs. Conner, this is what I love about you. No matter what, you see good in life, and you are so positive. I have said this before, if I could pattern my life after anyone, it would be you.”

“Well, my dear Julie, I pray you are better than me, for I do have my downfalls. I am human, you know, and I must repent and strive to do what’s right daily. That’s what keeps us on our knees.”

Getting up to leave, Julie said, “I’ll send you the information about the wedding. Thank you for agreeing to being my matron of honor, and let the boys know I expect them to play. My special day would not be complete without my precious extended family.”

After hugging Leah, Julie left. Leah was so touched by Julie’s invitation. Bowing her head, she prayed a prayer of thanks.

Around four o’clock, the boys burst through the back door. “Mom, where are you? Look what we have!”

As Leah came through the living room, the boys had brought in a set of drums. Behind them was Cody, smiling.

Stephen said, “A guy brought these into Cody’s store today. He doesn’t want them and told Cody he could do whatever he wanted with them. So, Cody gave them to us. Isn’t that wonderful? Now we have a new instrument to learn to play.”

Looking over at Cody, Leah asks, “Which one of you wants to play the drums?”

Cody spoke up, “I think they all do. They tried their hand at playing them, and actually did pretty good. I don’t think there is an instrument they can’t play. Besides, you can’t beat the price.”

Not sure about the drums, Leah asked the boys, “With all you have going on, when do you plan to practice?"

Benjamin chimed in, "Oh don't worry, Mom, we can take turns. Besides, in school, they have a band class. We could sign up for that. Won't that be cool?"

Shaking her head, Leah just said, "I suppose so." She never wanted to deny the boys access to music. Also, looking around, she wondered where they would put the drums. There were several pieces to it, and Leah had no idea if they needed all of them.

Daniel started picking up the drums and said, "In the living room by the piano would be a great spot." So, the boys started gathering up the drum set and headed to the living room.

Still in a state of shock, Leah stood still and thought, "A drum set! What will Nora and Nick think now when the boys start practicing?"

Trying to pull herself together, Leah walked into the kitchen. She was still thinking about the drum set when suddenly, someone was going to town playing the drums. Then the cymbals dinged. Closing her eyes, she said, "Lord, the violin and the banjo I thought were straining on my nerves, but we got through it and now it's sweet music. Please help me get through the drums. Also, may our neighbors find this addition to the boys' music a blessing, not a disturbance."

In a few minutes, Nora came through the kitchen door. "Leah, is that drums I'm hearing?"

Not realizing she was shouting above the drums, Leah said, "Yes, some man gave them to Cody, and the boys happened to be there so Cody gave the drums to the boys." Then the drum playing stopped and Leah, still shouting, said, "They will be adding this to their music."

"Oh, Nora, I'm sorry, I didn't realize I was shouting at you."

"Don't worry, Leah, I guess this is another adjustment for us. Care to go shopping when they practice?"

Shaking her head, Leah said, "When they practice, the whole street may go shopping or go somewhere."

"I'm going to go let Nick know. Knowing him, he would

probably come over and want to try the drums out himself. He is as big a kid as the boys. They are good for each other, that's for sure."

Soon, Cody, Nick and the boys were in Leah's living room with all their instruments, having a wonderful time. Leah went next door, got Nora and the two went to town.

As they were going down the street, Leah turned to Nora. "I pray no one calls the police and complains about the noise. It's been a few years since our neighbors have had teenagers around."

"Leah, one day, we are going to look back on this and laugh. When our girls left, we felt lost. Now, we have a full house, with music and laughter. We need to be happy and rejoice," replied Nora.

"You are right, Nora. The girls played the piano, but they also played their stereo music for everyone in the neighborhood to hear, if you remember. We have gone from stereo music to live entertainment." Laughing, they found a coffee shop where they could sit and relax.

Later in the evening, Leah and Nora made dinner at Nora's house. They called to let the guys know dinner was ready, but no one answered their phone, so Leah went over to her house and finally got their attention. When the music stopped, Leah was certain they would all have hearing problems one day.

The invitation came in the mail for Julie Knight's wedding. It was set for the second of October. Leah and the boys were so excited. Julie had enclosed a note with the color of dress Leah was to wear and some songs she wanted the boys to play. The wedding would be in one month and Leah was sure she would be able to find a dress by then.

After dropping the boys off at school the next morning, Leah and Nora went shopping.

"Leah, October is a perfect month to get married in. The leaves will be changing, the temperature will be much cooler, Julie couldn't have picked a better month. Do you know how many attendants she plans to have in her wedding?"

"No, to be honest, I don't know much about the wedding plans at all. What she sent me in the invitation is all I know. I think she must be planning on a small wedding."

Leah and Nora had gone to every shop in town and could not find anything that came near the color Julie had requested. Deciding to call it a day, the two headed home. As they drove down the road, for some reason, a roadblock was up, and they had to take a detour. Taking a different route, they passed a store where a lady was putting a mannequin in the window for display.

Nora yelled, "Stop, Leah, I saw a dress in the window back there. We need to look at it."

Leah turned around, found a place to park the car, and the two went to the window where the dress was.

"Nora, this is a secondhand store. I can't buy a dress for Julie's wedding in a store like this."

"Why not? If it works, who will know?"

"Nora, it's not exactly the right color, although it is pretty. Besides, it's probably not my size."

"We won't know till we go in and ask. Come on, Leah, what will it hurt?"

As soon as they stepped inside the store, a clerk came up to them.

"May I help you ladies?"

Nora spoke up, "Yes, what size is that dress in the window?"

"I believe it is a ten. Let me check to make sure. It is a beautiful dress and was worn only once. Yes, it is a ten. Would you like to try it on?"

"Go ahead, Leah, try it on," Nora coaxed.

Leah went into the dressing room, and when she came out, Nora was smiling from ear to ear.

"Let me have your phone, I will take a picture of you and send it to Julie. She will either say yes or no."

Waiting for a reply from Julie, Leah and Nora looked around. The clerk came up and said, "If you are interested in the dress, I have a pair of new shoes, size seven, that would go perfect with it." Leah wore a size seven, and when she tried the shoes on, they were a perfect fit.

Leah's phone pinged and it was Julie. "Love the dress. Please get it if it's not too expensive. I'll make some changes on my end. By the way, if possible, I would like the boys to wear fall-colored shirts. You have done so well with the dress, I'll let you decide on the shirts and ties. Thanks. I knew you would come through for me."

Leah, looked at the clerk, "How much are the dress and shoes?"

"We just got the dress in yesterday, let me see, oh, the dress is thirty dollars, and the shoes are five."

Leah and Nora looked at the clerk in disbelief.

"Yes, we will take both," Leah stammered.

When Leah had changed clothes, Nora asked, "What kind of material is this dress?"

Looking more closely at the material, the clerk shook her head. "The dress is not satin, but it has a little shine to it. The fabric is soft yet not anything I can remember ever seeing. It's different yet pretty."

Leah held it up, "Depending on how you turn, it has a little green, a dash of red, a hint of yellow, and a touch of orange. Not exactly what we had set out to buy, but strangely enough it is perfect for the fall."

"By the way, you wouldn't happen to have any boys' shirts, would you?" asked Nora.

"As a matter of fact, I have some in the back. Not sure if it's what you're looking for but you're welcome to look. You see, there was a store closing, and we were able to purchase several things in bulk to put here in my shop. Hold on, let me see where we put them."

In a few minutes, the clerk asked them if they would mind coming to the back. She had several boxes of shirts and wasn't sure what they were interested in. Leah and Nora followed the clerk to the back of the store.

"We need four shirts for young boys for a wedding. Also, in need of ties to match, if possible," Leah said.

"Well, the only thing I can say is, if we each take a section and start looking, hopefully, we will find what you ladies are looking for."

The three ladies had gone through several boxes when the clerk said, "Would something like this do?"

Looking at what the clerk had, Leah and Nora both smiled.

Nora picked up the package looking for a size. "This one will fit Benjamin. What else do you have?"

Soon they had a light green, pale yellow, burgundy, and burnt orange shirt. Each shirt came with matching ties. They were new, still in the wrapper with a nice price tag attached.

"Oh, don't pay any attention to the tag inside the shirt, that's what you would have paid if you bought it at that store. Here the shirts are two fifty each," the clerk said.

Leah looked at the clerk. "You mean they are only two dollars and fifty cents each?"

"Yes, are you interested in the shirts as well?" asked the clerk.

"Oh, yes, absolutely. You are a blessing sent by God. We can't thank you enough," beamed Leah.

Leah and Nora walked out of the secondhand store with a dress, a new pair of lady's shoes and four new shirts with matching ties for the wedding and had spent a total of forty-five dollars.

"Nora, I am so grateful you saw that dress in the window and more grateful for the roadblock. God knew what we needed, and He provided. We serve a loving and giving God. This day has certainly been a blessing."

October second came, the sun was shining beautifully, and Julie was beaming. Everything fell in place just like Julie had planned. The boys picked out gospel songs to play at the reception that Julie later said were her favorites. Before Julie and Jared left, Julie handed Leah a bag.

"Open this only when you get home, and again, thank you so much for everything. I hope to be wise like you some day and see in others the good that you see. You will always hold a special place in my heart." Giving Leah a hug, Julie and Jared left for their honeymoon.

When Leah and the boys got home, Stephen asked, "What's in the bag, Mom?"

"Oh, I nearly forgot. Julie told me to open it when I got home. Let's see what's inside."

Taking out a small box, it had Daniel's name on it. The next box had Stephen's, the next Benjamin's, and the next Caleb's. The last box had Leah's name on it.

"Well, we all have a little something. You boys open yours, and then I'll open mine."

Opening the boxes, the boys gasped when they saw what was inside. They each had a knife with their names engraved on it and on the other side was the date. Caleb noticed something else in the box. Beneath the cotton that held the knife in place was a hundred-dollar bill, along with a note.

Thank you not only for today, but for who you are. Through you I have learned a valuable lesson. I pray if I ever have children, they will be just like the Conner boys.
Love forever,
Julie

Each boy had the same in his box. They were happy about the money, but the knives were what really meant so much to them.

"Open your box, Mom. Let's see what you got. Did you get a knife too?" the boys all asked.

Opening the box, Leah held up a cameo brooch. It was pinned to a handkerchief trimmed with lace and the initial LC embroidered on it in a mixture of fall colors.

"What are you going to do with your gift, Mom?" ask Daniel.

"I'll wear the pin from time to time, but the handkerchief I'll carry in my Bible. I use my Bible every day, that way I'll always be sure to pray for Julie and Jared."

"Mom, can we show Nick our knives?" Benjamin asked.

"Of course. I'm sure he may have a few knives himself to show you guys. Don't stay too long."

With that, the boys were out the door.

Twenty-One

Diane pressed the number under Paul's name. Please answer, I need your help, she said to herself.

"Hello."

Diane asked, "Who is this?"

"Who would you like to speak to?" was the reply.

"Iris, is this you?" Diane asked.

"Yes. Diane, is this you?"

"Yeah, I want to talk to Paul. Would you put him on the phone?"

"Diane, Paul's not here at the moment. Can I help you with something?"

"No, well not exactly – I need – you see – oh, when will Paul be home?"

"He should be here in about thirty minutes. Call back then if you want or can he reach you at this number?"

"Iris, as soon as Paul gets home, have him call me. I need to talk to him right away."

Then the line went dead. Iris thought to herself, Diane has not changed a bit. It would be too much trouble to say, "Nice talking to you" or just say "bye."

When Paul walked in, he went straight to his office. Iris went in to see how busy he was.

"Paul, have you got a minute?" she asked.

"Sure, Iris, what's up?"

"You got a phone call today. They want you to call them as soon as possible."

"Who did you say called?"

Swallowing, Iris laid Paul's phone on his desk. She pressed the button on the phone to show the number. "That number belongs to Diane."

Looking up at Iris, "Diane called? Here? Today? What did she want?"

"Paul, I don't know. She only wants to talk to you, and she said as soon as possible."

"Do you have any idea how many years it has been since we have spoken? The last time I tried to call her, she hung up on me and told me to mind my own business, that she didn't need me in her life."

"I know, Paul, but she is the only sibling you have. You could at least call and see what she wants."

"Iris, I'm sure she wants something. I'll think about it. I'll call her later."

Turning his chair around toward the window, Iris knew Paul was praying, so she left him alone.

Paul had just turned back around to his desk when his phone rang. It was Diane. It rang several times, then he finally answered it.

"Hello."

"Oh, Paul, I'm so glad you answered. I'm needing to talk to you."

"How are you doing, Diane? It's been a while since we have heard from you," Paul said.

"Well, I'm doing okay. I have a favor to ask of you."

Taking a deep breathe, Paul asked, "What might that be?"

"Paul, you know it's just us, and I am missing my family. I know it's been years since we have been together, and for some reason I feel we need to spend some time together. I was wondering if it would be alright if I came out to visit you. Are you still living in Nebraska?"

"No, Diane, we moved years ago. We are in Wyoming now."

"Oh, I didn't know that. But that's alright, I can come to Wyoming. If you don't mind, I happen to have some time this week, I could fly out on the next flight coming your way. I'll check with the airlines and let you know when I will be arriving. It will be so good to see you again, I can hardly wait."

Paul cleared his throat. "Diane, before you plan your trip, remember we have rules here, and you will abide by them. You may be an adult, but in my house even guests follow the rules. If you don't, you will find yourself in a hotel waiting on a flight back to Virginia. Do you understand?"

"Paul, you were always the serious one. You know I will be on my best behavior. I'll call the airlines and see when I can get a flight your way and then I'll call you back."

"Diane, don't you think you will need to know where in Wyoming I'm living?"

"Yes, I totally forgot. I'm just so excited to see you that it slipped my mind."

"We live in Laramie."

"That's great, I'll book a flight for Laramie."

Paul shook his head. "Diane, the closest international airport is in Denver, Colorado."

"Oh, how come they don't have one in Laramie? Is that far away? Will you be able to meet me at that airport?" Diane was becoming upset with what Paul was telling her.

"Diane, find out when you can get a flight out here, and either Iris or I will meet you at the airport. I have a lot going on, so it depends on when you're coming as who will pick you up."

"But, Paul, I had rather you pick me up. Nothing against Iris, but I would feel more comfortable with you."

"Like I said, depends on your flight. Just let us know."

"Oh, okay."

Diane hung up the phone. Paul walked outside where Iris was sitting on the porch.

"Well, I just talked to Diane. She plans on coming for a visit. Said she had some free time this week."

"So does she plan to stay a few days, or what?" Iris asked.

"I don't know. She basically invited herself. I hate to say this, but I think she is not telling me everything. Which wouldn't surprise me. I did tell her she had to abide by our rules, which she stated was no problem."

"Paul, maybe your sister has changed. That would be such a blessing and an answer to a prayer."

"Call me a doubting Thomas if you want to Iris, but I don't think she has. She sounded too much like the same ole Diane to me. Guess we will find out in a few days."

"Paul, did you mention the boys to her?"

"No, thought it best to wait till she came. Not sure how she will take it, but no matter, those boys mean more to me than she does."

Two days later, Diane used the last of her money to purchase a plane ticket to Denver, Colorado. When her plane landed, she was looking for Paul, when she saw Iris.

"Hey, where's Paul? I told him I wanted him to pick me up."

"Hello, Diane. Good to see you. Paul had a meeting that he could not miss, so here I am."

"Couldn't you have gone to the meeting in his place?"

"No, not hardly. It has to do with things for the ranch. That's his department. I do the cooking, housework and errands when needed."

Diane looked at Iris. "Did you say a ranch? Do you guys live on a ranch?"

"Yes, Diane. It's nice and quiet where we live. Neighbors are a mile or so away."

"How long does it take you to go into town?"

"Well, we don't go into town often. Only when it's necessary."

Looking puzzled, Diane asked, "Do they deliver pizzas out to a ranch? Do you ever go out to eat or go see a movie?"

"No, Diane, those things are seldom done. We stay busy at the ranch and don't have time for all that. We raise and grow what we eat, so there's no need to go into town for dinner. We live a simple life."

"You mean a boring life. I need to talk to Paul and try to get him out of this rut he is in. Why did you do this to him? Do you not want a social life, either?"

"Diane, we do have get-togethers. Our neighbors come over, or we go to their place, have square dances, picnics, and all sorts of fun things. We really have a great time. You will have to come and visit us sometime when we are having one of our shindigs."

"By any chance, Iris, do you and Paul have a car I could use to go into town? I don't think I can handle hanging around the ranch all day. I would be so bored. I didn't come out here to be bored."

"Diane, you will have to take that up with Paul. After dinner tonight, maybe the two of you can talk."

"Trust me, I have plenty to talk to Paul about. I feel so sorry for my brother. I had no idea what he was going through."

The rest of the trip to the ranch was quiet. Iris could tell Diane was making a mental list of things to discuss with Paul. If only she knew what was ahead of her.

When they arrived at the ranch, Diane was amazed at the size of it. Iris showed Diane which room she would be sleeping in and told her she was going to start dinner. Diane never offered to help.

When dinner was ready, Iris rang a huge dinner bell that hung outside at the end of the back porch. Diane came downstairs to see what was wrong.

"Iris, what was that noise?"

"That's the dinner bell. This is to let the workers know the meal is ready."

"You have people working here and you feed them? How many workers do you have?"

"We try to keep around ten, but right now we have twelve."

"Where do they stay?" Diane asked.

"They stay out in the bunkhouse. We have it all fixed up, and they actually enjoy it. Gives them some time to themselves."

Just then, Paul walked in.

"Oh, Paul, it's so good to see you. We have so many things to discuss. On my way here from the airport, I made a mental note of things to go over with you."

"It's good to see you, Diane. Hope you will enjoy your stay. It's a beautiful day, so we will be having dinner outside. Also, you can meet our boys."

Diane was thinking of meeting the men that worked there, but when she walked outside, she was shocked at what she saw. She even gasped.

"Paul, those are boys. Where did they come from?"

"Diane, these are our boys. As you can see, we have all ages and love them all. Come, sit down at the table, and they can introduce themselves to you."

Diane leaned over to Paul and whispered.

"Paul, I don't enjoy being around kids. They are such a pain."

"Well, Diane, you have a choice. Adjust to our boys, or we can put you on a plane back to Virginia. Which shall it be?"

Looking around at all those faces staring at her, Diane slowly made her way down to the picnic table where the boys were seated.

One little boy spoke up and said, "Would you like to sit here beside me?" and scooted over to make room for Diane to sit down.

After Diane took the seat, the little boy smiled and held out his hand.

"Hi, my name is Charlie. What's your name?"

Diane tried to turn to one side to avoid him.

"I guess you are shy, but that's okay. After a few days working in the field, you get over it. We've never had a girl worker here before. What did you get in trouble for?"

Diane turned and looked at him. "I won't be working in the fields, and I am not in any trouble. You need to mind your own business."

Paul walked over to Diane, "As soon as you have finished your meal, we will have that talk. But right now, the boys will introduce themselves to you. This is what we do when we have someone new come in."

As it came their turn, each boy stood and introduced himself. When they had finished, Paul turned to Diane.

"Now if you would be so kind to stand and introduce yourself to the boys."

Diane felt like she was in school. She stood, with a frown on her face, looking at the boys replied, "I'm Diane Baker," and sat down.

One boy at the end of the table stood up, and everyone bowed their heads. When he finished praying, he sat down, then they started eating.

After they had finished eating, the boys started gathering things off the table. Charlie looked at Diane, "Since this is your first day here, I'll take your plate till you know what your job is."

Having no clue what Charlie was talking about, Diane sat and watched while the others put things away and started doing dishes. Paul walked over to Diane, "We will have that talk now. Let's go sit on the front porch."

As soon as they sat down, Diane turned to Paul. "I have several things on my mind, first of all,"

Paul interrupted Diane, "You may have several things to say, but first you need to hear what I have to say. You are welcome to stay as long as you want, but like I said on the phone, we have rules, and you will go by them. I have no idea why you decided to call us after all these years of wanting nothing to do with us, but you are here, and we hope your stay is a pleasant one. While here, you will help with the work. Iris could certainly use it. She will let you know what she needs help with, and you are expected to do it. The boys rise every morning at five, breakfast is at five thirty. You will need to be dressed and in the kitchen to help Iris by four forty-five. Before you leave your bedroom, your bed is to be made and everything in place. The only time the boys do the dishes and clean-up is in the evening. Do you follow me, so far?"

Diane just looked at Paul in disbelief.

"The boys here are our boys. You are to respect them, and they are to respect you. They have jobs to do, and you are not to interfere with what they are doing. We might go into town twice a month and then only when necessary. Any questions, Diane?"

Taken back by all that Paul had said, Diane wasn't sure what to say.

Finally, she asked, "Are all these boys yours and Iris's?"

"Yes and no. No, we didn't give birth to them, but yes, we have taken them in. Some had some issues at home, some lived in a foster home, but for a certain reason they could no longer keep them, so they are here. Our goal is to help them and prepare them for adulthood. Some of the boys may stay a year with us, others stay a little longer, depending on the situation. Oh yes, before we eat, the blessing is said. We take turns, and when it comes your turn, you are expected to bless the food. We have church over at John Leighton's place every Sunday."

"I guess I'm expected to go to church also?" replied Diane.

"Yes, you are. Here we set examples for the boys. We don't ask anything from them that we don't do ourselves. That is why I said on the phone we have rules here, and you will go by them."

"Paul, how come you only have boys here? Don't you like girls?"

"We felt it best to have either all boys or all girls. When we started, we had more boys that needed our help. Barry Hawkins and his wife Betty, who live over in the next county, set up a place for girls on their ranch."

"Paul, I would like to stay here for a while if that's alright with you and Iris. This all seems so interesting."

"Diane, why don't you be honest with me. You have no place to go but here. So, what happen back in Virginia? Are you in some kind of trouble? What are you running from?"

"Paul, what makes you think I'm in trouble? We haven't seen each other in years. We need to spend some time together and get reacquainted."

"Diane, Iris said you only had a small bag with you. If you are planning on staying for any length of time, I would think you would need a little more clothing. It will soon be winter here, and I'm sure you don't have a coat or clothes for our kind of weather. Today has been a warm day, but our nights can be cool. With what you have on, you're going to freeze. So now, tell me what made you leave Virginia."

"Honestly, Paul, I only wanted to come and see you and Iris. You two are all the family I have. Isn't that reason enough?"

"To be honest, coming from you, no. You have an agenda. It will eventually come out, and then we will know the truth. Sorry to be so harsh, but remember, I grew up with you. From what little I have seen today, you haven't changed, and I will leave it at that. If you stay, you will take orders from Iris and will not give her a hard time. You can make your stay here pleasant if you so choose."

Getting up from his chair, Paul walked into the house. Diane was wondering if coming here was a good idea after all. She had no other choice for now. Also, how was she going to get out of blessing the food and going to church? Seemed like everywhere she went she came across some holy rollers. The world was infested with them, including her brother and Iris.

When Paul went into the house, Iris followed him into his office. Closing the door behind her, she asked Paul.

"Don't you think you're being a little hard on Diane?"

"No, I don't. If I don't set the ground rules now and stick by them, she will cause us more grief than we care to deal with."

The next morning, the breakfast bell was ranged. Diane was fast asleep upstairs when she heard the bell. Sitting up in bed, she couldn't figure out what was going on. She headed downstairs to the kitchen. Iris was coming in from the back porch when she saw Diane.

"I do believe you overslept this morning. Paul is outside making sure everything is set up for the boys."

Heading for the door, Iris spoke up, "Before you go outside, you might want to change your clothes. I don't think Paul will be too happy if you go out in your pajamas."

"Paul will just have to get over it. I'm on vacation. I'm not punching a timecard this morning." And out the door Diane went.

When she walked out onto the back porch, the boys were coming in from the bunkhouse. Paul turned to see Diane standing there in her pajamas, and he could feel his blood pressure rising.

"Diane, around here we dress appropriately. Don't you ever show up around any of us dressed like that. Now go get some decent clothes on and meet me in my office."

Diane turned to go in the house, then turned and said, "Who in their right mind rang that stupid bell this morning? Do they not have any respect for those trying to sleep?"

Paul walked over to Diane. "I rang that stupid bell to let everyone know breakfast was ready. I do believe last night we discuss you helping Iris with breakfast this morning. Now, go change and meet me in my office. Do you think you can do that?"

Going into the house, Diane was mumbling something, but Paul didn't really care. He had plenty to say when they met in his office later.

When Diane came back down, she started to go outside to fix her a plate of food. The coffee and bacon smelled so good. Iris was at the sink doing dishes.

"Diane, excuse me, but Paul is expecting you in his office."

"Oh, he can wait a few more minutes. Smelling breakfast has made me so hungry."

"I'm sorry, Diane, but breakfast is over. Everything was eaten. There is some coffee left if you would like a cup?"

"You mean you didn't save me a plate of food? How can you be so cruel? When I finish my talk with Paul, I expect to have bacon, eggs, biscuits, and coffee waiting for me. Do you understand? I'm Paul's sister, not your hired help."

Diane did not realize Paul had walked in behind her. He cleared his throat, and Diane turned around.

"Paul, can you believe nothing was saved for me for breakfast?"

"I suggest in the morning you wake up on time, come down properly dressed and help Iris with the cooking, like you were supposed to do this morning. I'll see you in my office now."

Turning, Paul walked toward his office, with Diane following him.

He took a seat behind his desk and motioned for Diane to sit across from him.

Before he could say anything, Diane leaned forward and said, "Paul, I am not one of your hired hands. I expected to be treated a little better and as for your wife …"

Blood pressure on the rise again, Paul stood, leaned across his desk, and said sternly, "Don't you say one word about Iris. If you're halfway smart, you will take a few lessons from her. We are not here to take orders from you. This is our home, and as long as you are under my roof, you will do as we say. You are to show Iris respect and do exactly what she tells you to do. She will never ask you to do anything that she herself will not do. Sorry you missed breakfast this morning, but hopefully you will be on time for lunch. Should you miss that meal, we plan to eat at five thirty this evening. If you're late for that one, I suggest you set your alarm to come down in the morning to help with the preparation for breakfast."

"You mean, if I'm late, I don't get to eat? That's cruel, Paul."

"Diane, we have twelve boys here. They are always on time, and I don't go around reminding them of what they are expected to do. They know the rules and they abide by them. You will help Iris today with the chores and you better not give her any lip. Also, I have asked Iris to look at what clothes you have. I don't want you showing up again in anything like you had on this morning. If this is all too much for you, I will gladly buy you a plane ticket back to Virginia. Do you understand, Diane? I don't want to have this conversation with you again."

"Paul, you don't have to get so worked up. Just tell me what you want me to do, and I'll do it."

"We tried that last night and somehow it didn't work. Let's pray it sinks in this time. Now go see what you can do to help Iris."

When Diane walked into the kitchen, Iris was gathering up some gloves and other things.

"Paul wants me to help you. Where shall we start?"

"Well, this morning, I have to go to the barn. We just got a call that the milk truck will be running behind today, and they want us to go ahead and get the cows set up for the milking."

Diane looked at Iris. "We have to milk cows?"

"Oh, don't worry, it's nothing like it used to be. We have machines that do the milking for us. We just have to get everything set up. Come on, you can help me."

Following Iris to the barn, the closer they got, the worse the smell. Diane thought, at the hospital, you came across some bad smells, but this was a little much.

The cows were already outside in the pen, ready to come inside. Iris was busy setting things up, and all Diane could do was hold her nose, thinking she was glad she had missed breakfast.

"Okay, Diane, when the cows come in, we lead them to a stall, secure them and then wipe them down before putting the pump on. This cleans them so no dirt or anything is on them before placing the pump in place. I'll show you how on this cow, and then you can do it. We have ten stalls, so we can each do five. When they have finished milking, we lead the cow out and bring in another one. It's easy. Once the milk truck arrives, we can leave, and they will take over."

Iris led her cow to the stall, secured it and started wiping her down, then secured the milking machine. "That's all you have to do. Now you try it."

Diane started to walk out to get a cow, but the cows were already coming in and walking up to a stall. Iris had to close the door to keep them out till they were ready for them. The cows knew what to do, but Diane was so unsure of handling them. Iris handed her the bucket of cleanser. Taking the cloth, Diane just held it.

"I don't think I can do this. I feel like I am violating this cow."

Iris laughed, "They go through this every day, they don't mind. Go ahead, once you do it, you will be fine."

Slowly, Diane reached over to wipe the cow down. Then taking the milking machine she placed it like Iris had said, and the suction held it firm.

"How do those cows produce milk?" Diane asked.

"Well, a cow cannot produce milk until it has given birth to a calf. These cows are Holstein."

"Sorry, to me a cow is a cow. Do you ever kill these cows for beef?"

"Yes," said Iris, "They provide meat for our table."

"What about the udder? Do you eat that too?"

Iris laughed, "The udder is a solid muscle. In France, I have been told, if you can find it, it's often cooked and sold by the slice."

"Should I ever go to France, I'll try to remember not to eat any meat." Diane made a terrible face at the thought of eating it.

They had all ten stalls full when the milk truck pulled up. "Sorry, Iris, had a flat tire this morning, then hadn't got far down the road and another one went flat," said Joe.

"That's okay, we didn't mind getting things started for you."

Diane had walked outside and spotted a baby chicken. Walking over she picked it up. It was so soft and cute. Iris came out and saw Diane with the baby chick.

"Diane, put that chick down, now!" But the mother hen was already on her way to Diane. When Diane heard the hen and saw her coming toward her, she started running, holding on to the baby chick. The next thing Diane knew, the hen was right on her heals.

Iris was hollering for Diane to put the baby chick down. Finally, Diane let go of the chick but kept running. When the mother hen stopped chasing her, Diane was almost to the house. Iris ran up to Diane.

"Did you not hear me say to put the chick down?"

"Yes, but what was wrong with that other chicken?"

Iris looked at Diane, "The chick you had was that mother hen's baby. She was trying to protect her baby."

"Why didn't you tell me this sooner? Do you have any idea how I felt?"

"Wonder what the mother hen thought when she saw you pick up her baby and walk away," was Iris's reply.

"Let's go check out what clothes you brought with you. I notice you have on the same clothes you had on yesterday. Paul will be going into to town tomorrow, and if you need anything, that will be a good time to go shopping."

"Paul is going into town tomorrow. Oh, that is great. There are several things I know I will need."

"Diane, if you want to go into town with Paul, I advise you to be on time for a meal and do what he wants you to do around here. When you go against what Paul asks of you, then when you want to do something, the answer will be no."

"Oh, don't worry, I won't mess up. I want to go into town for sure."

The rest of the day went smoothly. Diane did exactly as Iris asked. The next morning, Diane was up and in the kitchen before Iris.

"You're up early this morning. Did you sleep well last night?" asked Iris.

"Yes, I did. I also want to go into town with Paul today. He was agitated with me yesterday, so I knew I had better not push my luck with him today."

"Diane, I'm so glad you realize that. Paul will only take so much, and you do have a way of pushing his buttons."

After breakfast was over and the kitchen was cleaned, Paul came in and said, "I'm ready to go into town. Do you have your list ready for me, Iris?"

"Yes, here it is."

Diane walked up to Paul, "Iris said yesterday you were going into town today. There are a few things I need to pick up. Is it possible I can go with you?"

Looking up from the list, Paul said, "Diane, you can be nice. This blesses my heart. I would be happy for you to come along. Working beside Iris is a good thing, after all."

The ride into town took at least an hour. When they arrived, Paul told Diane he had some banking to do. He pointed out different shops and other places where she might enjoy shopping. At noon they were to meet at Cooks, a little restaurant down the street.

Diane looked at Paul, "there are some things I need, but I used nearly all my money on the plane trip here. Until my next paycheck comes in, can I borrow some money?"

Shaking his head, Paul handed Diane some cash. He had a gut feeling she had no money and there would be no paycheck coming in.

At noon Diane met Paul at Cooks. Paul opened the door as John Leighton was walking out.

"Hey, Paul, great to see you. I had planned to drive over to your place today. I wanted–" he began, then stopped speaking when he saw Diane. "Peyton? Peyton, I can't believe it's you. I have thought of you so many times."

He walked over and gave her a big hug. With his hands on her shoulders, he stepped back. "You haven't changed a bit. I can't believe you're here."

Paul spoke up, "John her name is not Peyton. It's Diane. This is my sister."

"Your sister?"

"Yeah, she came out a few days ago to visit with us. Why did you call her Peyton?"

"That's the only name I know."

"John, where did the two of you meet? Diane hasn't been around any since we moved here."

"Oh, it's been a while. I may have her name mixed up with someone else, but I do remember her." John kept his eyes on Diane. "Sorry, if I called you by the wrong name."

"No harm done," was all Diane said.

"I'll not hold you guys up any longer. Enjoy your lunch and I'll catch up with you later, Paul. How about I come over to your place later this evening?"

"John, why don't you come over for dinner? We always have enough and I'm sure the boys would enjoy seeing you, as would Iris."

"Sounds good. See you both later."

John headed down the street. Paul turned to Diane and asked, "Why did he call you Peyton?"

"Like he said, Paul. He had my name mixed up with someone else."

"But he said he remembered you. Where did you meet John?"

"Paul, I have no idea. I worked in different places in Virginia. From the hospital to working in a restaurant. Could have met him anywhere. He probably saw me and remembered me for some reason."

Doubting her story, Paul decided to question John. Yes, Diane was hiding something. He was sure of that.

John came a little early for dinner that evening. He needed to go over some things with Paul. Diane did all she could to keep her distance from him. After dinner, Diane asked Iris about who John Leighton was.

"John is single, never married. He has no idea how much he is worth, owns about two hundred acres. Every single female around has tried to attach themselves to him, but no one has succeeded. As you can see for yourself, he is drop-dead gorgeous and well- mannered. Whoever snags him will be one blessed lady. He turned his life over to Christ about three years ago. We have church at his place. John and some other men around here all pitched in and built the church, even purchased a piano for it. One of the girls that lives with Barry and Betty Hawkins plays the piano for us on Sundays."

"John had a church built? He gave his life to Christ, did you say?"

"Diane, his place is beautiful, and where he had the church built is perfect. That man has the most giving heart. When someone is in need, John goes out of his way to help them. He looks only for the good in people. Wish we had more people like John."

All Diane could think of was John gave his life to God. What was going on? Everyone she seemed to care for was turning their life around for this man named God. For the life of her, she couldn't understand what kind of hold this man had on people. They were giving up having a good time, and all they wanted to do was talk about blessings, going to church, reading the Bible, and all. This was so sad. Why can't these people see what they are doing? she thought.

In the office with the door closed, Paul and John were going over some things. They needed to move a water line around to service both properties. The existing one could not carry the amount of water needed.

Leaning back in his chair, Paul asked, "John, how do you know Diane?"

"I was afraid you were going to ask that. You could say I made her acquaintance a good while back. I was at a meeting in Virginia, and our paths crossed. Your sister is attractive, and you don't forget one as beautiful as she is."

"Mind if I ask what kind of meeting?"

"A man had contacted me about some property. At first it seemed like a good deal. Then when I investigated it more, it wasn't as good a deal as the man had led me to believe."

"So how did you meet Diane?"

"Like I said, our paths crossed while I was staying at a hotel. Why all the questions about your sister? Did you ask her about me?"

"Yes, I did, but I don't put much into what Diane tells me. I wanted the truth, that's why I asked you."

"I take it, you don't have much confidence in your sister. May I ask why?"

"You don't know her like I do. If she should decide to hang around for a while, you'll soon understand why."

The two men went out on the porch to sit and have a cup of coffee. Charlie came running up to the porch and said, "Eric is not feeling well. Can you come to the bunkhouse?"

Both men got up. Paul looked at John, "We'll need a thermometer. There's one in the bathroom upstairs, in a cabinet above the commode. Could you get it for me? I'll go on to the bunkhouse."

John hurried upstairs. He found the thermometer in the bathroom and was coming down the hall when Diane came out of her room. When she saw John, she turned to go back in, but John caught her arm.

"We need to talk."

"We have nothing to talk about. Please let go of my arm."

"This is not the place where we can talk. I'll figure out a place and let you know. I'm sure Paul will have you in church Sunday, so I'll let you know then."

Letting go of Diane's arm, John turned to go to the bunkhouse.

Twenty-Two

To Leah the years seemed to be flying by. Daniel was now seventeen and would soon be graduating. Stephen was fifteen and soon would be getting his driver's license. One car was not going to work. Cody had gotten Daniel a job at the music store which was not far from the high school. If it was pretty, Daniel walked to work, and Cody brought him home in the evenings. If the weather was bad, Cody would pick Daniel up at school. With Stephen turning sixteen soon, a second car would be nice. Daniel and Stephen would have to share it, which she didn't think would be a problem, because the boys all got along so well.

Leah decided to go car shopping while the boys were in school. She had Nora go with her. They went from one car lot to another.

"Leah, I had no idea cars were so expensive. Nick and I haven't bought a car in twelve years. I thought they were high then, but the cost of even a used car is more than we paid for a new one."

"Nora, I think what I will do is buy a used car that is only a few years old and give the boys my car. An SUV will be nice to have. But I need to do some more praying. I had no idea what I would be up against when I decided to purchase another car."

That night when it was time for devotions, Leah told the boys she had an unspoken request. It was Caleb's time to read from the Bible, and he chose 1 Peter 5. After reading the scripture, they bowed their heads as he prayed.

"Dear heavenly Father, we want to thank you for all the blessings you have given us. We ask that, Father, You be with those who are sick, whether it be at home or in the hospital, those who are facing tough decisions about work, home, life. For those that don't know You, that someone will be able to reach them so that their life can be complete. Be with the homeless and our churches. Father, be with each pastor, teacher, and in each service may your Spirit fill the rooms. Help us that we will always do your will and never be afraid to stand for You. We pray for our mom; she has an unspoken request tonight. Father, your word says to cast all our cares on You because You care for us. Whatever is on our mom's heart, we lift up to You. She always says, 'God knows what's best, take your burdens to him and He will answer them in the way it will best benefit us.' Again, Father, we thank You for your many blessings on us. Amen."

Each one came to Leah to give her a good night hug and kiss. As Caleb hugged Leah, he said, "Mom, God has got this. Whatever is on your heart, God will take care of it."

As the boys went to bed, Leah sat there thinking of the scripture Caleb had read, wondering why he had chosen that particular scripture. Smiling to herself, she thought, God does work in mysterious ways.

A month had gone by, and Leah still had not decided on what to do about a car. She had looked in the paper, and still nothing appealed to her, but she knew she was going to have to decide soon. She even put on the prayer list at church that she had an unspoken request. The next Sunday after church, Kit Mason came up to Leah.

"Leah, will you be home this afternoon? I would like to talk to you about something."

"I plan to be home, all afternoon. The boys and Cody are going somewhere, so come over anytime."

"Thanks, Leah. Once Tara and I get the kids fed and settled, I'll head your way."

About two-thirty the doorbell rang. Sure enough, it was Kit.

"Come on in, Kit, and have a seat. Care for a cup of coffee or a glass of tea?"

"No, thanks, Leah. Your home is still as warm and loving as I remember as a kid. I always enjoyed coming over after church or when you and David had parties here for our Sunday School class. How are Abigail and Anna? I haven't seen them in ages."

"They are doing fine. Like you, they have families of their own now."

"Time does go by quickly. Anyway, what I wanted to talk to

you about is, as you know, my mom passed away three months ago. My sister and I have been slowly going through some things, and we came across something that we would like to give you. Our parents were well off. Dad sold his business right before he had his heart attack. Which was good, for that was one less thing that our mom had to deal with. Anyway, with what they have in the bank, and selling their home, my sister and I are well taken care of."

"Kit, I know losing your parents has been hard. You were so close to them, but they are together now, and I'm sure much happier than we are."

"Losing them was hard, but we have to look at the big picture. God knows what's best and He never makes a mistake. Anyway, our parents left two nice cars. One is a 2020 Lexus SUV and the other is a 2018 Honda. They are in excellent shape. The Lexus has low miles, and the Honda has low mileage also. They bought the Lexus about six months before Dad had his heart attack. Mom only drove it around here in town after Dad passed, and I would go over and drive the Honda a little just to keep the battery charged. My sister and I want the cars to go to someone special. We prayed about it, and my sister said after she finished praying you came to her mind. I knew this was what we were to do because as I prayed, you came to my mind also. We felt like this was what God wanted. You took four boys in when they were little, gave them a home and a lot of love. They are now at the driving age, or at least two of them are. So, we want you to have both cars. Like I said, we don't want you to buy them since our parents left us financially well taken care of. You have a heart of gold, and it shows in those boys. So, to help you out, just like you helped those boys in a time of need, we are giving you both cars."

As Kit was talking, tears began to roll down Leah's cheeks. She knew then why she was having a hard time deciding on what kind of car to get.

"Kit, I can't thank you enough. You are an answer to a prayer. I knew we needed another car, and I've been praying what to do. Nora and I went and looked at cars, and I found an SUV that I liked but didn't want to spend the money on it. I have seen your mom's car, and it is much nicer than the one I looked at. Please let me pay you something."

"No, they are a gift. If you have any extra cash, put it in the offering plate at church. God will direct it where it needs to go. As you know, He is always a few steps ahead of us."

Standing to go, Kit hugged Leah.

"The cars are at my house. We can get together tomorrow to change the title over to you. You and the boys can pick them up then."

"Kit, again, thank you. You will never know what this means to us."

When Kit left, Leah went into her bedroom and got down on her knees. Through her tears, she tried to give thanks to the Lord. She felt so unworthy of such a wonderful gift. She cried and prayed till almost time for church that night.

The next day, Nick, Nora, and Leah went to Kit's house after the boys left for school. Kit was outside working when they pulled up.

"Good morning, Leah. Hey, Nora, Nick. We have the cars around back. I got up early this morning to go over them. I wanted to make sure they were clean and shiny for you."

Leah looked at Kit. "I don't think I have ever seen those cars when they weren't clean."

Kit laughed. "They always kept them in the garage and you're right, if it rained on them, Dad would wash the car as soon as the sun came out. They both have a full tank of gas and all the manuals, and service records are in the glove box. Tires are in great shape, and I even had the cars serviced for you. I wanted to make sure they were in tip-top shape and ready to be driven."

With tears forming in her eyes, Leah walked over to hug Kit. "I still can't thank you enough. God will bless you for your love, generosity, and thoughtfulness."

"Leah, I truly believe God directed this. We prayed, you were praying, and God answered those prayers. His love is so overflowing that it flows down on us, his children. You know in Hebrews it talks about having faith. Also, in Mark 11:24 it says, 'Therefore, I tell you, whatever you ask for in prayer, believe that you have received it, and it will be yours.' But then, I know I don't have to tell you this, for you were the one in Sunday School many years ago that taught this to me and so many others. You are a wonderful teacher, and your love shows in all you do. I don't know anyone more worthy than you. Look at what all you and David gave to others over the years. Just this morning as Tara and I were getting the kids ready for the day, I told her that if we could be like you and David, what a wonderful life we would have. You two set an awesome example of what a Christian life should be. Thank you, Leah Conner."

Leah's tears were overflowing by now. Nora and Nick both agreed that if anyone deserved help, it was certainly Leah. Nora went over to Leah, and the two hugged and cried.

Kit led them to the cars, which looked brand new. Leah drove the SUV home, Nick drove the Honda and Nora drove their car, for she said she felt more comfortable driving her own car.

Leah's garage was only built for two cars. Where were they going to put a third vehicle?

Nick spoke up. "I can move my truck into our house garage, and we can put the Honda in there. Whoever drives the Honda, I will give them the garage code, and that way the car will be inside and out of the weather."

"Oh, Nick, I don't want you to go to all that trouble. We can figure something out here. Maybe we can build a carport and put a canopy over it."

"No, Leah, I have already made up my mind. The Honda will go in this garage. Now that all this is settled, I'm hungry. What's for lunch, Nora?"

Leah hugged Nick. "You and Nora are the best neighbors. Have I told you both how much I love you?"

Smiling from ear to ear, Nick said, "Leah, the feeling is mutual. Nora and I can't imagine not having you and those boys around. You have no idea what those boys have come to mean to me. I'm their Uncle Nick, and I love it."

Soon the boys were home from school. Leah and Nora were grilling out for dinner that night when Daniel came out and asked, "Whose car is in the garage? Did you go buy a new car today, Mom?"

"No, the Lord supplied us with a much-needed extra car."

Caleb overheard Daniel and Leah talking about the car, and he went into the garage to see it. When he came out, he looked at Leah, "Mom, that was your unspoken request, wasn't it? I have been praying so hard for God to hear your request, and yesterday when I prayed it was like I didn't need to pray anymore, and now I know why."

As if Leah had not cried enough, she realized how much those boys were into praying and believing. Closing her eyes for a moment, she had to give thanks to her heavenly Father.

Leah explained how the car came about and showed the boys both cars. Daniel wanted to drive the Honda, and Stephen said he was fine with driving Leah's old car when the time came, and she would drive the SUV. Then they moved Leah's old car into Nick's garage and put the Honda in the garage next to the SUV. Nick and the boys spent the rest of the evening looking over the cars and discussing things under the hood. Leah and Nora sat on the swing outside listening to them.

Leah leaned over to Nora, "I'm so glad Nick is here to help the boys with things like a car. All I know is when a light on the dashboard comes on, I need someone to look at the car. I do watch the gas gage and know how fast I'm driving."

Twenty-Three

Sunday morning, Iris was up extra early in the kitchen. When Diane came in, Iris not only had breakfast underway but was cooking lunch.

"Morning, Iris, how come you are cooking lunch this early in the morning?"

"Today we are having dinner at church after the service. Everyone brings a dish or two. It gives you an opportunity to talk to your neighbors and find out how everyone is doing. Being new here, it will give you a chance to meet others. Everyone around here is so nice and friendly. I'm sure you will have a great time."

"Iris, I'm not exactly feeling well. I hope you and Paul don't mind if I stay home today."

Looking up at Diane, Iris knew she didn't want to go to church. "That's between you and Paul."

About that time Paul walked in. "What am I between?" Paul asked.

"Oh, Paul, I got up this morning not feeling so good. Thought it best if I stayed home this morning."

Paul walked over to Diane and placed his hand on her forehead. "Well, you're not running a fever, so go ahead and get dressed for church. Dr. Wilson will be at church this morning. If you're still not feeling well by the time we arrive, I'll have him look at you. He is a great doctor. You can tell him your symptoms, and he can let you know what your problem is. He may have you go into town to his office for some tests but most of the time, he already knows what the problem is. We are fortunate to have him."

"What kind of a doctor is he exactly?" Diane wanted to know.

"He's a family doctor. He treats anything that needs treating. Like I said, he is good. little gets past him."

"Paul, I don't want to bother him. I possibly have a twenty-four-hour bug and will be better by tomorrow. I'll stay home just to be on the safe side.”

“Nothing doing. You are going to church this morning if I have to pick you up and carry you the way you’re dressed. You have no fever, your face is not flushed, and you’re not pale. If you are sick, I’ll have the Doc check you out. Subject closed.”

Paul walked outside and left Diane and Iris to finish cooking. After breakfast, Diane reluctantly got ready for church. When she went downstairs to get in the car, she received a shock.

“What is that wagon for?” Diane asked.

Tommy walked up to her, “We, we, we, go to to ch-ch-church in the wa-wa- wagon.”

Looking at Tommy, Diane said, “I’ll go find someone who can talk plain. You need to stay away from me till you learn how to talk right.”

Diane walked away irritated at Tommy and wondering why Paul would want a boy like that around. Tommy looked to be about eleven. Diane walked over to Paul. “Why do you have the wagon out today?”

“Because we are going to church. On days when it’s pretty, this is what we take.”

“You ride in a wagon? Have you lost your mind? You had me to go to town to buy a dress for Sunday, and now you want me to ride in a wagon?”

Paul laughed, “The fresh air and ride will do you good. The boys don’t mind. In fact, they look forward to it.”

“Well, I’m certainly not riding in no wagon. I’m going in the car.”

“Diane, in case you have forgotten, you don’t have a car. So, looks like you will be riding in the wagon with the rest of us. Do you want me to help you up?”

“No. Here just take this food and I’ll get in myself.”

As Diane started to get in the wagon, Paul said, “Excuse me, I drive the wagon and Iris sits beside me. You will ride in the back with the boys.”

Diane looked at the boys standing around the wagon, waiting to see what she was going to do.

"This is just great. First, you make me go to church when I'm not feeling well, and now I have to go in a wagon and sit in the back with a bunch of kids. Thanks, Paul, you really know how to make a person feel welcome."

"Diane, have you noticed you are the only one complaining? You should be grateful that we don't walk to church."

"Walk? No one in their right mind would want to walk to church. Paul, you have spent way too much time in the sun. What brain you had is fried."

As Diane made her way to the back of the wagon, the boys gathered around to offer her some assistance should she need any.

"Get away from me, I don't need your help," Diane spat out.

Waiting patiently, the boys stood still till Diane got up in the wagon and found a seat. Then they each climbed in and sat down.

Iris came out with a cart with several dishes on it, and they placed them at the end of the wagon. Then Paul helped her onto the seat, and off they went.

One little boy named Micah was sitting near Diane.

"My name is Micah. You are a pretty lady. Do you have children?"

"No, I don't. Kids are a waste of time."

"Mr. Paul and Miss Iris love kids. That's why we are here. They are the best."

Looking at the boy, Diane said, "How come you are not living with your parents? Guess you were so mean they couldn't stand you and wanted rid of you."

Micah looked down and then looked back up at Diane.

"God took both my daddy and mama home to heaven. They were in a bad car wreck while I was in school. Mr. Paul and Miss Iris came and got me, and I have been with them ever since. Miss Iris said that God needed them in heaven right away. I'm not mad at God, for Mr. Paul said God never makes mistakes, and besides, him and Miss Iris was looking for a boy just like me."

Not sure what to say, Diane just swallowed hard and turned her head.

Micah leaned over to Diane, "Would you like a hug? I like

hugs. They make me feel better.”

Taking a deep breath, Diane looked at Micah and said, “No, thanks. I’m not into hugs.”

“Maybe you should try them. They make you feel so good. Miss Iris gives really good hugs.”

Wishing the child would hush, Diane tried to turn in what little seat she had away from him. As she turned there sat Tommy.

“Mic, Mic, Micah is right. Hu-hu Hugs fe, feel go-od. We-we al-all like hu-hu-hugs.”

Diane thought to herself. Just my luck to be stuck back here with a wagon full of brats. She refused to talk to them the rest of the way to church.

When they finally arrived at the church, Diane noticed others had come in wagons and a few in cars. A pavilion outside near the church had tables lined under it, and women were placing the food they brought in certain places. As soon as the boys were out of the wagon, they gathered the dishes Ms. Iris had prepared and took them to the pavilion. Micah and Tommy were standing at the wagon to help Diane down. When she started to get down, the boys held up their hands to help her.

“I don’t need your help. I am capable of getting down by myself,” Diane barked.

Micah looked at Diane and replied, “A gentleman is supposed to help a lady down. Mr. Paul said it was only right.”

“Well, all I see is two boys, no men are in sight, so I’ll do my best to get down.”

Diane got down, and as she walked over to the church, she wondered how she was possibly going to get out of going inside. Then she decided she would stay outside around the food to make sure no one bothered anything. Just as she turned, she gasped.

“John, I didn’t see you.”

“Good morning, Peyton, I mean Diane. How are you today?”

“Oh, I am just fine. Now if you will excuse me, I’m going to go over and help the ladies with the food.”

Taking her arm, “No need for that. Since this is your first Sunday here, you are not required to help set up. Now, let’s go in and find a seat, shall we?"

"John, I really need to help Iris. She cooked for an army this morning."

"Nonsense. Iris is used to cooking for a large number of people. So come on. Do you prefer a seat toward the front or are you a back row person?"

Paul walked up as John was going to lead Diane into the church.

"John, good to see you this morning. If you plan on sitting with my sister, be sure to make her behave. If you blink, she may not be beside you."

"Morning, Paul. Don't worry about your sister. I'll keep an eye on her. Besides, I have Tommy and Micah here to help me."

Looking at Diane, John motioned with his hand for them to go inside the church. The closer Diane got to the door, the more she could feel her heart beating double-time. She did not want to go inside.

"Let's sit at the back, John, I don't do well up front or in the middle. I need at the back so I can be near the door and can get fresh air."

John and the boys started laughing. "Diane, the church is air conditioned. I don't believe you will have any breathing problems. Follow Micah and Tommy, and we will sit with them," John replied.

Going inside, taking a seat, Diane started perspiring. Her whole body became clammy. Then everyone was asked to stand to sing. Micah handed her a book and asked, "Do you like to sing?"

Refusing the book Diane shook her head no. All she could think of was how to escape. When the song was over, Diane decided she needed to go the bathroom. She asked John where the lady's room was.

Smiling at her, he leaned over to whisper in her ear, "The church has not installed one yet, you will have to go to the outhouse. I'll take you."

Shocked by his answer, she said, "In that case, I'll wait," for she knew John would bring her back inside the church.

Finally, the service was over, and Diane had no idea what the preacher had talked about, since she listened little. When they gathered around the pavilion for the pastor to bless the food, Iris walked up to Diane. "If you need to use the bathroom or wash your hands, the bathroom is downstairs. You can go through that side door over there, it's much easier to get to from here, and you won't have to go back through the church."

Looking at Iris, Diane said, "You mean you have indoor plumbing here? I thought you had an outhouse?"

"Heavens, no, Diane. We may be out in the country, but we are not primitive. Why would you think that? The church is air-conditioned. Why wouldn't we have running water?"

Turning, looking for John, Diane had a few words to say to him.

As soon as the preacher said "Amen," Diane started searching for John. He was with a whole gang of kids, playing with them.

Diane walked up to John and said, "Aren't you afraid you might get your hands dirty, since there is no running water?"

John just smiled. "So, who told you?"

"Iris informed me if I needed a bathroom or wanted to wash my hands where I could go. Odd, she knew about the bathroom, and you didn't!"

"Diane, I didn't completely lie to you. We do have an outhouse. When I bought this property, it had an old run-down house with an outhouse. I left the outhouse standing while we tore that house down and built my home. Later I donated some of my property for a church. The outhouse was used during that time also. I own a lot of land here, and when I got saved, I felt it only right to donate land for a church. Everyone around came and helped build it. It's a beautiful church, don't you think?"

Diane looked at the church, "To be honest, I haven't paid much attention to how churches look. A church is a church to me. Guess we had better get in line before the food all gets gone."

Diane expected the kids to make a run to the table of food, instead they kept on playing.

"Are they not going to eat?"

"They will, but around here, the men go first. After they have gone through the line, the ladies help the children. After the children are fed, then the ladies eat."

Surprised by what John said, Diane wasn't sure if he was telling her another one of his tales or if it was the truth. Looking toward the pavilion, Diane saw that only men were going through the line. If they needed anything, the women were close by to help.

"Why are the men the only ones to go through the line first?" Diane asked.

"Men are to be the head of the house. They are served first and then the children. Men work hard all day to provide for their families. It's the wife's place to make sure he has a meal to eat when he gets home. Our women are not slaves by any means. We respect them for the things they have to do."

"Do these ladies not hold public jobs?

"We have some who do, but the majority of the wives work at home. The younger women, women not married or women that are married but haven't started a family yet, work in town."

"Oh my, what a boring life. If I stay here, I will probably move into town and get a job. I need to be where the action is."

"Diane, you may not realize it, but there is plenty that goes on here. By the way, I understand you enjoy holding baby chicks!"

"That is not funny. That hen scared me to death. How was I to know not to pick up that chick?"

Laughing, John said, "What I would have given to have seen you with that baby chick. From what I heard, you should be a track star."

Finally, it was time for the women to eat. John went in front of Diane, and she was surprised at the amount of food still available.

John had a blanket for them to sit on while they ate. Then he asked,

"What are your plans for this afternoon?"

"I really don't have any."

"Good, I'll hitch up my buggy and pick you up around three o'clock. I'll drive you around and show you some of my property and where some beautiful spots are."

"Don't you have a car?" Diane asked.

"Yes, I do. But why drive a car when you can go for a buggy ride and enjoy the fresh air and the beauty of God's country?"

The boys were soon after John to play ball with them. He went, changed his clothes, and soon was playing ball, acting like one of the kids.

One of the girls came over to Diane. "Hello. You must be new around here. I don't think we have met. My name is Rose. What's your name?"

"My name is Diane. Don't you want to go play?"

"No, I like to go around and visit with everyone. Why are you sitting here by yourself? Don't you have any friends?"

"I prefer to be alone, if you don't mind."

Sitting down on the blanket beside Diane, Rose said, "I'll be your friend. Everyone needs a friend."

"Who are your parents? Don't you think they may be looking for you?"

"My mama is Betty. She knows where I am. I told her you look lonely, and I was going to go visit you. Is your mama here?"

"No, my mother is dead."

"I'm sorry. I don't know where my birth mother is, either. I sometimes wonder if she is with Jesus."

Looking at Rose, Diane said, "I thought you said Betty was your mother?"

"She is. When I was born, my birth mother had been doing drugs, and I was considered a drug baby. Mama Betty and Daddy Barry took me home with them, and I have been with them ever since. I love them, and they love me. I call them my mama and daddy because that's really who they are. They are now waiting on the adoption papers to go through."

"How old are you?"

"I'm five."

"You are a pretty little five-year-old and talkative."

"I just like people. Since you don't have any friends, I'll be your friend. Want to be pinky friends?"

"No, we can just be friends, okay?"

"Okay. Well, Mama is motioning for me to come, so I'll see you next Sunday. If you don't have anyone to sit with you, I will be happy to."

Going over in her mind what Rose had said about being a drug baby and then how she talked about it so casually made Diane wonder if it ever bothered Rose about her birth mother.

Iris came over. "Well, Diane, I think we have everything packed up. Are you ready to go?"

"Yes, John is supposed to come over this afternoon around three to take me on a buggy ride."

"Oh, Diane, you will enjoy that, especially if you are on his land. There are some beautiful spots and a ride in a buggy will make it more special."

"Iris, looks like he would get a convertible to ride around in. I'm sure the ride would be much smoother and more enjoyable."

Iris laughed. "Wait till you go for your buggy ride. I think you will find the experience gratifying."

At three o'clock, John rode up in his buggy. Paul greeted him and the two talked for a few minutes. When Diane came out to the porch, Paul wished them a good afternoon ride.

John took Diane to several sites and told her all about the land he owned. They rode by different rock formations, found a field of colorful wildflowers, even saw a few antelope. Coming upon a stream of water, John stopped the buggy for Diane to take in all the beauty when out of nowhere a moose came out and walked down to the water for a drink. Diane had never seen a live moose and was so excited.

"Is that a male or female moose?" she asked.

"That is a male moose."

"How can you tell from here?"

"When you see a moose with antlers, it's a male. If it doesn't have antlers, it's a female."

"Oh, well, I guess that makes sense. Never thought about looking at their antlers."

"Trust me, you don't want to find out any other way."

They continued down the road to a shady spot where John pulled over. He spotted a coyote and pointed it out to Diane.

"This is a nice place to talk, and we've got a good breeze, too. Diane, did you take the money I left you in Virginia and put it to good use?"

"Yes, and no. I didn't spend it the way you wanted, but it did help me."

"I tried to contact you after I left. In fact, I flew back to Virginia about two months later. I tried to call Bo, but some lady answered and said I had the wrong number. She told me the phone number was her late husband's number, George Mitchell. I googled the name, and when I saw the picture, I knew the guy was operating under a different name. I asked around if anyone knew a lady by the name of Peyton, and like Bo, that wasn't your real name."

"All you told me was your name was John. You didn't give me your last name."

"But I did tell you the truth. My name is John. Anyway, a friend of mine travels a lot and wanted to set me up with a hot date as he called it. He knew Bo and said he would take good care of me. Well, he did. After I left you that morning, I could think of nothing else. I played over and over in my mind us being together that night. I wanted so much to find you. I'm being honest. I have not been with another woman since that night. I had no idea you were Paul's sister. In fact, I didn't know Paul had a sister. I wanted so much to find you and bring you out here, away from the life you were living."

"Oh, John, I had no idea." Diane leaned over to kiss him, but John pulled away.

"Don't get me wrong, you are still in my heart, but I can't kiss you or hug you."

"Why, what's wrong? What's stopping you?"

"You see, I have done a lot of soul searching. I turned my life over to God and I promised him I would never touch any woman unless we were married. I know what it feels like to have you in my arms, and I can't let myself get that close to you. I'm human and a man, so I must refrain from temptation. But I want to show you what God can do for you, for us. You have my heart, but we need to get you right with God. We can't be unevenly yoked."

Looking at John, Diane wasn't sure what all he was talking about. This religion thing was really messing people's minds up. How was she going to undo this and have him back the way he was in Virginia?

Twenty-Four

Stephen was offered a part-time job as a mechanic. He was always helping Nick and word soon was out that he was quite good. He worked a few hours after school and half a day on Saturday. Like his brothers, he sang as he worked. One day, Caleb and Benjamin stopped by as Stephen was working and singing. So, they joined in. They also helped him with the car he was working on. Mr. O'Dell, the shop owner, came out and saw the three working and singing away. When they saw him, they stopped because they knew they weren't supposed to be working on the car.

Mr. O'Dell said, "I would like nothing better than to hire all three of you, but due to your age, I can't. If you guys worked on cars like you sing, I would have the greatest shop in town."

"Sorry, Mr. O'Dell, we stopped by to see Stephen for a minute. He was singing and we sort of got carried away," smiled Caleb.

"I know you boys didn't mean any harm, but until you get some age on you, it's too much of a liability. Now if you want to hang around and sing that would be great, but I can't pay you for that."

Caleb and Benjamin cleaned off their hands.

"Thanks, Mr. O'Dell, but we like to sing as we work," said Caleb.

The two walked off and said, "See you at home, Stephen."

A few days later, Stephen came home and went straight to his brothers. They were deep in discussion when Leah walked in.

"What are you boys up to? I can see some concern in your faces."

"Oh, Mom, it's just guy talk. Everything is alright," replied Stephen.

Leah walked away, but she felt it was more than guy talk. What were those boys up to?

It seemed they always had to go somewhere but said they couldn't tell her, not now anyway. Leah even ask Nora and Nick if they had any idea what those four were up to. They were of no help. Six months had gone by, and whatever they were up to was still a secret. They were spending less and less time at home. Not to mention churches from all around had been calling wanting them to sing for them.

When people asked for them to sing, they asked what name they went by. They were mostly known as Leah's Boys. Sometimes they were called "The Conners." They had calls from other counties, and soon other states close by were inviting them to sing at fundraisers. Yes, the boys were becoming quite popular. Nick and Nora always went wherever the boys were singing, for they needed Nick's truck to haul their equipment, plus they were always there for support.

Benjamin came running in the house one Saturday and said, "Mom, come out to the garage. We have something to show you, but you must close your eyes."

When Leah got to the garage, Benjamin made sure she had her eyes closed. He walked her outside and said, "Now open."

When Leah opened her eyes, she couldn't believe what she was seeing. "Oh, my. Where did you boys get this?"

Daniel spoke up, "A guy from the music store came by and asked if I knew anyone who could use it. It needed a little work, and he needed someone to take it off his hands. Stephen checked everything out. Nothing was wrong under the hood, so Mr. O'Dell gave us the name of a man that owns a paint shop. We went and talked to him, and this is what we have been working on for the last six and half months."

Before Leah was a beautiful white van. On the side was painted "By Grace Quartet." Leah broke down and cried. The boys had needed something to put their equipment in when they traveled to singings, and here God had supplied that need. What was even more special, Leah's middle name was Grace.

The boys gathered around Leah and said they didn't have a name for themselves, but it was "By Grace" they were who they were.

Nick and Nora pulled up in their driveway and saw the van. They came over to check it out.

Nora asked, "Are you boys aware that Leah's middle name is Grace?"

Daniel spoke up, "Yes, and it was by God's grace she found us. We felt like this was an appropriate name for us to be known by."

Nora walked over to the boys and said, "Have I told you lately how much I love you? You four never cease to bless me." Then she gave them a hug.

They explained how they did the work themselves. "The guy at the paint shop showed us how to make repairs and taught us how to paint vehicles. We practiced on some old cars he had that were used for parts for other cars. We also reupholstered the inside here to make it look as new as possible. Putting our logo on was the tricky part."

Nick shook his head. "Just how did you boys pay for all this?"

Daniel said, "We had been praying about this for some time. Mom always said to take everything to the Lord. The van was given to me. We did a few fundraisers for the guy at the paint shop so that didn't cost us anything. The only cost was the logo. Not bad, don't you think?"

"Your strong faith in the Lord will carry you four guys to great things in life. Don't ever doubt the Lord. Always look for ways to serve him, and He will continue to bless you. I believe that with all my heart." Nick then walked over to the guys and hugged them with tears in his eyes.

In two weeks, they had a singing to do in West Virginia. As they proudly loaded up the van, they ask Nick if he cared to ride with them. Daniel had not driven that far yet and wanted Nick along to help him in case he had any questions. Leah and Nora followed behind in the car.

The school where they were singing was Parkersburg High and it was known as the second largest in the state. Unloading their equipment and getting set up, they noticed people had already started coming in. In no time, the auditorium was packed. Benjamin looked out at the crowd. He turned to his brothers.

"We have never sung in front of this many people before. I bet there are two thousand people out there."

Caleb peeked through the curtains. "Wow, this place is packed like sardines. It's standing room only."

Stephen also looked out. Turning to the others, he said, "Daniel, we need to pray."

As soon as everything was set up, the boys gathered in a circle to pray. They prayed for God to calm their nerves and to use them, praying that through their songs, someone would be blessed or saved.

When the curtains opened, the crowd stood clapping and cheering. Never had they experienced anything like this. As they started singing, some in the crowd clapped their hands, others raised their hands, and they could hear some amens. What a blessing the night had brought. After they finished singing, a preacher walked out, said a few words, and then asked if anyone needed prayer. People started coming forward and kneeling near the stage. The boys were so touched by the love they felt at that moment. low, they played "Amazing Grace."

As they were trying to put away their instruments, several people came up and ask if they had CDs to sell. Different ones wanted to shake their hands and all bragged about how much they enjoyed their singing and wanted them to come back as soon as they could.

Once they were in the van, Stephen said, "I never thought about us making a CD. What do you guys think?"

Nick turned in his seat. "They thought I was your manager, and I was able to get you more singing engagements. I think a CD is a great idea. We should have thought of that sooner."

"I'll check with Cody on Monday. I bet he can put us with the right person," replied Daniel.

When Monday came, Daniel explained to Cody what they were needing, and sure enough, Cody knew exactly how to help the guys out.

"Come to the store on Saturday around one, and we will get you fixed up."

By Saturday evening, the guys had made their first CD. The label would read, "By Grace Quartet." On Sunday, they went out with Cody to get some photos of them in different places to put on the cover. They couldn't believe how well-known they had become.

That night as they were getting ready to do their devotions, Benjamin looked over at Leah.

"You know, Mom, when we first came here, I was a little scared. We had never had a home, a bed, or three meals a day. We didn't know what it was like to bathe or get hugs. Things here were so different. You have given us so much and without you, your faith, love, and support, we wouldn't be who we are today. Standing on that stage Saturday night, I had never seen so many people. It was scary. But when we started singing, all that went away. Those people were so happy. Through our faith, we were given peace. This is what you taught us.

"I thought of some scripture you had read to us in the Bible from Romans 5:1-5, 'Therefore, since we have been justified through faith, we have peace with God through our Lord Jesus Christ, through whom we have gained access by faith into this grace in which we now stand. And we rejoice in the hope of the glory of God. Not only so, but we also rejoice in our sufferings, because we know that suffering produces perseverance; perseverance, character; and character, hope. And hope does not disappoint us, because God has poured out his love into our hearts by the Holy Spirit, whom he has given us.'"

Benjamin continued saying, "I just want to say 'thank you' for what you have done for us, for the path you made available. Looking at those people that night made me glad that our songs touched them."

Daniel spoke up. "Some of my friends from school play guitars and other instruments, and they are always after me to come play for them, but their songs are not Godly songs. I listen to them, and that's not who you taught us to be. When I studied the words to their music, it was trashy. I didn't want to be associated with that. Had we not come here, that's probably what we would be listening to. I want to say, 'thank you' for guiding us in the correct way."

"I think all four of us feel the same way," added Caleb. "Stephen and I were talking today at the choices we have in life. Seeing so many people come down to the stage the other night, crying, praying, reaching out for help, it was touching. It made me feel good, that God had allowed us through his songs to speak to their hearts."

Stephen said, "All I can add to what they have said is, 'Amen.'"

Leah blinked back the tears in her eyes, knowing in her heart God had his hands on these boys. "All I can say is to stay on this path. When the day comes that God calls me home, I pray you four will continue this journey with God. Don't do it for fame or money, but for the glory of God."

Then Stephen read some scripture, and they had prayer before turning in for the night. As Leah sat on the couch thinking about what the boys had said, she wondered how a mother could walk away from four precious boys. Did she not realize what blessings God had given her? Yes, God had taken her David away from her, but in return, he blessed her beyond measure with four handsome and wonderful sons.

Twenty-Five

Diane was unhappy with the way things were going with her and John. She had been with Paul and Iris for eight months, and each day, she had hopes of changing John's mind. No matter how hard she tried, he would not give in to her desires for him. She went to church only to please him, but her heart was not in going. She would let her mind wander about different things during the service, sometimes singing a song in her head to tune out the preacher.

After helping Iris in the kitchen with breakfast, Diane went outside. The day was so beautiful, so she decided to go for a ride. No one was around so she saddled up a horse herself. She took off in a direction she had never been before, wondering what she might see. After about two hours, she decided to turn around and go back home. Then a thought struck her. Wonder how fast the horse could go and would he be able to jump the rocks and stumps out in the field?

She took off trying to get the horse to pick up more speed. Suddenly, the horse reared back, and Diane fell off. Her leg hit a rock, and with a popping sound, pain shot up her leg to her hip. The horse then took off, leaving her behind. She called out for help but didn't see anyone around. She noticed her leg was bleeding, and the pain so unbearable. She knew she could not walk back home, and she was not sure if anyone would know where to look when she didn't show up for dinner.

The hot sun was beating down on her. She had no water and knew she needed to find some shade but moving was too painful. She was now soaking wet from the sun and not sure if she was even on Paul's land or on John's.

Then the sun began slowly going down, and Diane was afraid she was going to have to stay out there all night. Closing her eyes, she began to cry. Then before she realized what she was saying, she said, "Please Lord, send someone to help me. I don't want to die out here." That was the last thing she remembered.

Paul was working near the barn when his horse came walking up. Surprised to see a saddle on him, he wondered what was going on, for he thought his horse was in the corral. He went to check on the boys to see if they knew anything about his horse being saddled and out. No one knew anything.

It was near dinner time, and when Iris rang the dinner bell, everyone gathered in but Diane. Paul realized then that she must have taken the horse out for a ride, but what had happened to her? He got up and called John to see if he knew anything, but he hadn't seen Diane all day.

"I'll head over your way, and hopefully we can find her before dark."

While waiting on John, Paul gathered the boys that were good with horses, and he felt safe in sending them out. They had their horses saddled up and were laying out plans for who to ride where on the land when John arrived.

Micah and Tommy rode out with Paul, and after a while they split up and were to meet in one area at a certain time.

Tommy was getting ready to ride back to meet Paul and Micah when he spotted something in the grass. It was a rocky area, and although he thought Diane wouldn't be around those rocks riding, he went to check it out anyway.

Sure enough, there lay Diane. Tommy quickly dismounted and checked Diane, but she did not respond to his call or touch. He could see that her leg was broken. Running back to his horse to go for help, he didn't realize Diane was coming to consciousness.

She tried to call out to him, but he didn't hear her. In her mind she thought, of all people to find her, it had to be Tommy. He would never be able to tell them where she was, and knew she was going to die here.

Tommy found Paul and Micah and told them about Diane. He also told Paul he would need his truck to be able to bring her back to the ranch, and they needed to call Doc Wilson, for he would need to know about her leg. Tommy was certain it was broken.

About an hour later, Diane could hear an engine. Looking,

she spotted a truck and began to call weakly for help. Soon, Paul, John and Tommy were by her side.

Paul and John began to secure her leg so they could put her in the back of the truck. Paul looked at Diane and said, "You have Tommy to thank for finding you. He told us where you were and that your leg was broken, and we would need the truck."

"He could have given me some water. I was dying of thirst."

"He didn't have any water to give you, or he would have. Besides, you were unresponsive, and he knew you needed help fast. Tommy was so scared; he was crying when he got to us. You need to thank him, Diane. Would it hurt you to be kind to him just once?" Diane only looked at Tommy but never said anything.

They took Diane into town to see the doctor. As Tommy had said, her leg was broken. After spending several hours in the emergency room, they were able to go home. Diane had a cast from her foot to above the kneecap. She was given crutches to use, but she stated she wouldn't need them. John put them in the truck anyway.

The next day, Paul brought Diane breakfast. "We are going to fix a room downstairs for you to sleep in till your cast is off. Getting you up the steps is too hard."

"I'm sorry, Paul, to be such a bother."

As Paul was setting up her breakfast tray, he asked, "By the way, what were you doing way out there on the back property? We are seldom out that way."

"I wanted to go for a ride since it was a beautiful day. I think something spooked the horse, and when he raised up, I fell off."

Paul looked at Diane. "That was my horse, and he doesn't spook easily. Also, the saddle wasn't fastened properly. It's a wonder you made it as far as you did."

Iris knocked on the door. "The bed is ready downstairs, if you're ready to help her down."

When they finally got Diane situated in her new room, Iris told her she would be back later to check on her. Paul had some errands to take care of, and Rose was coming over from the Hawkins ranch to help.

Lying in the bed, Diane was becoming bored. No television, no radio, no nothing. Then someone knocked at her door. Thinking it was John, she said, "Come in."

When the door open, it was Tommy. He had brought her some wildflowers he had picked that morning. Walking over to Diane, he handed them to her. Thinking about what Paul had said, Diane took the flowers and said, "Thank you, Tommy, this is thoughtful, and thank you for saving me yesterday."

"I'm glad you are okay. I was really scared yesterday when I found you. Do you need anything before I leave? I need to get back to work."

"You could put these flowers over on the dresser. That way I can see them. The vase you put them in is also nice."

"I borrowed the vase from Ms. Iris. Hope the flowers brighten up your room for you. Well, I better go. I hope you get to feeling better soon."

Tommy started out the door and Diane said, "Tommy, you're not stuttering. What happened?"

"Doc Wilson said he thinks it's because I got scared yesterday. When I first saw you, you didn't move. I thought you were dead. Then I checked your pulse. I knew you needed help right away, and I rode to Mr. Paul as fast as I could. Doc Wilson says sometimes a traumatic shock can do that. In trying to tell Mr. Paul about you, the stuttering went away. Thank you for helping me."

Diane looked at Tommy and couldn't believe it. "You sound so much better."

Walking back over to Diane, Tommy leaned over and gave her a hug. "I hate that you got hurt, but I'm so glad I can talk normal."

Taken back by Tommy's hug, Diane didn't know what to say. Then Tommy turned and walked away.

Later that evening, John stopped by to see how Diane was feeling.

The door to her room was open, but he knocked anyway. "How is the cripple doing?"

"Oh, John, this has been the longest day. I have nothing to do but lie here."

"Looks like someone came by to visit with you?"

"No one but Iris. She brought me my food and asked if I need anything. There is no television, no internet, no radio in here. I need something to do!"

"So, who brought you flowers?"

"Oh, just Tommy. Hey, do you know he doesn't stutter anymore? Apparently last night he was so scared, he forgot about stuttering."

"Diane, you need to be grateful to Tommy. He found you, then came and told us exactly where you were, and that your leg was broken. He also checked to see if you were alive and told us he thought you had either passed out from the heat or the pain in your leg. That boy cares about you. Why can't you show him some respect and be thankful?"

"You sound like Paul now. Did he send you in here to say that?"

"No, besides, I like Tommy, I care. By the way, I have a gift for you."

This perked Diane up. "You have a gift for me? John, you are so thoughtful. What is it?"

John handed her a box. When Diane took the lid off, she just looked at it.

"Well, what do you think? I don't think you have one."

Diane wasn't sure what to say. This was not what she was hoping to receive.

Finally, she took it out of the box. "No, I don't have a Bible. You even had my name put on it. That was thoughtful."

John took the Bible from Diane. "I will come by every night that I possibly can, and we can read and pray together. Let's start tonight in the book of Psalms, or do you have a favorite scripture?"

"No, I can't think of one at the moment. How about you? Do you have a favorite?"

"Oh, I have many. In time, I hope you will have many, too.

So, do you want to read first or shall I?"

"No, you read tonight. I will listen."

"No problem. When I come by tomorrow, you can tell me what you have read and what your thoughts are on the scripture. Soon, you will have some favorite scriptures yourself."

Diane laid her head back on her pillow. This was not what she wanted, and she didn't want John to read to her, especially from a Bible. What is it with these people? Can't they understand she wanted nothing to do with their so-called God? How was she going to endure these nightly readings?

John read the first chapter. "Do you have any thoughts or comments on what I read, Diane?"

"No, I'm good."

"Do you know where the book of Psalms is in the Bible?"

"No."

Holding the Bible out to Diane, "The book of Psalms is in the center of the Bible. Do you know what the first book is in the Bible?"

"No, and I really don't care. Why couldn't you have brought me a romance book?"

"Because I wanted you to have the best book that was on the market. If you read the book of Ruth or the book of Song of Solomon, you might find that interesting. There is no greater book than the Bible. If you don't read it, then when I come over, I'm going to read it to you."

"Isn't it enough that I go to church every Sunday and sit with you? Do you have to keep pushing this stuff down my throat?"

John took Diane's hand in his. "If you want us to ever be together, then you will have to accept Christ into your life, and I will have to see some changes. Christ is number one in my life and always will be. He should be number one in yours also. Without him, we have no future."

Laying the Bible on the bed, John got up and left. Diane could feel the tears rolling down her face. She wanted to be with John but not like this. Why did things have to change?

Iris came in to see if Diane needed anything. She thought she might want to get up and try to take a sponge bath. Looking at Diane, Iris asked, "Why the tears?"

"Iris, I hate life. It's just not fair. Everyone wants me to change. I'm not the problem, but no one can see that."

Iris sat down in the chair by Diane's bed. "Diane, you bring the majority of your problems on yourself. You can't see it, but you want to put the blame on everyone else. Nothing is ever your fault. You need to be able to meet people at least halfway. No longer than you have been here, you blame all of us when things don't go your way. We all make mistakes, but you don't want to admit that you are ever wrong. I'm sorry about your leg, and we want to help you, but your attitude needs to change. Behind every dark cloud, there is a rainbow. Until you admit some things, you are always going to be a miserable person. You are fortunate that John Leighton cares about you. You have no idea how many single women around here would love to have his undivided attention. He's nice to everyone but has never shown any of them the time of day, and here you come in, and you can't help but notice he's crazy about you. Get your act together, or you might lose him. Now, do you want that sponge bath tonight or in the morning?"

Several days had passed, and John hadn't stopped by to see Diane nor had any of the boys. Diane saw only Iris. Even Paul had not stopped by to see how she was. She knew he was home because she had heard his voice. Finally, Diane asked, "Why is everyone staying away? I broke my leg, it's not like I was diagnosed with a terrible disease."

"I think everyone is giving you some time to do some soul searching. Like I said the other night, we are not your problem. You are your own worst enemy. You can get up from your bed and use your crutches, but you would rather lie here and have everyone come to you. I notice John brought you a Bible, but you haven't touched it. You have plenty of time to read, and he gave you the best book to be bought."

"I didn't ask for a Bible. That was his own doings."

"See, your attitude is your problem. Starting tomorrow, if you want to eat, you will have to get up and come to the kitchen for your meals. Also, you need to figure out a way to bathe yourself. I don't mind helping you dress, but it's time you started trying to do a few things on your own."

"So now you're turning against me, too?"

"No, you have laid here and felt sorry for yourself long enough. We have choices in life, and you can choose to get up or lie here. The choice is yours. It shouldn't be too difficult for there's only two choices."

"As soon as I can travel, I'm leaving here. I thought when I came, you guys would be happy to see me and want to have me around. Looks like I was wrong. It was a waste of my time and money coming here."

"Again, Diane, we have choices," Iris said. "No one can make them for you. Have you stopped to think why you are so bitter? What brought all this bitterness inside you? No matter where you go, it's not going to go away till you figure some things out. Paul, John, nor I can do that for you. John gave you the best guide for your life. Again, you can read it; if you don't understand, ask. The Bible says in Matthew 18:12-14, 'What do you think? If a man owns a hundred sheep, and one of them wanders away; will he not leave the ninety-nine on the hills and go to look for the one that wandered off? And if he finds it, I tell you the truth, he is happier about the one sheep than about the ninety-nine that did not wander off. In the same way your Father in heaven is not willing that any of these little ones should be lost.' Diane, you are that little lost sheep that has wandered off. How long are you going to keep straying away?"

Iris gathered up some things and walked out, closing the door behind her, praying for Diane as she went.

Twenty-Six

Graduation day came for Daniel. He was so excited to be walking across the stage to receive his diploma. Leah, Stephen, Caleb, Benjamin, Nora, and Nick were all excited for him. Nora and Nick bought Daniel a new guitar for graduation with his name on the neck.

"This is so awesome," said Daniel, giving Nora and Nick a big hug.

"So, what are your plans now that you have graduated?" Nick asked.

Daniel looked around at everyone and smiled. "I have been offered a manager's job at Sam's Music Store. He is thinking about retiring, and if all goes well, I will buy him out. He wants to make sure I have a full understanding of the store, and of course, he said he would always be available if I had a problem with anything."

Leah gasped. "You mean you will soon have your own music store?"

"Yes, and the good part is, I am going to hire my brothers to help me. We all can play just about any instrument we want, and we can always give lessons. Not sure if I want to change the name of the store yet. Had thought when it was mine, I'd name it Conner Brothers Music Store, but that will come in time."

Leah said, "Conner Brothers Music Store. Oh, my. You guys just keep on blessing me. I wish so much David was here to share in all this. He would be so proud of you boys."

Stephen hugged Leah. "We want to make you proud of the name you gave us. From all we have been told, he was a godly man. People looked up to him and respected him, and our plans are when you hear the name Conner, you know it's a name of worth."

Not a dry eye could be found among them.

Two years had gone by, and the boys had taken over Sam's Music Store. They changed the name to "Conner Brothers Music Store." One morning Leah went over to visit Nora.

"Got a few minutes to spare, Nora?"

"Sure, I just put on a fresh pot of coffee, and I have a cinnamon cake in the oven that should be done soon. Looks like you have something on your mind. What's up?"

"Nora, I don't feel the boys need me as much as they used to. They pick up after themselves and even help with the laundry, and I have always let them help in the kitchen. Now they can cook without my help. They keep the cars clean inside and out. The lawn is mowed, edged. They even weed my flower beds. When they go off to the music store, I have hardly anything to do."

"Leah, look at how far they have come. They could go out on their own and do well. You have taught them so much; they are even cautious about their spending. You have a lot to be proud of."

"Don't get me wrong, Nora, I am so proud of them, but I don't feel as needed anymore. I don't have to ask them to do anything, they just do it. Caleb even looked in the cabinets to see what we were low on, made a list and said, 'I made a grocery list. Anything you want to add to it?' I looked it over, and I had nothing to add. Then he told me they would stop at the store on the way home, if I decided I needed anything to give them a call."

"Leah, those boys need you still. If something were to happen to you, they would be lost. You are their safety net. The rock they lean on. Give it some time, and you will see how much you are needed."

"I don't know, Nora, the girls went off to college, got married, moved away, had families of their own. David passed away and then soon, I got the boys."

"Leah, you still have your church activities. I think the problem is that you're missing the boys not being home as much as they were. Why don't you cook lunch for them and take it to the store? Not every day but surprise them every now and then.

Who knows? You might find something to do at their store. This is something to put on our prayer list.”

“Oh, Nora, that’s a perfect idea. I knew talking to you would help. Now, where’s that coffee and cake?”

The next day as soon as the boys left for work, Leah went straight to the kitchen to prepare them lunch. She fixed steak, gravy, mashed potatoes, green beans, corn, rolls and a chocolate pie. As she was getting things ready to take to the store, she remembered she had some iced tea. She filled one cooler with some heat wraps she had and in the other cooler she put her tea and chocolate pie. After gathering up paper plates, napkins, eating utensils, and cups, she headed for the music store. She drove around back and let herself in. They had a small kitchen with a small table. Leah started placing the food out so they could come in and eat.

Benjamin walked in. “I thought I could smell food. Mom, what are you doing?”

“I know you boys need to eat. I made you a little lunch so you wouldn’t have to order out.”

Benjamin looked at all that was on the table. “Mom, that’s not a small lunch, but I’m not one to complain. Since I’m already here, I’m going to eat.”

As Benjamin was eating, Caleb walked in. “Mom, what are you doing here, and hey, Benjamin, where did you get this food? Were you not going to tell us about it?”

Benjamin grinned with a mouth full of food. “I was going to come get you guys just as soon as I was finished. We all can’t eat at once because someone has to be out front.”

Caleb looked at Leah, “Mom, did you do this?”

“I know you boys must eat, and I wanted to help you. This way, you don’t have to order out.”

Caleb looked at Benjamin. “I’ll be right back.”

Soon he was back. “I told them I was going to take a lunch break. Didn’t give them time to ask questions. Besides, they were with customers.”

Just when they were ready to go back to work and let Daniel

and Stephen come eat, Leah said, "Oh, I almost forgot. I made a chocolate pie."

Benjamin said, "Mom, if it's alright, can we save the pie for this afternoon? What you brought was so good and filling. I could go for a nap right now, but better let the other two come back."

Benjamin and Caleb gave Leah a hug. "Mom, what would we ever do without you?"

Though they didn't realize it, those words were music to Leah's ears.

When Daniel and Stephen walked in, they were so surprised. Daniel laughed, "Benjamin said we had a surprise in the kitchen. Looks like he and Caleb found the surprise first."

"Now, don't worry, I have kept your meal warm. Here are the plates, I hope you enjoy it," replied Leah.

Like the other two, they ate till they were stuffed. Leah brought out the chocolate pie and Stephen said, "Mom that's going to have to wait. You outdid yourself with this meal. But don't worry, if you leave it, I'll be sure to sample it this afternoon."

Daniel and Stephen both gave Leah a hug. "You are the best. We love you so much."

As they went back out into the store, Leah looked at what she brought. little was left. She felt so happy. After cleaning everything up, she quietly left and went home. That night when they got home, Leah had made them chicken salad sandwiches, a salad, and baked beans. For dessert they had an apple pie.

The next day, Leah made ham sandwiches, potato soup, chips, coconut pie and some drinks. While she was at the music store, she decided to look in the office. All four boys were busy with customers, and she didn't want to bother them. The office was a little cluttered. She remembered Daniel saying he was trying to get it organized but had been so busy. Wanting to help, she sat down and started sorting papers, putting labels on things and what she wasn't sure about she put in a folder with a sticky note on top, "Not sure about these papers." The phone rang a few times, and Leah decided since the boys were all busy, she would answer it to help them out.

Since she didn't know the answer to the questions from the phone calls, she found a tablet and wrote down who called, what time and the question they had. Not planning on staying long, she looked at her watch and knew she had to leave to make dinner for that night. The boys were still busy with customers, so Leah slipped out the back door and headed for home.

That evening, when they were sitting at the dinner table, Daniel spoke up. "Mom, we know you were at the store today. Stephen went to pick something up for lunch and found you had already been there. Thank you, the meal was good. Also, when I went into the office, the desk was so organized. Thank you for taking the phone calls. I called the people back before we left."

"I hope you don't mind what I did. I wanted to help you out. You always seem so busy. I had no idea a music store had that much business."

"We have been calling around trying to bring in more business. Buying the store from Sam has turned out to be a great investment. The county built a new school, and we got the contract for the instruments they would need for the band. We also work with other schools on their instruments plus music lessons. Stephen is setting up for us to have trophies, medals, ribbons and things for the school and some churches. Our business is growing, plus we have been getting more calls for us to sing."

"Oh, this is wonderful."

"Mom, we were wondering, how would you like to come work for us?" Daniel asked.

"Me? What would I do?" Leah exclaimed.

"We realized today that we could use you in the office. I can go over everything with you. You don't have to work a full day. If you want, you could work about four hours a day. You could take care of the mail, the phone, see to it that the bills are paid, and make deposits at the bank. This would all be a big help to us. That is, if you want to."

"I would love it. I could come in around eleven, bring lunch and work till three. That would give me time to go to the bank for you and be home in time to prepare dinner."

Caleb said, "Mom, you don't have to make lunch for us every day. We can eat a sandwich."

"We will see. There may be days I'm not up to cooking, then I'll stop and pick something up. So, when do you want me to start?"

After dinner, the boys told Leah they would clean up the kitchen. While they were cleaning up, Leah went next door to see Nora.

"Oh, Nora, I want to thank you for suggesting I make the boys lunch and take it to them. It has worked out better than I thought. Today, I went in the office, straightened a few things up and took some phone calls. Tonight, they offered me a job working with them. I only have to work about four hours a day, but I will be with them."

"Leah, that is wonderful. We have been praying that something would come about to where you could spend more time with the boys, and look, God came through again. He is so good."

Leah smiled, "Yes, He is! All the time. I start tomorrow, I am so excited."

The next day at ten forty-five, Leah slipped in the back door with the boys' lunch. When everything was made ready for them to eat, she went to the office. The phone rang almost constantly. She didn't leave till nearly four. Daniel walked in the office and said, "Mom, you were supposed to leave at three."

"This phone hasn't stopped ringing. We may have to come in after the store closes to go over things I need to do. You need to hire someone just to answer the phone."

"It's not like that every day. If you want to come back tonight, we can go over what we need you to do. By the way, we need someone to deliver some things from time to time. Do you think Nick would be interested?"

"Oh Daniel, I think he would love it. Ask him tonight when

you get home.”

Soon Leah was working in the office four to five hours a day, sometimes longer. Nick was in and out making deliveries, and if anything needed repairing, he took care of it. After work one evening when Leah got home, Nora came over.

“Okay, you and Nick have something to do, and I am left out. So, I have decided I will have dinner for everyone when you guys get off. It’s not right for me to be left out.”

“Nora, we didn’t mean to leave you out. I am so sorry.”

“Well, I can cook, and I do enjoy it so if you have to stay late, that will be alright. This way if you’re tired, your dinner will be ready when you get home.”

“This is so thoughtful of you, Nora. You have a key to the house, so if you need anything, help yourself. The boys keep the cabinets and the refrigerator stocked.”

“Yes, I saw that. I called to ask if you had any butter before I ran out to the store, and you put me on hold, so I went to see if you had any. Leah, you have enough food to do you for several weeks. Are they afraid you might starve?”

“That’s what I was trying to tell you a few weeks ago. They go through and check out what we have and bring in what we need and what they think we need. So don’t go buy anything. Check out what we have in stock. It can save you a trip into town.”

“I’m going to have Nick make a sign that says, ‘Conner’s Grocery.’ Then we will have a music store and grocery store by the name of Conner’s.”

They both laughed.

Twenty-Seven

Paul took Diane into town. The cast was finally coming off. After wearing it for six weeks, when the doctor removed it the first time, she tripped on the steps as she was leaving and cracked her leg again. This put her in a cast for over three months. Diane was so ready for the cast to come off. She had gotten used to the crutches finally, but still was more than ready to part with them.

When Dr. Wilson removed the cast, he asked her, "Do you think you can make it home safely this time?"

Diane looked at him and said, "No offense, but I hope the next time I see you it will be at a social gathering and not in your office."

They all laughed, and Paul helped her out.

Diane told Paul, "My leg feels so light. It doesn't feel like my other one."

"That's because you haven't really used it on its own for several months. The feeling will come back, but you still need to be careful."

While helping Diane in the car, John Leighton walked up.

"Hey, Paul, how are things going?"

"John, good to see you. When did you get back in town?"

"I made it home yesterday. Hello, Diane, I see you have the cast off finally."

"Yes, just now. What's this I hear that you have been out of town, John? Guess that explains why I haven't seen you around."

"I had some business in Virginia to take care of."

Turning to Paul, John said, "I have some things I would like to run by you when you have some free time."

"I will be out your way in the morning, John. Would it be okay if I stop by then?"

"Perfect. I'll have a fresh pot of coffee waiting for you. Diane, take care of that leg." Then John walked off.

Diane wondered what business John had in Virginia. She was sure Paul didn't know, or at least not yet. If only she could ride with Paul in the morning to John's.

The next morning, Diane was up early to help Iris, and hopefully, Paul would let her ride with him to John's. As soon as breakfast was over, Paul told Iris he would be gone most of the morning, plus he had to stop by and see John.

Diane spoke up, "Paul, would you mind if I went with you this morning? With my cast off, I can get around so much better, and I haven't been anywhere in a while."

"Sorry, Diane, I have some things I need to attend to. John wants to see me about something, and I'm sure now that you can get around, Iris could use your help in a lot of ways. You ladies have a good day."

Diane wanted so much to find out why John was in Virginia. Finding out from Paul was unlikely, and she didn't want to come right out and ask John. Hopefully, Iris would know in a few days, and she would ask her.

Diane went outside to clear things up after breakfast when Tommy and Micah came up.

"How does it feel to have the cast off?" Tommy asked.

"Great. I can get around so much better. Tommy, I want to thank you again for helping me when I fell. I owe you a lot."

"Ms. Diane, we both helped each other. I think God was there for both of us."

"I don't know that God wanted me to break my leg," she said.

"Well, you were doing something that you shouldn't have been doing. God knew that, so He punished you. He knew I needed help with my speech, so He sent me to you."

"Tommy, God doesn't punish people!"

Micah looked at Diane. "Don't you read your Bible? It says when we keep on going against God's word, we will be punished. You have been doing that a lot since you got here, so He probably thought enough was enough."

"No, Micah, I don't think I have read that."

"Well, the Bible tells us a lot of things. Come down to the

bunkhouse some night. We all sit around, read, and study our Bible. You sure do learn a lot."

"Thanks, Micah, I'll keep that in mind. You two take care today. I need to get back in the house to help Iris."

Diane was surprised that the boys read their Bibles at night. She wondered if this was Paul's doing, and if this was another one of his rules.

At church on Sunday, John came up to Diane and asked if they could sit together.

"Only if we can sit in the back. I'm not ready to move up yet."

"Sure, no problem. Paul tells me you have been coming to church. I'm glad to hear this."

"Did Paul tell you he didn't give me any choice? That was my only outing for the week."

John laughed. "I'm sure it wasn't as bad as you let on. If you would listen, Pastor Morgan delivers some good messages. You could learn a lot from listening."

"I'll think about it. Say, did I hear you say you went to Virginia? If I had known you were going, I would have gone with you. It would have been good to see some of my old friends."

John looked at Diane. "One of your old friends is dead, remember? Or should I say your boss?"

Not finding humor in John's remark, Diane turned and went in the church to her back row seat.

A year had gone by, and as they were sitting in church one Sunday, Pastor Morgan announced they would be having a singing at the auditorium in town. There would be a charge, and the money would go to pay the singers for their time and travel expenses. When John Leighton was out of town and heard the singers, he had made arrangements for them to come to Wyoming. He said posters would be put up to let everyone know and suggested that everyone mark their calendars.

"Diane, I want you to go to this singing with me. You might enjoy yourself," John said.

"Isn't it enough that I go to church? Now you want me to go

to some singing.”

“You keep telling me you care for me. I have told you, until there were some changes, we have no future, only friendship. I think I have been more than patient with you. Now, I plan to go to this singing, will you come with me or not?”

“I’ll think about it and let you know.”

“You have one week, and if I don’t hear from you by then, I’m asking someone else to go with me. Sometimes I feel I’m wasting my time with you.”

John turned and walked away. Diane stood there in shock. He can’t ask someone else. She thought he cared about her. Then she remembered something Iris had said to her. “There are a lot of ladies in this town that would give anything to have John Leighton pay them some attention.” How could she fake being a Christian? She was certain he would catch on. If not, Paul and Iris would. What was she going to do?

“Ms. Diane.”

There stood Rose.

“Hello, Rose. How are you this morning?”

“Ms. Diane, I am fine, but you look so sad. Would you like for me to pray with you?”

“What did you say?” asked Diane.

“I asked if you would like for me to pray with you. You look so sad. It always helps when I pray.”

Reaching up for Diane’s hand, Rose started praying. Diane wasn’t sure what to do. She looked at Rose and thought, “This kid is praying for me.” Diane had a feeling coming over her that she had never felt before. She needed to get away, but she couldn’t just walk away while Rose was praying. She heard Rose say, “Lord, we love Diane. She is our friend. We ask that you reach down and bless her and help her to smile and be happy again. We know that You can do this, and she really needs You. Put your arms around her and let her know You love and care for her, too, and that she is not alone.”

Diane had to get away. As soon as Rose finished praying and let go of Diane’s hand, Diane turned and ran toward the wagon.

She found herself fighting back tears. What was happening to her? This wasn't right.

She never said a word to anyone on the way home. As soon as they arrived, she got down out of the wagon and went straight to her room. She needed to get away from everyone and try to get her composure back. What was she going to do about John? Why did Rose want to pray for her? Diane fell by her bed and started crying and could not stop. What was wrong with her? What was happening?

Downstairs Paul went to Iris and said, "Did you see Rose praying for Diane today after church? It seemed to really get to Diane. Do you think its possible God is answering our prayers? That it is taking these children to get to Diane? First Tommy and now Rose."

"You know, Paul, God is slowly chipping away the wall Diane has built up. She has been through so much, and I'm sure she has gone through a lot in Virginia that we know nothing about. I wonder how many people she has met that have been praying for her. God is in control, and after a while, she will break. I hope it won't take anything drastic to open her eyes."

"I think God is slowly opening her eyes and heart. I hope that when that day comes, I will be there."

The next Sunday, as the people were gathering in for church, Diane went up to John. "I would like to go to that singing with you, if you still want me to go."

Smiling, John looked at Diane. "I would like nothing more."

Inside, Diane wasn't sure if she wanted to go, but more than anything, she didn't want anyone else to go with John. She would pretend to enjoy herself for John's sake.

Twenty-Eight

Business was picking up for the Conners. Seemed they were getting more and more orders for instruments, lessons, or someone was calling for them to schedule a singing engagement.

John Leighton was in Virginia on a business trip when a friend he was having dinner with told him about the Conners, saying, "You need to go by and see them. They are knowledgeable of all instruments."

So, John decided before he headed back to Wyoming to check the guys out.

John had rented a car and had plenty of time before heading to the airport, so he got directions to the Conners Music Store. When he walked in, he was amazed at the atmosphere. This was no ordinary music store. He felt like he had always been a customer there. He purchased an organ for the church, and Benjamin took care of the order. The price was much better than the price he had been given in Wyoming, even with shipping.

When John walked out to his rental car, it would not start. He tried and tried. Finally, he walked back into the music store. He explained about his car, and that until the car rental company could come out, which was going to be a while, the car would be parked in front of the store. He was sorry and hoped it didn't create a problem.

Daniel looked around for Stephen. "Hey, can you go check out this guy's rental car? Seems it won't start."

Stephen walked out, raised the hood, and started tinkering. While he was tinkering, he started singing. John was amazed at the boy's voice.

"Say, have you ever thought about singing in public?"

Stephen looked at John, "Now give it a try."

John got in the car, and it started right up. "What did you do?"

"Oh, I just did a little of this and a little of that, that's all," replied Stephen.

John, still amazed at the boy's voice, again said, "You never answered my question about singing? You have a great voice."

Smiling, Stephen looked at John. "Have you got a minute?"

"Sure," was John's reply.

They walked back into the music store, and Stephen walked over to a piano. When he sat down and started playing, his brothers picked up an instrument and started playing along with him, and then they broke out singing. John didn't know what to think. When they finished, he asked, "Have you ever thought about traveling to other places to sing?"

The boys grinned, and Stephen said, "We are known as By Grace Quartet."

"Would you guys consider coming to Wyoming to sing? We will pay all your expenses."

Daniel spoke up. "You will have to talk to Nick, our manager. He handles all that. He tells us where we are to be, and we go and sing."

"So where do I find this Nick guy?" John asked.

Caleb pointed to a man over near the counter. "That's who you need to talk to."

John and Nick talked for some time. When John left, he told Stephen, "Hope to see you guys soon."

About a month later, as they sat down to dinner, Nick came in with a letter from John Leighton.

"Do you boys remember the man from Wyoming?"

Stephen did. "Yeah, he's the guy with the rental car that wouldn't start."

Nick nodded his head. "Well, you boys have done some traveling but not as far as Wyoming. He wants you to come sing at an auditorium. Said it would hold about five thousand people or more."

"Wow, we have never sung at a place like that," replied Caleb.

"Well, according to this letter, you have never been offered this kind of money to sing before, either."

"What kind of money are you talking about, Nick?" Leah asked.

Nick laid the paper on the table. They all leaned over to try to see what the paper said.

Daniel picked the paper up. "Is this for real? They will pay this kind of money for us to come sing?"

"That's what the letter says, and he asks that you bring plenty of CDs," smiled Nick.

"When we sing, we do it because we enjoy it. That's why we sing at benefit singings. Never thought about charging," said Daniel.

Nora got up to get dessert. "You boys are better than what you give yourselves credit for. I know at some of the places where you have sung, the men would come up and slip you some money. Maybe you should consider charging. This could be the start of a new career for you."

"But what about our music store?" Caleb asked. "We all love working there."

"May I make a suggestion?" replied Leah. "Sam is always popping in and out of the store, and sometimes, I think he regrets selling it. Why don't you see if he would work when you have a singing engagement? I'm sure Cody could find you a few young guys to fill in also to help Sam during that time. It would help Sam and give some young guys a chance to work."

"Mom, that's a great idea. I know Sam would be happy to help us out. Like you said, he is always popping in to see how things are going and to talk to the customers. Mom, you're the best." Daniel went over and gave Leah a hug.

"So, I take it you boys want to go to Wyoming?" asks Nick.

"Sure," they all said.

The next day the boys got together with Cody to make some CD's.

"About how many CDs do you guys want to make?" Cody asked. Caleb looked at his brothers, "Is four thousand too many?" They agreed that was a good start.

The next day Nora came in with decorations to put in the window. She had started coming by to decorate for whatever the holiday was. While she was working at a window, a lady came in.

"Excuse me. Do they sell used pianos in here?"

Nora pointed to Stephen. "That young man can answer any questions about a piano you have."

The lady thanked Nora and walked over to Stephen.

"Excuse me, I'm looking for a used piano but in good shape. By any chance, would you have one?"

Extending his hand, Stephen said, "Yes, we do. My name is Stephen. What kind of piano do you have in mind?"

"It's for my daughter. I don't want to spend a lot of money till I know for sure she is serious about playing."

Smiling, Stephen said, "I totally understand. By the way, I didn't catch your name."

"Oh, I'm so sorry. You gave me your name, and I simply brushed it off. My name is Missy Taylor."

Stephen froze when she gave him her name. In fact, Daniel and Caleb did too.

"Excuse me, young man. Are you okay? You look like you just saw a ghost."

Trying to regain his composure, Stephen felt like the floor was pulling him in.

"Did you say your name was Missy Taylor?" Stephen asked.

"Yes, why?"

Stephen trying to think what to say, asked, "Do you live here?"

Caleb went into the office where Leah was and said, "There is a lady out front that says her name is Missy Taylor. Do you think it could possibly be?"

Leah got up and went to Caleb. "Go in the kitchen for a while. Let me see what I can find out."

Caleb went to the kitchen and Leah went out front close to Stephen.

"Stephen, let me take over from here," she said, then turned to the lady. "If you don't mind, could you come into the office?"

The lady wasn't sure what was going on. All she wanted to do was buy a used piano. She followed Leah into the office, and when Leah closed the door, the lady asked, "What is going on here?"

"Please have a seat and let me try to explain." Leah, quietly asked God to help her before she, herself, sat down.

"I apologize for this odd situation here, but I need to ask you a question. Do you have any other children besides your daughter?"

"Yes, I do. Why do you ask?"

"By any chance would your other child or children be boys?"

Again, the lady replied, "Yes."

Leah could feel her heart racing, but knew she had to continue.

"Do your sons live with you?"

"No, they don't. Please, why all the questions?"

"May I ask why your sons don't live with you?"

"I refuse to answer any more of your questions until you explain why," replied the lady.

Taking a deep breath, "You see, those four young men out there have no idea where their birth mother is. All they know is that her name is Missy Taylor."

The lady sat back in her chair, not knowing what to say. "I'm sorry, but those boys are not mine. I have a ten-year-old daughter, my sons are twins and are twenty-five. I was told after they were born, I wouldn't be able to have any more children. Then we received a surprise and had Libby."

Leah felt like she could breathe again but was unable to speak.

Mrs. Taylor spoke. "I can't imagine what those boys thought when I said my name. We are not from here; my husband and I are from Florida. My father passed away almost three years ago, and my mother moved here to live with her sister, who was a widow also. About a year later her sister passed away. My husband's company where he worked was going to transfer one of the men to Virginia. It was close to where my mom lived, so he asked if he could have the transfer. It was such a blessing. We live about thirty minutes from my mother, but soon she will be moving in with us due to health reason. The boys are going to college at Yale University. They want to become attorneys. Moving here also put us a little closer to the boys."

"Mrs. Taylor, I'm so sorry for questioning you, but I had to for the boys' sake. I'm happy for you and your family. I pray nothing will ever separate you."

"No need to apologize, if I were in your shoes, I probably would have done the same thing. Now if you will guide me to that nice young man, I'll see if he can help me in getting a piano."

When Mrs. Taylor and Leah walked out of the office, all four boys were standing on the other side of the counter, waiting to hear what Leah had to say.

"Stephen, this lady is interested in purchasing a used piano. They have moved here from Florida recently, so show her what we have and don't forget to let her know we offer lessons here if she hasn't already found a teacher for her daughter."

All four boys breathed a sigh of relief. Then Stephen took Mrs. Taylor over to the pianos.

As they were closing for the night, Stephen asked Daniel, "Do you remember what our birth mom looks like?"

"Stephen, I have tried to put her out of my mind. She may have given us life, but Leah Conner introduced us to an everlasting life. Leah Conner will always be my mom."

"I understand that, for which I am grateful, too, but today as I looked at that woman, the image of our birth mom just didn't come into focus. It's like it's gone."

"Stephen, you were, what, almost seven. I was barely nine. If anyone could remember her, it would be us, but when I think of her, I remember how she treated us. I want to forget all that."

Benjamin walked up and heard what his brothers were saying. "I can't remember our birth mom at all. But I do remember when we first went to Leah Conner's home. She fed us, bought us new clothes. We got to take a bath, brush our teeth, and we had a bed to sleep in that night. But the one thing that really sticks in my mind, that night before we went to bed, she let me sit in her lap and she put her arms around me. Those hugs and kisses on my forehead were heavenly. I know, Daniel, you hugged me close to you when things were bad before we met our mom, Leah, but there was something different about her hug and sitting in her lap. I didn't want to get up. I felt safe and happy."

Caleb said, "That hasn't changed, has it? We are happy and still feel safe. Let's just pray we never have an incident like this again."

When Leah got home, Nora called and asked her to come over. As soon as Leah walked in, Nora said, "Today when that lady said her name was Missy Taylor, I thought my heart had stopped. In a split second, a thousand thoughts went through my mind. Leah, you handled that perfectly. I don't know that I could have been so calm."

"Nora, I was not calm. I said a prayer on the way to my chair. If God had not been with me, I have no idea what would have happened. But the lady was nice and understanding. When Caleb came into the office and said a lady by the name of Missy Taylor was out there, the poor child looked like he had seen a ghost. He told me years ago he couldn't remember what his birth mom looked like. I'm sure it must have been hard on those boys."

"But they have you and are happy. I think her saying her name put everyone in a state of shock. For a few minutes, you could have heard a pin drop. The poor lady didn't know what to say or think."

"You know, Nora, I can't imagine what was going through her mind."

"Leah, I just wanted to talk to you before the boys came in for dinner. You know, I don't think I finished decorating that window. I don't even remember putting the things away."

"It's okay, Nora. I think the guys will understand. This hasn't been a normal day to say the least."

Daniel had talked to Sam about filling in for him when they had a singing engagement that would require them to be out of town. Sam was more than delighted to help. Then Daniel talked to Cody, asking if he knew anyone who would be able to fill in when they were gone and could help Sam out. In a week, Cody had three young men that loved music and were knowledgeable of musical instruments. Working part-time would be great for them.

Soon it was time to start planning the trip to Wyoming. The boys couldn't believe how quickly the time had gone by. Nick came into the store one day and gathered the four of them around.

"Received a letter from John Leighton in Wyoming. He wants us to stay with him on his ranch. Says he has plenty of room, and if we could stay a few extra days that would be even more perfect. They are expecting over four thousand people, and he said to remind you guys to bring plenty of CDs."

"I think staying on a ranch would be cool," replied Benjamin. "This is sounding better all the time."

Caleb turned to Benjamin, "We have never sung in front of that many people. We leave in a few weeks and have nowhere enough CDs."

Scratching his head, Stephen said, "Guess we had better call Sam and the other guys to come in and fill in for us a few days. We need to make different CDs with different songs."

When they got home that night, they were trying to sort through some songs that they felt people would enjoy and want to hear. Nora knocked on the den doorway.

"Have you guys got a minute?"

"Sure, come on in," they all replied.

Nora walked in with four big boxes. "These are for you guys."

When they opened the boxes, for a minute, they stood there looking at what was inside.

"Well, are you guys just going to stand there and look at the boxes?"

Finally, they each reached down and picked up matching coats and then pants, shirts, socks, and ties.

Daniel asked Nora, "You bought these for us?"

"Yes, Nick and I want you to look sharp when you walk out on that stage. Oh, your shoes will be here tomorrow."

"You know, you and Nick didn't have to do this. You two are the best. What would we do without you?" Daniel said.

"You four mean the world to us, and as far as we are concerned, we are family. When you have something going on, we will be right there. We have your back one hundred percent."

Twenty-Nine

John Leighton had asked Betty Hawkins if she could come over and help prepare his house for the Conners. He would need her to help with the cooking while they were there. Betty and three of her girls showed up two days before the Conners were to arrive. She wanted to take inventory of what John had and needed. She brought Carrie, who was nineteen, Mary Beth, who was eighteen, and Rose. Wherever Betty went, Rose thought she had to be with her mother.

John went over to see Paul and Iris the day the Conners were to arrive and asked Iris if she had a nice tablecloth he could borrow. Betty had told him his wouldn't do.

Iris laughed. "Yes, and I'll send it to you. I want to freshen it up before you use it."

Paul walked John to his car and asked how long the Conners would be staying.

"Well, Paul, I asked them to stay a few days after the singing. I would like to show them around. Something about those boys touched me. I can't explain it, but something tugged on my heart. Wait till you hear them. It's like something from heaven. That is the best I can explain it."

"John, do you think it might be possible that they could come over here one night for dinner? I'd like for my boys to have the opportunity to talk to them. The Conners don't need to know these boys are all from broken homes, but maybe in some way they might say something to give them encouragement. Iris and I do our best, but sometimes it takes an outsider to give them that little something."

"I'll see what I can do, Paul, and let you know. Now I had better get back to the ranch. Betty and those girls have my place looking like it has never looked before, not to mention the cooking they are doing. I have to stay out of my own kitchen for the aroma alone will starve you to death."

"See you tomorrow night, John."

John had returned to his ranch and had just gotten out of his car to tell Betty that Iris would be sending the tablecloth over when he saw a van coming down the road. He knew then it was the Conners. When they pulled up, John walked over to meet them.

Reaching out to shake their hand, John said, "Welcome to Wyoming and to the Leighton Ranch. It is so good to see you. I thought this day would never come."

Nick said, "Don't believe you have met these ladies. This is Nora, my wife, and this beautiful lady is the boys' mother. She is their backbone."

John walked over to both ladies. He shook hands with Nora, but to Leah he said, "You are one blessed lady. You can't help but be proud of these guys."

"Thank you for your kind words, and yes, I am blessed. Words cannot express how proud and honored I am to be their mother."

John took them into the house where Carrie and Rose had tea and soft drinks for them. After they had rested some from their trip, John asked if they were up to walking around. He showed them his barn and horses, and then they walked up a trail that led to something dear to John's heart. There in the clearing was a beautiful church. John explained that the people in this area didn't have a church close by, so he donated the land. He and area farmers got together and built the church. They made it bigger than what they needed, for it was built with the intentions of it growing.

They asked if they could go inside. "Stephen, this is why I wanted to buy an organ. One of Betty's girls plays the piano for us on Sunday, but we wanted an organ also."

"You have room for one. May I try out your piano?"

"You certainly can, Stephen. The piano may be a little out of tune."

"No worries, Mr. Leighton. If it is, I can take care of that before we leave."

As Stephen started playing, the piano didn't sound too out of tune. What a difference in his playing and Mary Beth's. Soon, the guys broke out in a song. Betty, Carrie, and Rose came rushing in. They stood at the back of the church listening. When the guys finished, they started clapping.

Betty walked to the front and introduced herself. "Hello, I'm Betty Hawkins. I don't think I have ever heard music from this church sound so good. You must be the Conners."

John looked at Betty. "How did you ever guess? Yes, these are the guys I have talked about for months."

"Well, John said you guys were amazing, and you are so right. I can't wait till tomorrow night. Now if you will excuse us, we need to get back to the house. Oh, these are my girls, Carrie and Rose."

After introductions, Betty and the girls left. Stephen went to the van and came back with an instrument and started tuning the piano.

When he finished, he played a song to see if they could tell a difference. A young girl walked in and walked all the way to the piano. "I wish I could play like that."

Stephen looked at her. "Can you play the piano?"

"I thought I could, but now I don't think so."

John walked over. "This is Mary Beth. She plays for us on Sundays."

Stephen scooted over on the bench and ask her to sit down and play something for him. She did but it didn't sound anything like how he played.

"Let me show you a few things that I think will help you."

"Oh, wait," she said, turning to John, "Ms. Iris sent this to you."

Mary Beth handed John a box that held the tablecloth he had wanted to borrow. Then she turned her attention back to Stephen.

The others went back to the house and left Stephen giving Mary Beth a few piano lessons.

After dinner that night, they all turned in early because it had been a long day. After the lights were out and everyone was in bed, the words of a hymn could be heard. The boys were singing "Amazing Grace."

The house fell silent as the boys finished all the verses in the song. John Leighton laid in bed with tears streaming down his face, overcome with thankfulness for this night and the precious song that was just sung.

The next day was a busy one. John took Nick and the boys to the auditorium so they could get all set up for that night. The boys could not imagine the auditorium being full of people in a few hours. But they were here to do God's work; it was about him, not them.

They ate an early dinner, for they felt it best not to eat just before going on stage. Nora had pressed their suits and shirts. She was more nervous than the guys were. She fussed over them, making sure everything was perfect, but they loved her for it. Just before they were to go out on stage, the guys knelt down and held hands. Daniel led them in a word of prayer.

"Our most precious Heavenly Father, as we come to You tonight, we ask You, Father, to be with every person that comes through that door. We ask that your sweet Spirit fills them and this building. Father, if there is one who is lost, maybe backslidden or dealing with sickness, or whatever the issue may be, we ask that they feel your power. Tonight, is not about us, it's about You. We sing to bring You glory, to lift You up. We are happy, Father, that You are using us; we are honored to be chosen to do your will. We ask that every song will bring many blessings. Again, Father, thank You for this night and for all that You have blessed us with. Our prayer is for You to receive all the praise and honor. Amen."

As they finished praying, each one received a text on their phone. It was from Abigail and Anna, letting them know they loved them and were praying for them and to text when they could on how the night had gone. The guys smiled because they loved their big sisters. Then they went out on the stage. For a few minutes, you could hear a pin drop. Then when they started playing their music and singing, it became a time of praise and worship.

John, Diane, Paul, Iris, Barry, and Betty arrived in time to get front row seats. The boys and the girls from the ranch sat in the second row. Diane felt she was the only one who was not enjoying this. She tried to focus her mind on everything else, but every so often, John would lean over and say, "They are so good. Aren't you glad you came?"

On the stage, Stephen spoke and said, "If anyone feels like they are alone and have no one to turn to, our prayer is that this song is for you. You see, my brothers and I can relate to this song. It says as you travel down life's road, God is in the valley that we walk through. Years ago, we four were in a valley and didn't realize it, but God was standing next to us. Just as the song says, He was in our midst and still is today, just as He is with you. You are never alone, just open up your heart and let him in. May this song bless you, and we pray that wherever you go, you can feel those angels camping all around you, for our Heavenly Father is truly in the midst."

There were few dry eyes in the building when the song ended. John looked at Diane and realize she wasn't even paying attention. How could she sit there and not feel God's presence? Leaning over to her, he asked, "How did you like that song?"

"Oh, John, it was beautiful. I really enjoyed it."

"What was the name of the song, Diane?"

Trying to remember, she couldn't even recall the words. "I don't remember the name, but they sang about going to heaven. It was touching, don't you think?"

"It was touching," he said. "You should have listened to it. It might have helped you." John sat back in his chair and wondered why she was so cold on the inside. What was it going to take to get through to her?

After a few songs, Daniel introduced the group to the audience. He mentioned Nick, their manager, Nora who oversaw their wardrobe and many other tasks, then Leah, their mom, who saw in them great things and gave them the faith and courage to do God's calling.

The guys sang for over two hours. Every time they tried to close, someone would call out to sing one more, and they couldn't turn anyone down. Then finally, they said they would sing one more.

Daniel said, "I feel someone needs this song and hope they would pay heed to the words. It talks about being in the palm of God's hand. I'm sure many of you have had a heavy burden and felt like you were sinking down. Tonight, are you searching for answers to all your troubles and strife? Then just give it all to Jesus, for He will certainly see you through. When you are in the palm of His hands, you know He has reached way down, that you are safe and secure with God's heavenly touch. Listen to God as we sing this last song."

Several people came down and knelt by the stage. You could feel God's presence everywhere. It was like being in a revival. John went down and thanked God for the blessings he had received. This night had blessed him more than he had ever imagined. When he went back to his seat, Diane was gone. He asked Iris, "Do you know where Diane went?"

"Said, she was going to go look for the ladies' room. She seemed put out."

John could not understand. How could she sit here and not feel something?

When they got back to John's house that night, everyone was so happy about how well the singing had gone. The guys sold all six thousand CDs they had taken, and they had made three different kinds.

Thirty

The next morning, John was up early, still feeling like he was walking on a cloud. He himself bought six CDs, one set for the house and the other for his car. Betty and the girls were coming in to prepare breakfast.

"Well, John, how do you think last night went?"

"Betty, I'm still feeling the effects of it. Never have I ever been in a service as touching, so affecting, so loving as last night. To be so young and have such powerful and spiritual voices. God has blessed them beyond measure. No wonder they draw a crowd. Once you hear them, you want more."

"I know, John. On our way home last night, the girls were singing some of the songs the guys sang. This morning while getting dressed I found myself humming to one of their songs. It definitely has an impact on you."

"Betty, those guys act just like we do. They don't place themselves up on a pedestal. They are so down to earth. Stephen is the one who worked on my rental car when I was in Virginia. Some singers, when they become known, act like they are someone special. Not these guys, and I hope they always stay that way."

As they came in for breakfast, Nora and Leah realized it wasn't quite ready, so they went into the kitchen to help.

Leah said, "Never turn down help in the kitchen. Besides, it will make Nora and me feel more at home."

Over breakfast, John mentioned that Paul Baker and his wife, Iris, would like to have them over for dinner. "They have a ranch for boys, also Ms. Betty here, she and Barry have a ranch for girls."

Caleb smiled, "That sounds great. How big is his ranch?"

"Paul's is not as big as mine, but we all help each other when it's time to harvest. That's what neighbors do. I'll send word over to Paul and Iris that we will have dinner with them tonight."

Later that afternoon, Micah and Tommy rode up in a wagon. They had put bales of straw in the back and then put blankets over the straw to sit on.

Daniel, Stephen, Caleb, Benjamin, Leah, Nora, Nick, and John got in. The boys were taking them on a tour of the ranches and then would stop at the Baker ranch for dinner. John pointed out some nice scenic views and what different areas were used for. The day was beautiful with the wind blowing just enough to be comfortable. Soon, they were pulling up at the Baker ranch.

Betty and the girls had left John's and gone over to help Iris prepare dinner. The food was spread out on the table under the trees. It looked like what you would see at a church function. It was amazing, and it all looked delicious. As soon as the blessing was said, everyone fixed a plate and soon found a spot to sit down.

Daniel, Stephen, Caleb, and Benjamin sat on a blanket on the ground with the boys from the ranch. They laughed and talked like they had been friends forever.

Charlie asked Benjamin, "Is it hard to play an instrument?"

"No, not really. It's best if you pick out one that you like. You should have Mr. Baker take you to town and look at all the different kinds of instruments and find what most appeals to you."

Charlie dropped his head. "That will probably never happen. We are here till someone wants to adopt us or until our parents straighten up."

Tommy laid his fork down, "My parents didn't want me because I stuttered really bad. When my stuttering stopped, they still didn't want me back because they had other things to do, and I would be in the way."

Micah smiled, "But Mr. Paul and Ms. Iris want us and said we would always have a home here with them. We are lucky to have them, but it's sad that our parents don't want us."

John and Paul were in earshot of what the boys were saying. They wondered what the Conner boys thought of the situation.

Daniel laid his fork down and looked at the boys around them.

"We understand what you guys are talking about. You see, our mother abandoned us, and Leah Conner took us in. She is the reason we are who we are today. She could have easily walked away from four small little boys like our birth mom did, but instead she wrapped her arms around us and filled us with love. Later she adopted us. Our birth mother was more into what the world had to offer, and our mom, Leah, was more into what God could offer us. Being here is your blessing from God. Always look ahead and never look back. From what I see, you guys are fortunate and blessed to be here," he said.

"So, your parents didn't want you either?" asked Tommy.

"Look at it this way, Tommy," said Stephen. "Mr. and Mrs. Baker needed you more. That's why God brought you here. You never know what plans God has for you. So always keep your eyes and ears open. Read and study God's word, you will be surprised at how He speaks and will guide you. In the book of Matthew 7:7-8, it reads, 'Ask and it will be given to you; seek and you will find; knock and the door will be opened to you. For everyone who asks receives; he who seeks finds and to him who knocks, the door will be opened.'"

Daniel held out his hand, and all the boys laid their hand in his. "We want you guys to know, we are going to be praying for you every day. We know what you're feeling, and we know the prayers you need. We may be several states away from you, but know that our prayers are with you, and we would love to hear from you. We will leave our address with Mr. Leighton so you can write or call anytime. You are our brothers in Christ and we love you."

Paul and John were so touched by what they heard. They had no idea the Conners were adopted.

John turned to Paul. "My meeting those boys was a plan from God. Them coming here to sing was in God's plan, also. I thought having them here was more for me than anyone, but God just showed me that those boys had the greatest need, and He used me as a steppingstone to fill that need.”

Paul patted John on the back. “God is always working. Even miles away, He can bring things together.”

Iris was talking to Leah about the boys and asked if they got their talent from her or her husband.

“The boys received their talent from God. I can’t take credit for any of it.”

“Well, you and your husband are certainly blessed. Our boys are all from broken homes. Barry and Betty Hawkins have a ranch, and it is set up for girls. These children needed somewhere to go and someone to love them. Your boys are so blessed to have godly, loving parents.”

“Mrs. Baker, my husband is in heaven. About a year after his passing, I came across these four boys. Their mother abandoned them in a store that I happen to be at, and she never came back. I took them in, and if you could have seen them, it would have broken your heart. Here I was a widow taking on four small boys that I didn’t have any idea who their parents were. The name they knew their mother by was all we had to go on, and we are not sure if that was her real name. But anyway, with the help of our dear sweet heavenly Father, those boys turned out to be a blessing for me, and I couldn’t love them more if I had given birth to them.”

“Oh, Mrs. Conner, I had no idea. You have done a wonderful job with those boys.”

“Well, I have been blessed with wonderful neighbors, Nick and Nora Perkins. Nick has been like a father to them, and Nora is like another mother. The boys often refer to them as their uncle and aunt. They support the guys totally and the guys love them.”

Benjamin walked into the kitchen. “Hey, Mom, I found Chester.”

“Oh, Benjamin, you know that’s not Chester. Where did you find him?”

“One of the boys here found him and kept him as a pet. He named him Chester. Great name, don’t you think?”

Leah laughed as Benjamin took the turtle back outside.

"Mrs. Baker, when Benjamin first came to live with me, he found a turtle. I won't go into the whole story, but anyway, he named him Chester. That has been many years ago."

"Oh, that is funny. Charlie found the turtle a few days ago, and said he wanted to keep him and was going to call him Chester. I thought that was an odd name for a turtle, but apparently not."

The night was coming to an end, and as the Conners were getting in the wagon to go back to John's house, Paul asked, "By any chance can we have one more song?"

Getting settled in the wagon, they whispered to each other and then sat back to sing, "Thank you, Lord, for your blessings on me." For the Conner brothers, this song was one of their favorites and hoped it would touch the boys at the ranch as well. How many times had they themselves said, "Thank you, Lord, for the blessing You have bestowed upon us."

The boys at the ranch knew the song was for them and as the Conners rode out of sight, they continued singing till the whole song was sung. As their voices slowly faded away, the boys huddled together and cried and thanked God for their newfound friends.

The Conners stayed on two more days after the singing and then headed home. It was hard to leave, for they had made friends with so many in that area, but the boys needed to get back to work.

Iris was in the kitchen humming a song she had heard the Conners sing. Diane walked in, and asked, "Why are you humming that song again?"

"In my mind, I can hear those boys singing that song. Having them here was such a blessing. I hated to see them go."

"What's so special about those boys?"

"Diane, they have a great testimony. They talked to our boys here, and it helped them so much. Did you talk to any of them?"

"No, I had better things to do with my time. I stayed upstairs in my room."

Iris shook her head. "I didn't realize it, but those boys were abandoned by their mother in Virginia. She just walked into a store and left them with a stranger and never went back for them. Can you imagine a mother walking away from her children?"

"Maybe they were brats, and she couldn't take it anymore."

"Mrs. Conner was a widow and took them right in. She didn't come right out and say, but I bet those poor children were hungry and probably dirty. I wonder if they had been abused. That woman is a godly lady, and the boys couldn't have been given to anyone better. Her neighbors accepted the boys and became another set of parents to them."

Being in a not-so-good mood, Diane said, "Well, praise the Lord."

Iris looked at Diane, "That is not a remark you should be making, especially when you don't mean it. Did you not feel anything from their visit?"

"Iris, I did not want to go to the singing, but I went because of John. Isn't it enough that I was there?"

"Oh, speaking of John, he is outside. He wants to talk to you."

Diane rushed out the door, and there was John sitting at one of the tables. "Iris said you wanted to see me. What's up?"

"Diane, I watched you the night of the singing and then that night when the Conners came over. I have done a lot of praying and to be honest with you, we don't have a future together. Your heart is cold as a rock. What I felt for you in Virginia and the way you are now, I'm sorry, you don't seem to be the same person."

"You don't have any idea what all I have gone through. I'm not like you, I can't go out and buy whatever I want or donate land to a church and then have it named after me. I'm a Baker not a Leighton."

"You can be whatever you want to be. If feeling sorry for yourself is what you want to do, then go ahead and drown in your own misery. I have God in my life, and He has shown me a much better way to live. Look at those Conner boys. They didn't have much of a life, but Leah Conner took them in, and they accepted a better way. I have tried to offer you the same thing, but you are too cold-hearted to want to change.”

Diane looked at John. “You know nothing about those guys.”

“Paul and I overheard them talking to Paul’s boys. They offered them some good advice. I’m so glad while I was in Virginia that I had the opportunity to meet them.”

“Where did you say you met them?”

“In Virginia. I can’t imagine a mother handing her children over to a stranger and walking away and not looking back. She must have been like you, with a heart of stone.”

Diane looked at John. “I can’t talk right now. I need to be alone.”

John got up and walked away. He didn’t know of anything else to say to Diane.

A week had gone by, and Diane went over to John’s house. When he came to the door, she said, “Please let me talk to you.”

John let her in.

Thirty-One

Leah was working in the office at the music store when Nick came in. "I just received a letter from the boys at the ranch in Wyoming."

"Lay it here, and I'll pass it on to the first one who comes in. Those little guys write every other week. I don't know what is in those letters, but our boys seen happy to hear from them."

Nick leaned against the wall, "Do the boys write them back?"

"Oh, yes. All four of them write letters and send them back in a few days. I'm so glad our guys have become a big help to them."

"You know, Leah, that was a wonderful trip. The guys have gotten several bookings since then, but I don't think any will ever top that trip."

"You're right, Nick, there was something special about that trip. Can't really put my finger on it, but God knows and that's all that matters."

"Well, I'm going to head home and help Nora with dinner. See you all later."

As they were getting ready to close the store, John Leighton walked in.

Daniel saw him first and said, "Hey John, what a surprise. It's so good to see you. Hey, guys, look who walked in."

They all came over, shook hands with John and began asking about everyone in Wyoming.

Stephen patted John on the back, "Need a musical instrument?"

"No, I'm here for personal reasons. Is your mom here?"

Caleb went back to the office to get Leah. "Mr. Leighton, what a surprise," she said with a warm, welcoming smile.

"Mrs. Conner, it's good to see you. How are you doing?"

"Oh, we couldn't be better. I was getting ready to leave, and I'm so glad I didn't, or I would have miss you."

"I'm glad you all are here. I need to talk to all five of you," John said.

Leah could see a concerned look on John's face. "Is everything okay?"

"I'm praying it will be," he said. "You see, several years ago, I was here in Virginia, and I met a lady who I became fond of. I went back to Wyoming and couldn't get her off my mind. I later tried to find her but with no luck. Then God got a hold of me and turned my life completely around for which I am so grateful. Then out of the blue, she showed up in Wyoming. Come to find out, she is Paul Baker's sister. Instead of the loving and caring person I remembered, she was now bitter and cold. I explained to her that I had given my life to God and things would no longer be the same between us unless she turned her life around. Unfortunately, she wasn't willing to do that."

Leah reached over and patted John's hand. "I'm so sorry."

"The night you guys came out to sing, I had asked her to go with me, praying something in one of your songs would touch her. But it did no good."

"John, you said she was Paul Baker's sister. I don't remember seeing her at his house that night. Was she there?" Stephen asked.

"Yes and no. She was there but kept out of sight. She didn't want to be around all those 'holy rollers.' She goes to church every Sunday but only because Paul insists. That was one of the stipulations he put on her if she stayed in his house. She only went to the singing for fear I would take someone else. It was a few days after you guys had left that I felt I was wasting my time with her. I went to see her and told her so. A week later, she came by my house and asked if we could talk. By looking at her, I knew something was going on. We talked for several hours, and by the grace of God, she turned her life over to the Lord."

"Oh, Mr. Leighton, that is wonderful. We are so happy for you," Leah said.

"Please call me John."

"Only if you call me Leah for that's what all my friends call me."

"Then Leah it is."

"So, are you two engaged? Do you need someone to sing at your wedding?" smiled Caleb.

"Not yet. I haven't asked her to marry me. There are some other issues that need to be addressed first. I brought Diane with me. I would like for you guys to meet her."

John walked to the door and asked Diane to come in. When she walked in, Stephen sucked in his breath. Daniel went pale. The closer she walked to them, the more Daniel backed up.

"You, you are not Diane Baker," replied Daniel. "What are you doing here?"

"Please let me explain," Diane said.

Shaking his head, Daniel was still walking backwards. "Your name is Missy Taylor."

John dropped his head. He was hoping they wouldn't recognize her, not at first anyway. Leah, Caleb, and Benjamin turned to look at Diane.

Daniel had tears running down his face. "How could you after all these years?"

Leah spoke up, "Daniel, let's hear what this lady has to say. It's only right to let her talk."

"Mom, you have no idea what she did to us. I'm the oldest, and I remember so much. She is not my mother and never will be. You are the only woman I'll ever call Mom."

With tears streaming down Daniel's face, he turned and ran out the back door.

Diane looked at Leah, "I came to make things right. I wanted the boys to know who I am, and I'm not the same person I was years ago. At that time, I had met a man I thought that really loved me. He made so many promises, and I believed him. Whatever he asked of me I did. He didn't want children and ask me to do something with my four sons. He said, if I couldn't, he would, that it was either him or them. I chose him because of all his promises, and I thought my life would be so much better. We were struggling at the time, and I thought if I could find them a nice home, things would be better. When I saw you at the store, you seemed like a nice lady, so I left the boys with you and never looked back. In the end, this man took everything and left with my best friend. By then I had blocked so many things out of my mind."

Stephen cleared his throat, trying to get the words out he wanted to say. "Daniel does remember more than any of us because he is the oldest. He looked after me, Caleb and then Benjamin. Do you even remember what all he had to do?"

"Stephen, I know I was a bad mother then."

"You think you were a bad mom. Let me say this, you were the worst mom in the world. Daniel would go out and try to find food for us. Sometimes, he would bring a half-eaten sandwich he found or scraps from a trash can. He would go into a store and steal milk for us to drink. He took rags that he found and used them as diapers for Caleb and Benjamin. We slept on hard floors over in a corner to not bother you and whoever you brought home that night. If we as much as whimpered, your guy friend would knock us around. Daniel took a black eye once trying to shield us. You would go off for days, and we had no idea where you were. You would tell us if we left the house, we would catch it. Sometimes you left us in a car for days at a time. Our clothes were nasty; we smelled. Even one of your men friends said that we were nothing but a bunch of stinking pigs. If my memory is correct, he also told you to get rid of us. That he couldn't handle us being around. Just before he left, he told you that when he came back that if we were still there, he would get rid of us, himself. So, you may want to refer to yourself as a bad mom, but I would think more of Satan himself. You don't even deserve the air you breathe."

Then Stephen turned and walked toward the door. "I'm going to go find my brother."

Leah asked Caleb and Benjamin if they could take John and Diane to the house. She was going after the other two, and she would be home as soon as she could.

Daniel ran till he couldn't run any more. Finally, he collapsed at a pole on Main Street. Crying uncontrollably, he was remembering all the terrible things that he went through as a child. He had buried them deep inside with the intentions of never remembering them again. It began to sprinkle rain, but Daniel couldn't move. It seems everything was rushing at him. Then he heard a clock. He looked up and there on the pole he was holding on to was a big clock. What was it his mom Leah said, "Never look back; keep pressing on for what happened a minute ago is gone, and you can't get it back. You can change what's ahead."

He couldn't change the past, and he saw that finding their new mom Leah was a blessing and a gift from God. A gift that had shaped not only his future, but the future for his brothers. Daniel cried out, "Oh, dear Lord, please help me. Help me to be strong. Help me to understand why, after so many years, this woman that is supposed to be our birth mom shows up. What does she want from us? What do we do? I need you, Father, so much."

Daniel remembered Leah teaching them that they should never touch a woman unless they were married because anything outside of marriage was a sin. Before they considered getting married, they needed to pray and ask God to send them the wife they needed. She told them that a woman that sleeps with a man and not married will face an unhappy life, for God will not be in it. The Bible is your guidebook, always follow it. Then he thought of Diane, the one who gave birth to him and his brothers. She was a sinful woman. How many men had she had in her life? Did she even feel anything for them? And what of the men? What kind of man will take a woman out and use her for his own pleasure?

The rain had picked up, but Daniel didn't notice. He was hurting so. Then, he felt an arm around him, an arm he knew so well. As he turned, he fell into Leah's arms.

"Oh, Mom."

"I'm here, Daniel. You're not alone. Remember the song you sing. 'He's in the midst of our storms, He's in the valley we walk through.'"

As it rained, Leah held Daniel in her arms.

Stephen got home only to find Diane and John sitting in the den along with Nora and Nick.

"Has Daniel made it home yet?"

Nora shook her head no. "Stephen, would you like something to eat?"

"No, I'm going to change clothes. These are wet. Are Caleb and Benjamin here?"

Nora pointed to their room. "I think they are waiting for you."

Nearly two hours went by. Finally, Leah and Daniel walked in. Both were soaked to the bone.

Nora jumped to get them some towels, not sure if she should say anything. They went and changed into some dry clothes and then Leah came into the den where Diane, John, Nora, and Nick were sitting.

Daniel and his brothers soon came out. They got chairs and sat as close to Leah as possible.

John spoke first. "It was not our intentions to bring you boys any grief. I think the world of you and would love to have you come back out to the ranch. But once I was told about some things, I felt it only best to get things out in the open. What Diane told me caught me off guard. I was not expecting to hear the things she had to say. I had to walk away for a bit and do some praying. Then I went back into my house, and we talked some more. I couldn't believe I had fallen in love with someone like her. Then I remember in the Bible about a story of a man named Hosea. He married a woman the Bible refers to her as a promiscuous woman. Hosea obeyed God, knowing what kind of a woman she was. Diane came clean about her past and that is what it is, her past. I was with her when I was living in the world, but when I got saved, I couldn't live that life anymore. That's what I told her when she came to Wyoming. No matter what she had done in the past, I must look at who she is now. As for Paul and Iris, they were not aware that Diane had ever had children. When they were told of all this, they were shocked and like me, they had to take some time to pray and let this all sink in."

Nick folded his arms and was looking at the floor. "Like Hosea, if God is leading you toward Diane, then you must heed his word. God has a plan in store, you need to follow it. As for these boys, they are going to need time to let God heal them. They can't do it on their own. What you two did today took great courage and that comes from God."

Diane wanted so much to say something to her sons but wasn't sure what. As she looked at first one then the other, she was so amazed at how well they had turned out. She tried so hard to remember their features, how they talked, everything about them. She wanted it imprinted in her mind. Would she ever see them again? Did they hate her? Would she ever be a part of their life?

As John and Diane got up to leave, she wanted so much to hug the boys but that was too risky at this time. They were in a fragile state, and she didn't want to do any more damage than she already had.

When John and Diane arrived at their hotel, Diane reached out and hugged John. "Thank you for helping me with this. I couldn't have done it alone." Then she walked to her room, and he went to his.

In time the boys were able to forgive Diane for what she had done. Daniel became a preacher; Pastor Greg Harrington developed some major health problems which opened a door for Daniel. A young lady by the name of Katherine came to visit the church, and Daniel knew the instant he saw her that she was to be his wife.

Stephen and Mary Beth stayed in touch, and finally he asked her to marry him. She had never been outside Laramie, Wyoming, but she knew God had brought her and Stephen together, and she was okay to move to Virginia.

Caleb met a girl in Indiana while on a singing tour. Soon, Dana was moving to Virginia to marry him.

Benjamin found the love of his life in North Carolina. They were on a singing trip, and a young lady had parked her car next to their van. After the singing, she discovered she had a flat tire. Benjamin changed it for her, and she stole his heart right there.

Leah was happy, all her children had godly spouses. Leah continued to work at the music store, just to be close to the boys. Nick and Nora were always close by.

One evening after work, Leah received a call from Abigail to let her know that they would be moving to Virginia. Her husband was being transferred and they would only be an hour away. About six months later, Anna called to let Leah know that they would be moving to Virginia also. They would be about an hour away, but in the other direction.

Leah was so happy. Now during the holidays, her home would certainly be full again.

John and Diane got married three years later. The boys went out to Wyoming to be in the wedding and to show off their brides and also to see Paul and Iris, their uncle and aunt. Nick and Nora went along for Nora was still overseeing their clothes. They had to pass her inspection before any singing engagements or functions they might attend. The Conners became well known, and soon they purchased a bus to travel in.

They were known as "The Conner Brothers" and "By Grace Quartet." They preferred being referred to as "By Grace Quartet," for it was by God's grace that they were the Conner Brothers and also it was their precious mom Leah's middle name.

About the Author

Vicki McBee Irwin was born in Maryville, Tennessee. She married her high school sweetheart, Larry. They have three children, nine grandchildren, and nine great grandchildren. Because of her husband's Air Force career, Vicki has been blessed to travel to all fifty states and to many places abroad. To this day, Vicki and Larry love to travel and enjoy seeing all the many beautiful places God has created. Besides writing and traveling, Vicki also enjoys scrapbooking, sewing, cooking, playing the piano, and, of course, spending time with her family.

If you enjoyed this story, please help Vicki encourage others to read it by writing a review. No matter where you purchased the book, you can post a review on social media, Amazon.com, and elsewhere. On behalf of all authors, and readers, thank you!